KIND NEPENTHE

matthew v. brockmeyer

BLACK THUNDER PRESS

ISBN: 978-1-7337783-0-5

PUBLISHED BY BLACK THUNDER PRESS

TWO EARLIER EDITIONS OF THIS NOVEL WERE PREVIOUSLY PUBLISHED BY BLACK ROSE WRITING

Printed in the United States of America

Suggested Retail Price (SRP) $18.9

MAXY AWARD WINNER: BEST SUPSENSE THRILLER

Praise for

Kind Nepenthe

"Riveting. Stephen King fans may have finally found a new favorite author in this haunting novel."
—*Best Thrillers*

"This is the kind of book that will make you start looking for excuses to cancel all your plans so you can stay home and keep reading. Atmospheric, suspenseful, well-written. But be forewarned: You may not feel entirely whole when you come out the other side."
—*The North Coast Journal*

"Thoroughly suspenseful and haunting. Brockmeyer's unsettling tale has an effectively slow buildup to an intense boiling point."
—*Kirkus Reviews*

"You don't often come across a debut novel that is so unique in the horror field, one that speaks of scarred humanity so elegantly. For that reason alone, Kind Nepenthe deserves five stars."
—*The Novel Pursuit*

"This story has twists and turns that will be a true pulling factor for thriller readers everywhere. With a building suspense, this novel gets darker and darker as the pages turn. 5 out of 5 stars."
—*Online Book Club*

"Matthew V. Brockmeyer's debut novel looks at life through an alternative lifestyle lens and has accomplished an ultramodern horror thriller. This is a definite five out of five read."
—*Media Bitch*

"Mesmerizing."
—*Horror News*

For Tara, who never gave up on the dream

KIND NEPENTHE

ONE

"Devouring time, blunt thou the lion's paws,
and let the earth devour her own sweet brood."
—Shakespeare, *Sonnet XIX*

"Ring around a rosie, a pocketful of posies,
Ashes, ashes, we all fall down."
—Children's Rhyme

1.

Rebecca Hawthorne couldn't deny it anymore. Her little girl had grown strange since they'd moved to Coyote's compound. And it wasn't just her obsession with ghosts and her refusal to use the outhouse. Or her compulsion to find all the dead ravens in the forest and play with them like they were toys. Stacking them up into shimmering black pyramids, their wings entangled, beaks hanging open.

No. It was something deeper.

A fog seemed to have settled on her, hazing her once lively five-year-old glow, the way a bright pane of glass might slowly turn opaque from the elements: her head always lowered, as though weighted down by thought, her eyes dull and haggard. And no matter how much Rebecca tried to cheer her up, that moody grayness remained.

Megan had always been full of questions, but lately they'd taken on a darker tone.

"Mommy?" she asked as they climbed up the trail, stepping through the patches of light and dark that fell on the forest floor. "Are we going to stay here forever and ever?"

Rebecca shook back her long auburn dreadlocks, pushed up her glasses, and tried to laugh the question off. "Don't be silly. Of course not. Only until we can make enough money to buy our own land. Somewhere we can grow our own food. Have chickens and goats. A flock of ducks. Wouldn't you like that? Your own land with some baby ducks to take care of?"

"Yes. But, Mommy, if there's no such thing as ghosts, why do people say this place is haunted?"

Rebecca pressed her bottom lip between her teeth, wondering where in the hell Megan had picked up all these stupid stories. Was Calendula feeding her this crap? Coyote?

"Oh, sweetie, people say all kinds of things. It's just a silly story. Ghost stories can be fun, but ghosts aren't real." She quickly tried to change the subject. "Those sure were some good huckleberries, huh, kiddo? We were lucky to find some this late in the season."

"Yeah."

"Maybe I'll make pancakes tomorrow morning and we can put the rest of 'em in. Sound good?"

Megan merely nodded, and returned her gaze to the ground.

Rebecca lifted her face to the breeze that swept along the river, over the mossy rocks and bracken ferns and up the steep hillside of manzanita and madrone. A storm was on its way, blowing in over the hills to the west. All the weather forecasts she'd been hearing on the little transistor radio were warning of an El Niño winter: warm Pacific currents from the south bringing heavy rain and wind.

"I think we're going to get some weather, kiddo." She gazed out at the tall redwoods and Douglas fir along the horizon, their branches stirring lazily beneath a gathering of dark clouds. Three buzzards circled far in the distance, honing in on something dead. "Yup, a storm is definitely coming. Feels like a big one, too."

Megan looked up at her, all brown eyes and a smattering of freckles, mouth a purple smear of huckleberry juice. "Should I be scared?"

"No, no, sweetheart." Rebecca stopped and put down her harvest basket. "A rain will be good. The forest will love it and it'll probably keep the frost out of our garden."

She knelt down to fix the collar on Megan's second-hand coat, straighten her frayed corduroy jumper, and gaze into those big eyes.

"Do you remember my Granny Kay?" she asked, licking her thumb and rubbing at the purple stains on Megan's mouth.

Megan nodded her head, squirming away.

"Well, she loved the rain. When it would rain hard at night we would cuddle up on the sofa, wrapped up in a big blanket, and tell each other stories."

"I have a story. Can I tell you my story?

"Sure, kiddo. Let's hear it."

"This is the story of the little girl who lived on a boat in the bathtub."

"She must have been very small?"

"Yes."

10

"Was she a princess or a faerie or something?"

"No. She was just a little girl."

"Okay, well, what's the story?"

"One day her mommy came to the bathtub and the little girl and her boat were so small that the Mommy didn't see them, and she pulled the plunger and—*swoosh*—the little girl on the boat went down the drain, and she was washed out to sea, where there was a bad war clock."

"A war clock?"

"Yes, a war clock. You know, a *boy witch*."

"Oh, a warlock."

"That's what I said, a war clock."

"Right. Yes. So, what happened next?"

"Well, the war clock was very bad and very hungry, so he ate her up."

"He ate her up?"

"Yes."

"Then what?"

"That's it. He ate her up."

"Oh."

"Don't you like it?"

"Well, yeah. But it's so sad. I like stories with happy endings."

"You think it's too sad?"

"Kinda."

"Well, I'll change it for you, Mommy." The girl looked off into the woods for a moment, utterly still. Wind rustled through the dead leaves. "So, then a magic owl came down from the crystal forest and rescued the little girl on the boat. Plucked her right out of the war clock's belly. And the war clock got filled with water and sank to the bottom of the sea. Then the magic owl took the little girl back to her mommy, who said, 'Oh, where were you? I was so worried, I thought I'd accidentally let you go down the drain.' And the little girl said, 'No, Mommy, I'm fine and now we have a new friend, a magic owl.' And the mommy, the little girl who lived on a boat in the bathtub, and the magic owl all lived happily ever after." She glanced up into her mother's face. "Is that better?"

Rebecca forced a smile. "Oh, yes, much better, sweetie."

The preschool teachers back in San Diego all agreed Megan was gifted. *What a good story.* Though it was a little dark, it would actually make a great children's book.

The magic owl.

Did Megan think of Calendula as a magic owl? Her mind clung onto that one positive aspect of the story. He did juggle for her. That was a type of magic. Wasn't it?

2.

The dog—a purebred shar-pei—was going apeshit as usual: snapping and growling at the end of its tether, its face an ugly knot of wrinkles and fangs.

"Shut the fuck up," Diesel said as he limped over to the cooler, bent down—careful not to put too much weight on his bad leg—and dug his huge mitt of a hand into the slush of ice and water. His knuckles were bloody from where he'd scraped them against the truck's underside, hauling on the socket wrench, trying to loosen up the rusty bolts on that old tranny, and the cold felt good. He relished it a moment before wrapping his beefy fingers around a Bud and pulling the beer from the cooler.

Goddamn, if that transmission hadn't almost slipped right out of his hands, tumbled off the jacks, and crushed DJ's head.

He splashed water on his face, cracked the beer open, and gulped down half of it. It spilled from the corners of his mouth and into his beard, now grayer than the fiery-red and pumpkin-orange it had been in his youth.

He'd gotten oil and transmission fluid all over his good flannel shirt and jeans. Amber was going to give him a world of shit about that. He should've worn overalls. Probably had a few pairs in the toolshed, buried in the back somewhere.

He pulled a pack of Marlboros from his front pocket, shook one out and lit it. He was a little spun; he'd been up for a few days. But he had it together. Just had to breathe and concentrate on relaxing. He wanted another bump, another hit, but he had to pace himself. And he *had* to get some sleep tonight. He knew where that lack of sleep brought you. Knew it all too well: that terrible, soul-shattering paranoia. Shadow people lurking in the corners. Scores of tiny insects crawling over everything. And he was never going there again. Never. Especially now. After he had gone so far, accomplished so much. This was his second chance and he wasn't going to fuck it up.

Maybe DJ had some Xanax. That's what he needed. Something

13

to take the fucking edge off.

3.

The path wound down through a patch of cedar. Megan ran ahead and Rebecca watched her scurry along, her little face so serious as she scoured the forest, searching for mushrooms and wild greens.

They were hiking along an overgrown logging road that had been carved into the hillside fifty years ago to haul out the ancient redwoods that used to dominate the forest. It was nothing more than a path now, meandering along above the Santaroga River, on the far-eastern border of Humboldt County, California, near the corner where Humboldt, Mendocino and Trinity counties meet. The Emerald Triangle.

Lichen draped the skeletal branches of the tan oaks like pale-green spider webs. As they walked along, the afternoon sunlight cut through the canopy in coppery shafts that brought Rebecca's mind back to an illustrated Grimm's Fairy Tales book she used to read as a little girl. She thought about Hansel and Gretel trying to find their way back home after the birds had eaten their bread crumbs and, indeed, that's how she felt now: lost.

A part of her was *so fucking over it* and wanted to leave this place. Just run away and leave behind this mess she had gotten herself into. But leaving would mean giving up on the dream. That dream of making enough money to buy their own land. That dream that made her heart flutter and had brought them to this dark corner of Northern California.

Calendula was so adamant that if they just pulled off one more marijuana harvest for Coyote, they'd have enough cash to buy their own property. Then they could start an organic farm and live off the land for real. But she didn't know if she could stay here any longer. All the compromises she'd been forced to make were too much, and Megan's moods seemed to grow more somber every day. She wondered what would happen if she just up and left. Would Calendula refuse to go? Could she leave him, after all they'd been through together?

15

And at this point, she wondered, what was there to go back to?

"Mommy, look!" Megan bounded off the trail and down the steep hillside. She slid quickly through the fallen leaves.

Rebecca nervously followed behind. "Careful, Megan. Careful."

As she watched Megan slip down the hill, Rebecca's heart pounded in her chest. She couldn't see the river from here, the land just disappeared, sinking down into nothingness, but she could hear it: a low murmur of cold water moving over rock.

She was always terrified that Megan would somehow fall into the river. That's what they said happened to the little boy, that he'd drowned here, back in the early seventies, when the place had been a hippie commune. Supposedly his mother had been tripping on acid when she found the corpse and had gone mad, and now his ghost haunted these woods.

That's what people said, but people said all kinds of things about this place. She doubted if half of it was true.

Megan came to a stop in a patch of whitethorn, excitedly pointing down at a brown and yellow clump of flesh that bloomed up from the carpet of decaying leaves. "Look, Mommy. Look!"

Rebecca slid down to her, careful to disturb the hillside as little as possible.

"Good eye, sweetie. Now, what's this mushroom called?"

"Chanterelle, Mommy. Chanterelle is the orange one and oyster is the white one that grows on the trees."

"Oh, you are so smart."

Megan smiled, eyes ablaze with satisfaction while Rebecca knelt into the damp leaves, her ropey dreadlocks falling over her shoulders. She pushed her glasses up her nose and gently broke the mushroom off at the soil line, placing it in her harvest basket. So far, they'd found oyster and chanterelle mushrooms, plantain and miner's lettuce. This was going to be a good lunch. Not only sustainable and healthy, but free, which meant a lot, because they were nearly broke and almost out of groceries.

They'd spent just about the last of their cash on diesel for the grow room. Coyote was supposed to have been back a week ago with money and supplies and they hadn't heard a word from him. Typical.

16

At least the pot was nearly done and ready to harvest.

"Let's get a move on, honey."

They climbed back up to the path and continued along the trail. The land began to plateau near the rusted skeleton of an abandoned excavator, an ancient relic from the logging days. They stopped in a small copse of bay laurel. Rebecca squatted and brushed her hand over a patch of crimson-and-green, clover-shaped foliage blanketing the ground.

"Now, what's this plant called?"

"Redwood sorry."

"Redwood *sorrel*. Taste it. Tangy, huh?"

They each put a few small leaves in their mouths. Megan made a sour face and spit out a green clump. Rebecca laughed and began to pick the greens in a delicate and random manner, gently thinning them so that it appeared none had been taken at all, careful not to pull up any roots.

She could make a spicy pesto with this, though it did have a trace amount of oxalis acid in it so she couldn't use too much. She would have to mix in the plantain, miner's lettuce and whatever other greens she could find. It was still too cold for dandelions. She found herself smiling. This is what it was all about. Teaching Megan to live off the land. Be one with nature.

Then, looking up, Rebecca saw that Megan was standing atop the rotten stump of a redwood, her back to her. *How'd she get up there so fast?*

The stump clung to the edge of the hillside, its exposed roots— dug into the crumbling rock and earth—the only thing keeping the bank up, erosion having washed away the land around it. The river lay below, a moaning maelstrom of rushing water. Megan swayed slightly, leaning forward so that she hung over the edge of the river bank.

"Careful," Rebecca shouted. She could see Megan's little fingers twitch as her hands slowly balled into fists. Megan eased further forward, a little stick figure framed in amber light, bent over the edge, seeming to hang in the empty space past the stump.

Rebecca gasped. *She is going to fall into the river.* She leapt up, basket tumbling aside, and frantically started to run.

Reaching the stump, panting, the coppery taste of fear flooding her mouth, Rebecca held her hands out and tried to keep her voice from trembling as Megan began to sway back again.

"Come on, honey, let's get down from there."

Megan mumbled something Rebecca couldn't make out, her eyes half shut.

"Megan? *Megan!?*"

Megan opened her eyes.

"Please come down from there."

"I'm just looking at the river."

"I know, but it's dangerous." Rebecca held out her hands.

Megan blinked twice, very slowly, then stepped off the stump and into her mother's arms. Rebecca clutched her to her chest then strode away, past the twisted hulk of metal and rust, trying not to squeeze her too tight, fighting to slow her breathing and stop her panting. Telling herself, *It's okay. Everything is okay.*

4.

Diesel Dan eased his bear-sized hulk down to sit on the cooler and concentrated on not grinding his teeth. He watched as his son, DJ, crawled out from under the F250. The boy gave him a curious look, and for a moment Diesel could see himself through his son's eyes: panting, water dripping off his face, beer foam hanging off his graying red beard. Keep it together, he told himself. Keep it together.

"You okay, Pops?" DJ asked.

Diesel took a deep breath. "Yeah, I'm okay. You get all them bolts in?"

"Yeah."

"Good and tight?"

"Yeah, Pops."

"All right then, lower down them jacks and get these tools put away."

DJ nodded, thin lips downturned, and did as he was told.

They had been working on replacing the transmission on the F250 for over five hours. The truck was a present to DJ from Diesel. DJ was soon to be a daddy. All he had to do was help change the transmission and the truck was his. The thing was old, a ninety-six, but in damn-good shape: the rear end recently replaced, the four-wheel drive just worked on. And it had a Reunel bumper with a wench. A nice, big, reliable truck for a new family. Lately Diesel had been trying to make amends. It was no secret what a shitty father he'd been.

DJ pulled the jacks out from under the truck and gathered up the tools. He was tall like his father—six foot three—but bean-pole skinny. Diesel studied him, and thought he dressed like a clown: baseball hat perched half on his head, the straight bill cocked at a goofy angle; several thick, gold chains hanging down over a shiny Lakers jersey; jeans slipping off his hips and exposing his boxers.

Diesel nodded disdainfully at his son's flashy basketball sneakers. "Where's your work boots?"

DJ pulled the socket off a wrench and placed it in the tool box.

"Those things are heavy. Pain in the fucking ass."

Diesel grunted, puffed on his Marlboro.

It wasn't just the annoying clothes bothering Diesel. It was the boy's attitude.

That tranny had nearly fallen right on DJ's head. Some seriously unprofessional shit. Diesel knew better than to be fucking around like that, with the tranny balanced up there on a couple of car jacks. He was a certified diesel mechanic and that was amateur hour.

Crammed under the truck, knuckles ragged, no room to move, for a moment Diesel had seen it clear as day in his mind: the transmission tumbling down onto DJ who stared up stupidly at it, socket wrench in his hand, mouth hanging open, hat on all dopey. Diesel had pictured the boy's face as the metal tore into it, crushing his head into a pulp of blood and bone in the gravel. But then Diesel had snapped back to the here and now, set his jaw, grunted, and hauled the heavy piece of metal back into place, ignoring the sting of sweat in his eyes as he aligned the holes and DJ drove home the bolts and wrenched them in.

All's well that ends well, Diesel supposed, slurping down the last of his beer.

He watched his boy lug the heavy toolbox back to the shed, smudges of oil and grit on his fancy jeans. He should have been there more for him, wished he'd been there more for him. Maybe he could have gotten him to finish high school, train to be a diesel mechanic, like he had. Maybe. Maybe not. But he could have at least been there to see him grow up.

Thinking about it left an emptiness in his chest, as if some inner part of him had grown hollow, like a rotten knot in a tree. He could remember holding him as a baby—so small, cradled in his thick mechanic's arms—and imagining their future together: father and son but best friends, running a diesel-engine-repair shop together. Teaching him the dynamics of a motor, how the pistons moved, explaining the combustion chamber cavity. He saw them in the woods, side by side, chain-sawing rounds of firewood for the coming winter. Up in a tree-stand hunting deer. But that was before that damn excavator had rolled over, crushing his leg.

What had he even been doing up in the cab of that thing? He'd been there to repair the hydraulics, but somehow decided to give it a test drive, drunk as hell. He was at the controls, spinning the house around, lifting the bucket up, and suddenly the damn machine was sliding down the embankment. Then toppling. Trees flashing by. There was the sky, blue and clear, then the ground, sky again, then the impact, and then pain. The pain that'd never really gone away. It took them two hours to get him out of that damn thing.

Because of the alcohol in his system he got no compensation. It only got worse after that. The pain pills, the anger, the bottles of Lord Calvert, the DUIs. Then that damn shoplifting charge, so fucking embarrassing he was ashamed to show his face anymore.

He'd been trying to smuggle a shopping cart out the back exit of the Safeway in Fortuna. And what had been in it? *Hustler* and *Penthouse* magazines, three bottles of Crown Royal, Pampers, a carton of Marlboros, and a remote-control helicopter.

Drunk, of course, and fighting with the cops. Screaming his innocence, and smashing a young CHP in the face with his fist, crushing his nose. Then jail.

That wasn't a one-time deal, either. Happened not just once, but over and over again. The years slipping by. And the meth. Always the meth. Sometimes making him so damn paranoid he sat on the roof with his AR-15 assault rifle and a glass pipe for days, catching people lurking in the shadows from the corner of his eye, seeing bugs crawling over everything.

But meth was a tool. It could be abused or it could be used wisely. It could help. It did help. It got things done. You just had to be careful with it.

Diesel earned his release from his last stint in county five days before his fortieth birthday—14 months for DUI, possession of a controlled substance, and driving on a suspended license. While he'd been inside, his own father, DJ's granddad, had passed on.

He decided he'd had enough. He felt older. Not so stupidly self-destructive anymore. He'd ruined a marriage, destroyed a family, squandered opportunities. It was time to make amends.

That was six years ago. Now he kept his partying in check,

made sure he slept. Ate right. Kept the anger under control. Now his son was going to be a father. DJ's seventeen-year-old girlfriend Katie was six months pregnant. I'm going to be a grandfather, he thought. Imagine that.

5.

Rebecca gazed at the ancient redwoods lining the horizon, already obscuring the afternoon sun. She pondered over how they always loomed out there, a reminder of the deeper, primordial forest, all darkness and shadows. She could hear the neighbor's dog barking out in the distance. It seemed to never stop.

Barking and gunfire. A constant barrage of gunfire.

When they'd first pulled up, what sounded like a machine gun was echoing through the valley. Coyote said not to worry about it, the neighbor—Diesel—was a gun freak. "But he's totally cool," he'd assured them with a lopsided grin. "It's people like Diesel that keep these hills safe. Be grateful we've got a neighbor like him."

But gunfire didn't make Rebecca feel safe. It made her feel uneasy and jumpy.

Paranoid.

And the worst thing was that she really had only herself to blame for being here. It wasn't like she didn't know what she was getting into. She'd worked for Coyote once before. Coming up here to join his crew of misfit hippies at harvest, trimming his weed for him: manicuring the pot, clipping off all the leaves so that there were only large clusters of female flowers, or buds as everyone called them.

She could still hear his smarmy voice, purring from her cellphone when he had called her two months ago: "Just consider it a house-sitting job, *Humboldt County style.*"

He told her he had to leave on urgent business and needed someone to watch over his "scene," explaining how the main responsibility was simply getting diesel for the massive, car-sized, hundred-and-twenty-five-thousand-watt generator: driving the beat-up Dodge Ram to the gas station/general store once a week to fill up the custom hundred-gallon fuel tank bolted to the bed. That and keep the nutrient tanks in the grow room topped off and pH neutral. Make sure the place didn't burn down. Keep the gate shut and locked.

She had been skeptical and very hesitant—something about

Coyote never seemed quite right. With his long, graying ponytail and ever-present, tie-dye T-shirt, he gave off the vibe of a friendly old hippie, always listening to the Grateful Dead or Hendrix. But instead of drinking organic local beer and driving a Prius like so many of his cohorts, he drove a brand-new, gas-guzzling Lincoln Navigator with leather seats, ate at McDonalds, drank Coors light and smoked Camels. And he was always *all* business. He lived in the woods but he was just there to grow pot. It was all money, money, money. And there was something about his hooded eyes and arrogant swagger she didn't trust.

When Calendula heard about the offer, he was ecstatic and immediately began to pressure her to take the job. He had always wanted to live in the woods and grow pot. And so had she, *but not like this*: in the winter, with a stinking diesel generator and some crazy hydroponic system that used chemical fertilizers and pesticides, on a supposedly haunted piece of land people called Homicide Hill.

"I can't just drop everything and go," she'd said, giving Calendula that dead serious, *I mean it* look.

"Why the hell not?" He'd met her gaze head-on with those confident blue eyes, just a touch of a smirk to his mouth. "How many times have you said you want to move to Humboldt? Get out of Southern California? Be in the redwoods? Isn't this the chance you've been waiting for? We can live off the land, be surrounded by nature, cash in off a crop we grew ourselves. You're always saying how you want to live off-grid. Now we have the chance."

They *were* off the grid. No power lines, no phone lines, not even cellphone reception. No TV, no internet. If she wanted to look at Facebook or check her e-mail she had to take her smartphone and drive Calendula's Outback up the bumpy dirt road to the top of the mountain where she could get reception.

She hadn't wanted to go, but Calendula could be so persuasive.

Calendula with his short, spikey, blonde dreadlocks.

Calendula, whose real name was Mark, who grew up in a nice Chicago suburb and used to listen to hip-hop before he went on Phish tour and decided to move to California and live the hippie life.

Calendula, whom she claimed to love but really hadn't even

known a full year, who seemed so different when they worked together at the co-op, kinder and always concerned about the environment and all the other causes that meant so much to her.

Calendula, who had grown strangely feral up here doing his mountain-man thing, always drumming his fingers, his eyes twitchy, no longer gazing into hers with that steady, confident gaze that had originally drawn her to him.

With her almond-shaped eyes and dark lashes, full lips, high cheek bones and long neck, she knew men were attracted to her. She'd catch their stares, even with the thick, black-plastic glasses she wore, thinking they made people take her more seriously.

At the co-op she'd felt their gazes latch onto her as she worked, their eyes lingering a little too long as she organized bundles of organic spinach, rearranged pyramids of mangos and guava. She'd look over her shoulder and see their eyes fall down to her ass, her legs. She'd even catch her boss, that hypocritical prick David, ogling her breasts as he talked to her.

But she had a blunt, fierce manner that scared most men away. She had firm beliefs about what was wrong and right—what she ate, what she wore, what she spent her money on—and when these beliefs were called into question her eyes would go icy cold, her jaw clenched, thick lips pressed till they were thin and bloodless. But Calendula actually seemed to like her fiery nature, agreeing with her strongly about the inherent evil of corporations, the risks of genetically modified foods, the righteousness of vegetarianism, and he never stared at her tits.

Most importantly, he had been there for her when she needed him: when all that shit went down at the Starbucks and those traitors called her crazy and threatened to call the cops or even sue her. During it all he stood resolutely by her side and even defended her.

When it was first announced a Starbucks was going to open in the little seaside town of Ocean Beach, people had been up in arms against it. There'd been a lot of community meetings. She'd gone to them all, denouncing Starbucks as evil. Organized protests followed and she went door-to-door gathering signatures and explaining how a Starbucks would shut down the local mom-and-pop coffee shops, how it would not only destroy the charm of their tiny hamlet, but the economy as well.

But even with all its surfers, bikers, hippies and punk rockers, San Diego was still a conservative, Republican place and she was met mostly with sneers or outright laughter. Once she even got called a terrorist before a door was slammed in her face.

The grand opening of the Starbucks went along exactly as planned. She—and a handful of other protestors—showed up, picketing. No one paid them any mind. Soon the coffee shop was a bustling center of social activity.

But the final blow came about a month after the shop had opened. She was walking down the sidewalk, coming back from dropping Megan off at preschool, and she looked in the large front window of the Starbucks to see some of her fellow protestors inside, chatting over their laptops, smiling as they sipped from steaming paper cups. And there was her boss David, that asshole who was always staring at her chest, sitting right there in the middle of them, stupid smirk on his face as he tapped away on his MacBook Pro.

Traitors. They were traitors and she had told them so. Storming in, knocking over their drinks—their white-vanilla-decaf mochas or whatever the hell they were drinking—splashing them in their faces as she screamed at them. Which was wrong, she knew that, she was a pacifist after all. It was just, *how could they?* And she certainly didn't mean for the coffee to get all over their laptops and tablets. She didn't mean for the MacBook Pro to suffer a meltdown. And who doesn't insure a laptop that expensive?

But Calendula stood beside her during the whole ordeal. Defended her. And she let herself fall in love with him.

Because she did love him, she told herself. She loved the silly banter they always engaged in, teasing each other in that funny, flirty way they had. And he was *so* good to Megan. So attentive and sweet, teaching her the lyrics to Grateful Dead songs so she could sing along with him while he played guitar. Already more of a father to her than that drunken redneck back home in Bakersfield who wanted nothing to do with his own child. That grease monkey changing people's oil while she was trying to find a new way of living.

26

So, when Calendula urged her to drop everything to come up here to Humboldt and take over Coyote's indoor for him, she finally just relented and said yes.

Now she wondered about that decision. She'd given up so much to come here. Could she hope to get any of it back if she decided to leave? Her job at the co-op, just when it was looking like she was going to get a managerial position and not have to work for that shit weasel David anymore. Her apartment. She'd worked so hard: moving from the city, finding an apartment she could afford that was walking distance from the co-op and the Montessori preschool.

She'd made so many compromises. She missed being able to walk everywhere, the convenience and sense of community. Now the nearest store was twenty miles away, a grubby redneck hangout called the Last Chance Market: half gas station, half general store, it sold groceries, ammo, and fertilizer. They didn't carry organic produce or the vegetarian foods she craved, like tofu and tempeh. There was a co-op in Arcata but that was nearly eighty miles away.

And she felt lonely. So lonely. A constant, dull, aching loneliness that rested in the pit of her stomach like a rock.

Not just loneliness. Paranoia. She was paranoid of cops. Paranoid of rip-offs. Paranoid that the generator was going to break down, that the hydroponic system was going to go screwy. Everyone at the Last Chance Market knew what they were up to, going down there once a week and buying all that diesel. They had to—all these weeks—it was obvious, and it must be obvious that they were nearly done, the crop just about ready to harvest. They knew. She could see it in their eyes.

She'd always wanted Megan to be surrounded by nature, in the forest, with trees everywhere. She loved teaching her about medicinal herbs, mushrooms and gardening. But the truth was Megan seemed to be getting weird out here in the sticks.

Megan hated the outhouse. It was a stinky, claptrap little shack up the hill, behind the cookhouse, and Megan would refuse to go to it, even after Rebecca had scrubbed it clean and hung My Little Pony posters on the walls. They had to force her to go there before bed, walking her up and holding the lantern. Talking her into sitting on the old toilet seat. She'd even peed the bed a few times, something she'd never done before. She had potty-trained easily and very early.

And then there was that strange thing she'd done the other night, sitting in the hallway, knocking on that locked door, in some kind of daze, a puddle of urine at her feet as she blabbered on about the ghost of a little boy.

—

As the path twisted around the bend, a clearing revealed Coyote's compound spread out in the valley below them: three small back cabins, and the large main house—the cookhouse they called it— where they lived with the big indoor-marijuana operation. There were also a couple of run-down outbuildings, the generator shack, a trash-filled chicken coop, the cyclone-fenced, hundred-foot-by-forty-foot garden straddling the river, a broken-down Chevy Malibu up on blocks, the rusted-out hulk of a decrepit VW van, and the clay packed road leading off into the hills.

As Rebecca and Megan descended, the path widening into a dirt road, the dull roar of the generator rose from the compound, that incessant drone which, mixing with the hum of the grow lights and buzz of the fans, seemed to permeate her consciousness. She hated that sound. She had come here to be one with nature, to listen to the birds and the whistle of the wind in the trees, not the grinding howl of a diesel motor and the whine of high-pressure sodium bulbs.

Then they were stepping out of the tangle of chaparral— whitethorn and bay—that marked the perimeter of the compound.

After it had been a hippie commune, a bunch of bikers had lived here and the place was trashed: beer cans everywhere, cigarette butts, plastic wrappers, broken toys. It was marshy and dank from always being in the shade of the trees. All of the cabins were covered in moss and in a state of disrepair, the cabin closest to the forest in utter ruins: roof collapsed, poison oak and whitethorn growing up out of it. The cabin beside it had been used as a motorcycle repair shop by the bikers. It had no door and the light that filtered in revealed a floor littered in bolts, brake pads, belts, a rusted motorcycle frame laying on its side. The third cabin was where Coyote lived. It had a brand-new, shiny-red Honda 3000 EU generator parked in front of it, a thick extension cord snaking its way in through a hole in the wall.

Rebecca could never understand why Coyote chose to stay back here, shacked up in this dilapidated back cabin. He claimed it had "ambiance." He'd sit out here for days, weeks, at a time. Brooding, mumbling to himself, staring at the walls, smoking huge joints, tripping on acid. Sometimes, when Rebecca was trimming for him in the cookhouse, she would have to come and get him, ask him for supplies or more weed to trim.

It was always weird and kind of scary. The forest loomed over the back cabins, keeping them in perpetual shadows, and as she stepped into the darkness she would hear Coyote's voice, talking to himself, sometimes laughing, sometimes shouting. He would send her to the store with crazy shopping lists and a wad of cash—crisp, new hundreds. The list would be pages long with obscure items like a magician's wand, a twelve-string guitar, once even "my true wife and children." It was funny, but also really creepy. He'd hand her the list and money and smile his sleazy, offhand smile of yellow teeth, his fat belly poking out of a dirty, tie-dye T-shirt. And she'd go to the store for him, buying disgusting things she wouldn't dream of eating: cheese whiz, marshmallows, candy bars, cans of processed meat, pre-made frozen hamburgers, liters and liters of soda, cases of Coors light, cartons of cigarettes.

Fucking Coyote, who couldn't do anything for himself, who paid local rednecks to set up his pot grows, who paid a young, wannabe-hippie kid to haul his trash to the dump, acting like his land, his weed and his money entitled him to think of all the desperate people around him as servants.

Walking past Coyote's cabin, she couldn't help staring into the large, dark window that faced the trail to the cook house and main road. Peering into its darkness, she imagined a face suddenly materializing there. A ghostly, pale face rising up to look back at her and meet her gaze with glowing eyes set in dark, black pits. The face of a drowned little boy—hair dripping swampy water, bloated lips blue and green. Her face flushed and pinpricks broke out on the underside of her arms. She always did this, freaked herself out. Imagining spooky things or dwelling on stupid stuff. This place just crawled under your skin and got to you.

Once she'd asked Coyote why people called this place Homicide Hill. He just laughed. "They call every hill around here Homicide Hill, and every mountain Murder Mountain. It's the Wild West, baby. Something or other's gone down on every piece of land out here."

She shrugged off a chill, tossed her long dreadlocks over her shoulder, and pushed her glasses up her nose. "Come on," she said to Megan, eager to get away from the creepy back cabins. "I'll race you to the garden."

6.

"All righty, let's give 'er a try." Diesel limped to the cab of the truck, opening the door and heaving himself inside. DJ sauntered over to the other side and pulled himself up into the shotgun seat. Secreting a Bud between his legs, Diesel cranked the engine over. It roared loudly. He gave a wink to his son, slipped the truck in first. "Here we go."

Diesel let out the clutch and gently eased the big truck forward, its tires crunching over the thick layer of gravel he meticulously kept his driveway and yard covered in.

"Aw, snap," DJ said, slapping his hands against his thighs, his sullen face finally cracking into a grin. "We did it."

"What'd you expect, boy? I'm a certified diesel mechanic."

"I know, Pops. I know."

They tooled the truck around the yard, then up the driveway, out the gate, and down the dirt road and into the hills. Diesel revved the engine and shifted gears, speeding up on the straightaways so that the motor groaned and the truck lurched, downshifting for turns. Satisfied, he pulled the truck to the side of the road and spun around. Draining the last of his beer down his throat he crushed the can and, stretching his hand out the window, tossed it into the truck bed.

"Know what? I thought that fucking tranny was going to fall right on your goddamn head. I shit you not." He laughed. "Woulda' been a fucking mess, too, I tell you what."

"I saw it slipping, yo, and damn near crapped myself."

They both chuckled.

"How you and Katie getting along?"

"We're good."

"Ready to be a daddy?"

"Yeah."

"Yeah?"

"Yeah, Pops."

"Laying off that fucking meth?"

"Yeah, Pops." DJ looked away, out the window to the fog

draped firs looming behind the rolling hills.

"That shit will drive you fucking crazy, son. I tell you."

"Well, you should fucking know."

"That's right. I fucking do. I fucking do." He grunted, sighed, found himself unconsciously grinding his teeth. "You got any of them Xanax?" he asked, catching his reflection in the overhead rearview: beard untrimmed, disheveled hair sticking up, oil smeared across his forehead. Look like some kind of lunatic Paul Bunyan, he thought.

"What's wrong, Pops? Can't sleep?"

"Yeah, you could say that."

"Sure, I got some bars." DJ pulled an amber prescription bottle from his pocket, unscrewed the top, looked in, and rattled the bottle. "Maybe fifteen of 'em. Here, have 'em."

He passed the bottle to Diesel, who tucked it in his front pocket beside his Marlboros. "You need some cash?"

"Naw, don't worry about it, Pops."

"How's your mother doing?"

"She's fine. Doing fine."

"Still up in Eureka with that asshole?"

"Still up in Eureka with that asshole."

Diesel chuckled and clucked his tongue.

—

They rolled down the driveway to Diesel's property, past the wood chipper and four-wheeler, both neatly covered in tarps secured with tie downs, past Diesel's own truck, a red F350 dually, and pulled up beside the toolshed, its sliding wooden doors open and exposing a neatly hung line of chainsaws, an acetylene and oxygen tank in the shadows, draped with coiled green tubing.

Diesel eased the truck to a stop beside the old transmission.

"Righty, boy. Now help me get this old transmission in the back of yer truck."

"What am I going to do with it, Pops?"

"Ain't my fucking problem, just get it out of here. Shit, I leave that thing here Amber'll never let me hear the end of it. Calls me a fucking hoarder."

They got out of the truck and went to stand on either side of the transmission, Diesel limping and DJ's lanky body moving with a jaunty gait, nodding his head to some hip-hop song only he could hear.

"On three, boy. You ready?"

"Yeah."

"Kay, one, two, THREE."

They heaved up the heavy hunk of metal and slid it into the bed of the truck, its shocks groaning under the weight.

Diesel slapped his hands together. "Now let's go see the gals." He threw his arm around his son's shoulders, gripping his neck and giving him a little shake as they made their way to the porch steps. A rush of pride went through him. He'd built this whole house up from nothing but a shack, with his own goddamn hands.

He'd inherited the house from his father. It was nothing but a hunting cabin then, passed on from his grandfather. The first thing he'd done was build the large shed for all his tools. Then he replaced the decaying post-and-beam foundation with cinder blocks, ripped off the old, leaky tin roof and put on a new one with the finest composite roofing he could find.

The next year he covered it in gleaming white aluminum siding and wrapped an elaborate deck around it, installed a beautiful, custom, wood-and-stained-glass front door. After Amber showed up, he added a bathroom: put in a septic and a big whirlpool tub. Then he started building a massive great room on the back side, which was now just an unfinished and elaborate skeleton of two-by-sixes.

It was a work in progress, but compared to some of the clapboard shanties on the mountain, it was a palace. His palace.

Pushing the door open, he thought to himself, Ain't it a good goddamn day?

7.

Listening to the rhythmic glug-glug of fuel slurping into the rusted tank, Calendula watched Rebecca and Megan race down to the garden, his left eye twitching as he nervously rubbed his thumb in circles against the wart that'd recently grown on his index finger. From where he sat, perched atop the large fuel tank that led to the generator, pumping diesel into it from the tank welded to the back of the old Dodge Ram pickup, he'd been able to see them perfectly when they appeared out of the woods by the back shacks.

Diesel fumes wafted up and he rubbed at his eyes with his free hand. His head ached. It always did. He didn't know if it was the roar of the generator or the electrical discharge of the grow lights but this humming had started in his skull that he couldn't seem to shake.

He topped off the tank, replaced the cap, and hopped down to the ground, his spiky blonde dreadlocks bouncing to and fro.

Stepping into the dilapidated generator shack, he set about making sure the lines were secure. The generator—a bright-orange, 125,000 watt MQ WhisperWatt, roughly the size of VW van—coughed and sputtered twice, belching out dark, sulphur-reeking clouds of exhaust. His heart skipped a beat before it loudly began to purr once more. That the generator would stop running was one of his biggest fears. Keeping the fuel tank full had become an obsession. Coyote had warned him that if it ever ran out, it would be hell getting the bastard started again.

He checked the control panel: water temperature, oil pressure, engine microprocessor, frequency, amps, volts. Everything looked good. He'd changed the oil last week, cleaned the air filter. The lines seemed tight. Satisfied, he stepped out of the roar and stink of the shack and headed towards the wood pile.

Two ravens fighting over the guts of something dead paused for a moment to caw at him as he made his way across the trash-strewn yard. As he came abreast of them, the big black birds shrieked, beating their wings into a fury before flying off to the safety of an oak branch and staring contemptuously down at him.

The place was ruled by ravens. They were everywhere. They survived off trash, turning over garbage cans and tearing into the garbage bags, gulping down scraps of food and strewing the trees with bits of shiny refuse: foil, tuna fish cans, bottle tops. There were dead ones all around, too, their black bodies littering the ground like pockets of shadow. It was a weird thing—all the dead birds—something Calendula thought might have to do with the pesticides Coyote used. Several times they had found Megan playing with them. Making little piles. Stretching out their dirty wings so that they appeared in flight. It never failed to freak the hell out of Rebecca.

Pulling the tarp off the wood pile, Calendula watched Rebecca and Megan working in the garden behind the industrial, six-foot-tall chain-link fence. The fence stood out amid the squalor because it was shiny and new, well maintained. Anything that had something to do with pot growing Coyote kept pristine. That was his way. Everything else he let rot and crumble.

Seeing Rebecca and Megan shuffle about with their harvest baskets caused a sensation of warmth to flood Calendula's body. Rebecca, with her long dreadlocks and curvy body, looked unspeakably beautiful, and Megan was so fun and smart and cute. Having a kid around was a real joy, something he hadn't expected.

He loved them devotedly, ferociously. Inside himself he burned to shelter and guard them, watch over them, but also to claim them. To own them. Protect them the way a dog might fight off other dogs from a bitch in heat. A selfish love full of pride. He wished his suburban, wannabe-gangsta friends back home could see him now: a hot, dready girlfriend and full responsibility for a major pot grow.

The grow.

Sometimes it was all he could see. He'd find himself losing focus, his mind lost in imagining those big fists of lime-green colas, swelling, stinking, dank. Rebecca would snap her fingers at him. "Hello? McFly? Anybody home?" He'd smile, "Yeah, baby, what's up?" But even though he would be smiling and looking at her, his mind would still be on those long rows of herb stretched out under the grow lights. He would stay in the grow room until his face burned red and his eyes began to ache—pruning leaves, staking branches, checking meters, marveling at it all. O.G Kush, New York Sour Diesel, Girl Scout Cookie, Green Crack. Say what you wanted about Coyote, but the man knew his herb and got only the best, trendiest strains. The ones guaranteed to sell and make your head spin.

Calendula gathered up an armload of firewood and started down the trail back to the cookhouse. Because his and Rebecca's bedroom was connected to the grow room it never got cold, but the rest of the house, including the back room where Megan slept, would get freezing if they didn't keep a fire going in the old top loader: the funny, antique wood stove, which was actually a converted coal burner.

He made his way past the random junk that lay strewn everywhere: a truck axle, hub caps, a shot-to-shit tube television on a stump, stacks of plastic five-gallon buckets, a couple car batteries, cases and cases of empty beer bottles. The path snaked past a row of mismatched solar panels leaning against a shaky wooden frame Calendula had constructed. When they'd first gotten there the panels were lying on the ground, covered in oak leaves.

"What's up with the solar panels?" Calendula had asked Coyote.

Coyote had taken a sip of his beer, scratched his belly, and puffed on a cigarette. "Nothing's up with them."

"Can I hook them up?"

"Do what you want with them, just don't fuck with the roof. That's why they're there. Guy I had working for me a while back put 'em on the roof and made the damn thing leak." He gestured with his can of Coors Light over to where a tarp was draped over the roof. "Right over the grow room, too. What a fucking idiot. The water shorted out the lights and almost burned the place down."

"Well, we could build an array on the ground, over there where there's less shade."

"Whatever. We gotta 125,000 watt generator running damn near all the time, so I don't even see the need."

"Every little bit counts, right? Reduce, reuse, recycle. You know, I am a permaculture designer, and alternative energy systems were part of my certification process."

Coyote gave him a strange look, as if he didn't know what the hell he was talking about and didn't care, then shrugged, grunted, and walked away.

Calendula made the wooden frame for the panels out of scrap lumber he found lying around, but when he tried to assemble everything he discovered someone had looted parts of the system. There was a breaker box, and four big L16 batteries, but the charge controller and inverter had been pulled out and were missing, the wires that went into them ripped up and exposed. He thought about trying to rig up some sort of DC system, maybe just a reading light and a radio, but finally came around to Coyote's thinking: there's a generator running all the time, what's the use?

Slick, muddy patches lay on the trail from where the frost had melted that morning, and as he passed the old chicken shack, its wire-encased pen filled to the brim with raven-pecked bags of garbage, his sneakers slipped in the mud and he fell hard on his ass.

"Damn it," he muttered, thinking that as soon as he got paid he was going to buy a pair of heavy-duty lumberjack boots like all the local rednecks wore and scrap the baggy corduroy pants for warm, tough, double-kneed work pants. Maybe even a camouflaged jacket and a wool cap to hide his dreads in, so he could fit in and not be such an eyesore at the Last Chance Market.

He awkwardly got back up, backside soaked, steadied himself, and hauled the armload of wood past the chicken shack and onto the dilapidated screened-in porch, moss-covered strips of screen hanging off the frame. Pushing the door to the cookhouse open with his shoulder, he stomped through the kitchen and into the tiny living room.

It was called the cookhouse because it had been the mess hall for the logging operation that ran out of here back in the sixties. The three back rooms down the hall, one Megan's bedroom, one where Rebecca had set up her herbal business office, and the other a storage room Coyote had padlocked off, had been the cooks' quarters. The enormous grow room, whose entrance lay in the master bedroom where he and Rebecca slept, had been the dining hall, where rows of tables once fed crews of loggers. There was a tiny living room where the top loader sat, and a large kitchen with two double sinks and a huge range with eight burners.

Calendula added his armload of wood to the pile beside the old top loader. Getting it started could be tricky, having to reach down into its soot-caked opening, so he liked to always keep some coals burning. He opened it up and poked a stick down into the ashes, stirring up a few glowing embers. He pushed a couple of twigs in, adjusted the damper, and watched as a tendril of fire crept up and curled around the kindling. Adding larger pieces as the flames danced and grew, his eye began to twitch again. He hadn't had an eye twitch this bad since high school. Senior year. When he began to suspect that his supposed homey Brian Evans was fucking his girlfriend, Chelsea Beaumont.

Ever since he'd gotten here he felt nervous and twitchy. But also utterly ecstatic, like he was on some kind of amphetamine. As he watched the fire catch and roar into life he once again nervously ran his thumb over the scales of the wart on his finger and thought about his situation.

He had to convince Rebecca to stay for another run.

He'd mastered this grow room and wasn't going to let all his hard work and new-gained knowledge go to waste. Nine grand: that was what they were going to get for the last nine weeks, and what was that? Nothing. But Coyote had promised them half of the next grow if they stayed for another run. Half. You could get ninety pounds easy out of that room, easy, maybe even twice that if the crop came out perfect. Now that was some cake. If they could walk away from here with close to a hundred grand that could be their nest egg. All they'd need to make a start, put a down payment on a piece of land. He had to convince her.

The hum of the grow room permeated the building, saturating the air, making the walls tremble. *The grow room.* It was always there: the buzzing of the lights, the churning of the fans, and very faintly, beneath it all, the hydroponic solution slurping through tubes, circulating like blood in a body. A click and a whoosh as a sensor triggered the air conditioners to life. It was truly a living, breathing

thing. It was alive.

Rebecca didn't like it. Though she was quick to say how good the plants looked and what a good job Calendula was doing, she would rarely go in, and often complained about all the plastic and chemicals, about the way it sucked up such huge amounts of diesel and fertilizer. But to him, it was a thing of utter beauty: an exquisite, mad scientist's laboratory, like something from a monster movie with tubes and wires running everywhere, flashing meters and sensors, one wall covered with panels of breakers and timers, labyrinthine heavy-duty electrical wires running from humming ballasts, CO2 tanks standing on the periphery.

In the beginning Calendula had been overwhelmed by it all. The first time he entered the cavernous room, Coyote casually swinging the door open with that usual look of bored disdain in his hooded eyes, and Calendula had been stupefied. For one the room was so huge. It was hard to tell from the outside of the house that there was a room this big inside it; it seemed impossible. And the set up: a hundred high-pressure sodium, thousand-watt lights, air-cooled and connected with ducting, hanging on adjustable chains from the ceiling over a maze of three-gallon blue containers connected to two-inch white pipes. Each container held a one-gallon basket of orange lava rock with a two-foot-tall plant growing out of it. Twelve hundred plants in all. The plants' canopies all touched, making a sheet of green which glowed preternaturally under the intense white light. The tubes connecting the containers snaked their way across the floor and up to eight two-hundred-gallon tubs of nutrient solution that lined the far wall, bubbling and gurgling, faucets, drains, aerators and heaters poking out, wires running down into the solution from wall mounted pH and ppm meters.

"I know what you're thinking," Coyote had said, "but it's not as complicated as it looks. It's basically self-regulating. You just got to keep an eye on the pH and ppm meters, adjust the fertilizer mix week to week."

That was over two months ago and now Calendula knew that room, that laboratory, inside and out. Intimately. He was constantly checking the pH and ppm. He'd meticulously followed the fertilizer schedule, gradually increasing the phosphorous, lowering the nitrogen, adding aminos and catalysts. Then, as the buds swelled and the hairs darkened and shriveled, he'd finally flushed the whole system with flora clean, and for the last week had kept it running with nothing but water. Over half the hairs on the plants were dark now, the calyxes bulbous, coated in a thick blanket of glistening white crystals. He spent hours every day pruning back the lower branches, plucking large fan leaves that shaded parts of the plant, making sure every flowering branch received direct light.

Even when he wasn't in the grow room it permeated his consciousness, filling his brain, controlling his thoughts. Staring down into the open top loader, thumbing his wart, his left eye twitching, he grinned an idiot's grin and giggled quietly as he wondered: Who serves who? Do I control the grow room, or does the grow room control me?

8.

As Diesel and DJ came in the door, Amber began to frantically shout at them. "Shoes, boys, shoes!" She came from Tennessee and had a thick, Smoky Mountain drawl.

She'd come out here for the Redwood Harley Run a couple years back, met Diesel in a bar in Garberville—the Branding Iron—and never left. She was a pretty woman with long dark hair, high cheek bones and kind, warm eyes. But the skin on her face was stretched too tight, giving her a gaunt, skeletal look, and her teeth were a brown and yellow mess, littered with black, empty gaps.

She was wearing a black Harley shirt that had been custom cut into elaborate fringes, and sat cross-legged on a brand-new, white, L-shaped sectional sofa, smoking a cigarette and pointing a remote at the eighty-five-inch flat-screen television that dominated the far wall. Two glass display cases, which didn't match, were crammed in the corners on either side of the television, jammed full of random knickknacks.

Beside her sat Katie, a sweet-looking girl who appeared more fourteen than seventeen, gazing at an iPad perched on the mound of her pregnant belly.

"Yeah, yeah, we know." Diesel squatted down onto a stool by the door to unlace his heavy, black-leather logger boots. DJ slipped easily out of his basketball sneakers and gave Katie a curt nod when she turned and shyly smiled at him.

"Look at y'all," Amber said, "a filthy couple of grease monkeys." She crushed her cigarette into a large, Christmas-themed ashtray with a smiling Santa Claus that sat on the end table nearest her, amongst a clutter of porcelain figurines. "Y'all are just gonna ruin this here sectional. Let me get a sheet for y'all to sit on." She disappeared down the hall and returned a moment later with a sheet which she draped over the sofa, patting it and smiling. "There you go, boys."

Diesel grunted and limped past a stack of boxes given to him by customers looking for a good deal on meth: a George Foreman grill,

41

a stereo receiver, walkie-talkies, Legos. His trusty AR-15 leaned against the pile, the black metal well-oiled and gleaming. He made it to the sofa and eased himself down onto the sheet. "How you like that iPad, Katie?"

Katie looked up, her face a glow. "I love it, Diesel. Thank you so much." She really was a pretty little girl, Diesel thought, giving her his best fatherly smile. She was going to make one damn-good-looking grandson for him, that's for sure.

"Katie, you're family now. I want you to call me Pops like everyone else around here."

She blushed and looked down for a moment. "Okay, Pops."

Amber pulled her legs back up onto the sofa, curling herself around her knees, and flicked the remote again. "How'd it go with the transmission?" she asked absently.

"Good," DJ said. "Got her in there and she's running great."

"Well that's wonderful, honey. I just knew you boys would get 'er in there." Her eyes never left the screen as she continued to flick the remote, finally stopping at QVC.

"Damn straight," Diesel said. "I am a certified Diesel mechanic."

DJ sighed loudly and Amber patted Diesel's thigh. "We know, honey. We know."

Stretching out a bony hand, Amber picked up her lighter—encased in a black-leather case—lit another Newport 100, and blowing a blue jet of smoke from her mouth, leaned conspiratorially over to Katie and whispered, "You see that little elf they got for sale there? Now, isn't that the cutest thing? That darling little elf there?"

"It really is," Katie said.

DJ rubbed at a spot of grease on his jeans. "I saw Coyote's new workers yesterday down at the Last Chance Market. Bunch'a dread-locked super hippies."

Diesel said, "Yeah, I seen 'em around, too.".

"They was filling up on diesel."

"I'm sure they were."

"Driving *your* old truck. The Ram with the custom tank."

"I said I seen 'em."

"Well aren't you going to do something? That fucker owes us

42

fifty grand."

"Owes me, boy. *Me*. Now mind your own business."

"Bullshit, Pops. I helped set up that grow room. I wired it. We put in that whole hydroponics unit."

"You'll get what's coming to you. Now quiet it up."

"That Coyote shouldn't even be over there anyhow. That should be our land. Now this Coyote has got a parade of freaks coming through there. Blowing the whole mountain up, in front of God and everybody."

Diesel reached over and took his son's thin shoulder in his big hand, giving a firm, steady and mildly threatening squeeze that he could feel DJ recoiling from.

"I said, it's none your business, *boy*. Listen, this is the best my life has ever been. I'm not going to risk going back to prison for something stupid. I don't want any trouble. Now let it rest."

He relaxed his grip on DJ's shoulder, and DJ violently shrugged the hand off, his face twisted into a look of utter contempt.

"And I don't want you getting yourself in any trouble either, son. Specially on my account."

"Yo, I'm only trying to look out for *you*, Pops. It ain't right."

"Well, it is what it is."

"Shit, I've got my own forty acres. Land I bought with my own damn money."

"I know that, son. I know. And I'm proud of you, too. Damn proud." Diesel's brother, Steve, who lived down in Sacramento now, had sold DJ the last of his inherited land at a good price, to keep it in the family. Whenever Diesel got on DJ's case about anything, the boy was quick to bring up how he had bought his own hunk of property. "But I can handle my own problems."

The two stared at each other in uncomfortable silence for a moment. Then DJ stood up, brushed something from his shiny basketball jersey, now stained in grease. "Come on, Katie, we gotta get going."

"Kay," she said, pushing herself up from the sofa.

Diesel looked at his boy's face. Eyes narrowed, jaw clenched. He hadn't meant to make him angry. He pushed himself awkwardly up and limped to the corner, carefully setting his rifle aside before he started rummaging through the mound of merchandise piled up there. "Now, Katie, I got a case for that iPad over here somewhere, one of them good Otter cases to keep that thing protected. Ahh, here it is."

He limped up to the doorway and offered her the cover. She took it in her small hands and looked up at him—a little-girl face with big, wet eyes.

"Thank you, Pops. For everything, the truck, the iPad, everything." She threw her thin arms around his hulk, pressing her cheek into his chest and pushing her swollen belly against him, squeezing.

"Well you're sure as shit welcome, sweetie." He swallowed her up in his arms, gently patting her back. "You're a wonderful addition to the family. You just take care of that little one you got in you. That's my grandson in there."

"I will," she said, wiping tears from her eyes.

DJ pulled on his basketball shoes. "Come on, Katie," he said, opening the door.

As they walked out to the truck, the dog barking and snapping, Diesel stood in the doorway. Katie climbed into the passenger seat, and he called out, "I already got a whole mess of clothes and toys for the little critter when he gets here."

DJ hopped in the driver's seat, turning the loud diesel engine over. Katie waved as the truck lurched forward, its tires kicking up a small shower of gravel.

"Watch the fucking gravel!" Diesel shouted as the truck pulled up the driveway. He watched the pick-up move away up the driveway and into the hills.

He had to admit, DJ was right. They *had* put in that whole indoor setup. Wired it. Gotten Coyote the generator at a good price and tuned it. Installed all the lights. Set up the hydroponic system. Even got the lazy, hippie fucking bastard the clones. And the fat, hood-eyed, weasely fucker still owed him fifty grand. And Diesel didn't like people bringing outsiders here anymore than anyone else. Especially with a little girl. She couldn't be older than five or six. That was no place for a child. That place was so hot if you spit it sizzled. Who knows how many bodies Spider had buried out there. He'd taken care of a lot of people before getting taken care of himself, gunned down right there in the back cabin.

Diesel had been in prison when Spider was murdered. Apparently there was a big hub-bub and lots of commotion with the cops and their murder investigation. But nothing ever came of it. Nothing ever did out here. When he got out of the slammer that joker Coyote had somehow bought the place. Diesel never had a chance to get it back to his family. DJ was right, that land really should be theirs. It had been in the family for years. He had a deal with Spider, too, to get that hundred acres back. Spider had owed him. Diesel was probably the only one who *hadn't* wanted that dirt-bag dead.

Back in the day, Diesel's family had owned all the land out here. His cousin Bobby was the only one left with a big chunk: a five-thousand-acre cattle ranch. But Bobby was getting old and Diesel had no doubt that when he died his kids would subdivide it up and sell it for maximum value. They had no interest in ranching.

His grandfather had been the one who leased the land to Pacific Lumber, then grazed sheep in the meadows. They called them meadows back then, not clear cuts. His grandfather had brought the first hippies out here. Sold them the land for their commune. That crazy old hippie commune. Grandpappy thought they were neat-o. No one wanted that land anyway, a steep and rocky hundred acres: no good for sheep or cattle, and he sold it for twice the price that it should have been: fifty bucks an acre instead of twenty-five. Crazy how cheap land went in the old days. But it wasn't *that* bad a piece. It had that old cookhouse—which was a big, solid structure—those back cabins, and good water with the river there.

He could remember being a little boy and seeing his grandpappy at the Last Chance Market, in overalls and a Caterpillar baseball hat, holding court with all the locals, defending his decision to sell the hippies land.

"They're nice kids. Let 'em have it, see what they do. If they can make something out of it, good for them. Genepool's too fucking small out here anyway."

Diesel had known the little boy that drowned over there—

Tommy. They were the same age and had played together. He couldn't really remember him, couldn't even put a face with the name, just remembered being told: *You used to play with him. Before he drowned.*

Now all Diesel had left was this two-hundred-acre piece which used to be his dad's, right fucking next to the old hippie commune. It was crazy the way this place was subdivided up. When he was a kid you could just walk and walk for miles and miles. Nothing but hills and cattle. Find hidden creeks, patches of spooky woods. Now it seemed every forty-acre piece had somebody on it, growing herb, and no one wanted anybody walking around anywhere anymore.

DJ's truck disappeared into the hills and the last bit of dust faded up into the gathering storm clouds. Diesel was unsure just how he should go about laying down the law with the boy, especially now that he was full grown. He had never been there to discipline him when he was a child, had never been much of a father to him at all. He grappled with how to make things crystal clear now, how far to take it. He had to tell him not to meddle in his business, had to let him know who was boss, but he had to control his anger, too, that rage that he always felt brewing within him, that rage he was always struggling with, that rage that always drove him wild and got him in so much fucking trouble.

And there was that other thing. That thing that sometimes woke him up at night, making his heart pound, knowing he wouldn't get back to sleep: DJ had once watched Diesel beat his mother to the ground. DJ couldn't have been older than six or seven at the time.

Diesel and DJ's mother—Ella—were arguing. He couldn't remember why. He couldn't remember much of it at all. He was blacked-out drunk, of course. Woke up in jail. But later he had seen the bandaged face, purple, blue and yellow bruises, arm in a sling. Seen it when she got her stuff and finally left him for good, taking DJ and moving to Eureka, getting an apartment and a job at the new Target store out where the Montgomery Wards used to be.

Though his recall of that night was mostly blurred at best, one thing stuck stubbornly in his mind: DJ, up and out of bed, in his pajamas, staring at him. Not crying, or screaming, just standing there, staring. Ella on the floor, whimpering. Sometimes he awoke at night and that was the image in his head, little DJ, just staring at him.

He sighed. Ran a hand down his face, through his tangled beard, and went back into his palace.

9.

Running down the trail, Rebecca slowed and let Megan pass her and reach the garden gate first.

"Beat you, Mommy. Beat you."

"You sure did, kiddo. When'd you get so fast?"

"I've always been fast. You know that."

Rebecca laughed, undid the latch on the door and swung it open, Megan scurrying in and running off down the center path. Putting her hands on her hips, Rebecca surveyed the damage from the spate of frosts they'd had. Lettuce brown and wilted. Broccoli and cabbage starts she'd lugged all the way up here from San Diego lying dead, flat on the ground.

At least the kale looked good. And the fava beans had all germinated, their thick green sprouts rising robustly from the earth. Four twenty-foot rows, *a lot* of fava beans. She should have an excellent crop in the spring, *if* they were still here then. She could make all kinds of soups and stews, and if you dried them out, favas kept real good. She should end up with jars and jars of them. *If she stayed*.

She pulled up all the wilted broccoli and cabbage and carried it over to the compost. Two ravens sat atop the fence, squawking at her in their weird, frog-like croaks.

"Go on, get!" she motioned at them with her arms, but they stayed their ground, staring sullenly down at her. God, how she'd learned to hate these fucking birds.

She draped the vegetable matter over the top of the compost, covered it in a thin layer of straw, and mixed it all up with a pitchfork. The ravens shifted their weight from one foot to the other, never taking their black eyes from her.

She leaned the pitchfork against the fence and turned to see Megan at the far side of the garden, leaning against the fence, staring down the embankment at the river.

Rebecca came up from behind. "Whatcha' doing, kiddo?"

"Mommy, who's Spider?"

"Spider? Like the bug?"

"No. A man named Spider. Did a man named Spider live here?"

"I don't know, sweetie. Why?"

"Just wondering."

"Where'd you hear about this Spider?"

"Dunno. I think I dreamed about him."

Rebecca was struck silent, the hairs on the back of her neck tingling. She *had* heard talk of a Spider who once lived here. Not much. None of it good. Coyote refused to talk about him, except to say he was the biker who owned the place before him. *Where could Megan be getting this stuff?*

"Come on, honey. Let's pick some mint for tea. Wouldn't you like some hot mint tea?"

Megan nodded and silently turned from the river.

—

Pushing open the front door of the cookhouse, Rebecca looked down the hall to see Calendula in the little living room, staring down into the top loader at the crackling fire. He didn't even notice her walking up behind him.

"Hello? Ground control to Major Tom?"

He started and looked up with a weird, spooky glare in his eye, like he didn't know who she was for a second. "Oh, hey, baby. I didn't hear you come in."

"Yeah, I noticed. What were you doing?"

"Thinking."

"Thinking about what, pussy cat? The mouse that got away?" She put her hand on her hip and cocked her head at him playfully, until that warm, confident grin she loved so much finally spread across his face.

"How much I love that pouty face of yours, is what." He strode up to her and cupped her chin in his hands. "Oh, look at those stubborn, stubborn lips." He leaned in for a kiss.

49

"Uh-uh, mister." She gently pushed him away, then finally relented and let him give her a peck on the lips. "Observe the earth's sweet bounty," she said, proudly displaying her harvest basket full of greens and mushrooms.

"Impressive, but nothing compared to your sweet kisses." He pushed himself up against her, nuzzling her neck and looping his arms around her back.

"Oh, gross. Are you guys making out?"

"We're not making out, Megan. Just expressing our love. And where'd you get that word from, anyway? Making out?"

"It's two words, Mommy. Making and out."

"Okay, smarty pants, take the basket and put it on the counter in the kitchen with the mint."

Megan picked up the harvest basket and lugged it into the kitchen.

"She is something," Calendula said, nuzzling Rebecca's ear, his hands dropping down to cradle her ass.

"And so are you, mister. Stop that."

He gave her rump a gentle squeeze. "Earth's sweet bounty indeed."

She pushed him away and tossed her dreadlocks back with the flick of her head, gazed at him over her glasses which had slipped down her nose. "Hey, did you tell Megan about Spider?"

"Spider? Who's Spider?"

"The guy who lived here before Coyote."

"Nope. Never even heard of him."

"She was talking about him. In a really creepy way. Says she dreamed about him."

"Huh. Well, you know kids. Imaginations always working overtime. She must have just picked up the name somewhere."

"She also almost fell off a stump into the river."

"She did what?"

—

Megan sat at the kitchen table, working on her puzzle. First finding all the flat pieces that made up the edge, then the ones that fit in-between. She could hear Calendula and her mother talking in the other room.

She knew the little boy was in the cupboard under the sink. She didn't know *how* she knew this.

She just knew.

Just like she knew he'd been in that locked room the night she'd peed herself.

She got up and went to the cupboard, bent down, and slowly pulled open the door.

It was dark in there. But she could seem him, crammed into the far back corner, behind a few scattered mouse traps: a tuft of black hair over large, sad eyes. He wore only a tattered pair of cut-off jeans, cinched with a frayed piece of rope.

"I can see you hiding in there."

"I know," he said.

"Why are you in there?"

"I like it here. I come here to hide."

"Why are you hiding?"

"Just am. Listen, we can be friends. But you can't tell anyone about me."

"Why not?"

"Just can't. Promise?"

"Okay."

"I can teach you a song. My favorite song. Do you want to learn it?"

"Sure."

"It goes like this, 'The leaves are all brown...'"

He sang with a sweet melodic rhythm that sounded beautiful to her ears. She repeated the words, trying to get the same sound out of them that the boy had, but then Rebecca was coming down the hall and the boy was suddenly gone.

She quickly shut the door and backed away. She knew her mother wouldn't want her playing in there. Not with all the mouse traps Calendula was always setting. His "trap lines." She'd also promised the boy she wouldn't tell about him, and a promise was a promise. She went back to the table, studying the puzzle.

—

Rebecca began to wash the kale and mushrooms in the big kitchen sink. "Hungry, kiddo?"

"Yeah. Mommy, do you know this song, 'The leaves are all brown.'"

"Sure. 'California Dreamin'.' But you got the lyrics wrong."

"Oh," Megan said, going back to her puzzle pieces.

Rebecca put a pot of rice on to steam. Calendula had gone back to the grow room to check on CO2 regulators or something, but she could hear him stomping back out through the bedroom now. He came into the kitchen, planted a kiss atop Megan's head.

"CO2 tank is empty."

"Hmm," she said. She didn't see the need for putting carbon dioxide in the air anyway, there was plenty naturally already, and it wasn't sustainable. Wasn't that the beauty of plants to begin with? That they turned carbon dioxide into fresh oxygen? But she wasn't going to bring it up. She knew it got on his nerves when she complained how unsustainable the grow room was. The size of its carbon footprint. Knew he'd just say, "When we get our own land we'll do it right."

Calendula started poking around in the lower cabinets, murmuring to himself, looking at the mouse traps. He made his way to the cabinets below where Rebecca was dicing the mushrooms.

"Excuse me, baby. Just checking my trap lines."

"Can you please not do that now. It's totally gross."

"That is so weird," he said. "It happened again. Five traps set off and missing bait, three just gone. Gone. And no sign of any mice at all. It must be something big like wood rats or something sneaking in here somehow and taking off with them."

"Ugh, Calendula, please."

"Country living, baby." He gave her a little pinch. "You better toughen up if you want to make it."

"I warn you, I'm holding a knife."

"I thought you were a pacifist."

52

"Only politically, mister, not personally." She softly elbowed him in the ribs. "I've always stood up for a woman's right to defend herself."

"Typical, liberal hypocrisy." Growling, he playfully snapped at her ear.

"Will you get out of here, you old bear? I'm trying to cook us lunch."

He gave another growl, kissed her cheek and went.

Rebecca dry-fried the mushrooms and steamed the kale and chard, throwing in a handful of raisins and pine nuts. When the mushrooms stopped secreting water she tossed in a bit of diced garlic and ginger.

She took out three plates, placing a pile of rice on each one. Atop this she placed the mushrooms, draping them with steamed kale and chard. She scattered raisins and pine nuts over it all, sprinkled a little blend of herbs she'd mixed up to boost the immune system, and added a bit of redwood sorrel as a garnish. She still had half a loaf of her homemade rosemary bread left and she cut a thick slice for each of them. She poured boiling water into three mugs filled with mint leaves and plopped a metal straw into each.

"Presto! Look at *that*," she said. "Healthy and cheap." It was cheap, too. She'd bought the organic rice in fifty-pound bags for a bulk price. The most expensive thing was the pine nuts but she allowed for this luxury for she was constantly making some sort of pesto creation out of wild greens. Walnuts were cheaper, but not the same, so she gave herself this indulgence.

Rebecca watched Calendula gulp down his food, staring absently at his drumming his fingers. Was he even tasting it? When he was done, he rinsed his plate, set it in the rack to dry and immediately started back to the grow room. Rebecca called to him as he headed out the doorway of the big kitchen. "Calendula, can we talk?"

"I gotta get to the grow room, baby. The pH has been really fluctuating."

"I know, I've just got to talk to you for a minute. It's important."

He rolled his eyes. "Can't it wait?"

"Okay, but when you're done in there we have to talk. We

haven't heard from Coyote in weeks and I'm getting worried."

"Give me a couple hours and we'll talk. Deal?"

10.

As Diesel eased himself down onto the sofa, Amber said, "Wasn't that nice? I really like that Katie. She seems like such a good, sweet girl. Not like me when I was that age." She laughed to herself, lifting the lid on an ornate wooden box that sat surrounded by Christmas themed figurines on the end table, and pulled out a slender glass pipe and a small glassine bag. Gingerly, she removed a small shard from the baggie and dropped it into the blackened bowl. She put the stem to her lips and ran a flame in a circular motion under the pipe as she breathed in a hit. Holding the smoke in her lungs, she offered the pipe to Diesel.

"No," Diesel said, glancing at her sideways. He shook his head. "Nope. No more for me today. You know you ain't never going to get to sleep tonight if you keep doing that."

"Maybe some of us don't feel like sleeping just yet." She hit the pipe again and then set it in the ashtray, careful that it sat right and the hot end didn't burn the cluttered end table.

"What about your beauty sleep?"

She curled up against him, lifting her face to his so that their noses nearly touched.

"Don't you think I'm beautiful?"

He winked. "Oh, darling, you're the most beautiful thing ever walked this earth."

"You always say the right thing." She pressed her lips against his. "Are you ever going to finish building me my great room?"

"Did I put in a septic and give you a warm place to sit that sweet ass of yours?"

"Yes, you did."

"Then I will sure as shit finish your great room."

Her smile grew larger and she pressed her lips to his again. "Now, did DJ give you any of those Xanax's?"

"He sure did," Diesel said, patting the front pocket of his shirt.

"Oh goody." She took one of his big hands in both of hers. "Look at those poor, bloody knuckles." She gently kissed the ragged wounds. "I'm going to have to fix you all up. Now why don't you get out of those dirty clothes and let me make you a bath? I know how you love a hot bath."

Diesel didn't particularly like hot baths. That was all Amber. She was the one who had insisted he install the big jet whirlpool. She just liked mothering him, mixing in bubbles and lighting candles around the tub. But he ached and right now a hot bath did sound like just the thing.

He took out the bottle of Xanax, unscrewed the lid and took out a bar. Cracking it in two, he handed one half to Amber and popped the other in his mouth, grinding it with his back molars. Settling down into the sofa, he felt the bitter drug sink into his system and almost immediately start relaxing him.

Then the security system started buzzing: *Vehicle approaching-vehicle approaching.*

He sighed and grumbled, rummaging for his iPad. Amber shifted back to the other side of the sofa, picked up the glass pipe again. He hit the security-app icon on the screen with his beefy finger and a fuzzy image of a Chevy Silverado idling at his gate filled the screen: a thin face with a goofy fishing hat atop it, leaning out the window and waving at the camera.

"It's Andy." He tapped an icon and the gate began to swing open.

Amber blew out her hit, set the pipe back in the ashtray, and flicked the remote.

"Will you please do your business in the kitchen," she said. "That man always has the dirtiest feet."

"Yes 'um." He got up from the sofa and lumbered into the back bedroom: king size waterbed, framed pictures of galloping horses, a big peace pipe mounted to the wall with feathers hanging from it. He made his way to the closet. The left side was supposed to be his side, but Amber always had her stuff piled up here: running shoes and sweaters she never wore, expensive, designer sweat suits. He pushed her stuff aside and started spinning the dial on the big six-foot-tall safe bolted to the floor, then swung open the door.

The left side was filled with rifles and shotguns: a Beretta M12 that was worth a small fortune, a camouflaged Mossberg twelve gauge, a 30.06 with a Leupold scope, an M1, and his trusty, black tactical shotgun: a sawed-off Remington with a pistol grip.

The right side of the safe was shelved and crammed with boxes of ammunition, bundles of cash he hadn't had time to count, a stack of paperwork: deeds and pink slips. There on the bottom was a gallon-sized Ziploc freezer bag half filled with clear shards of meth, a digital scale and a little .22 caliber pistol he liked to keep tucked in his pants when doing business.

He picked up the meth and the scale, eyed the .22. He wasn't going to need that with Andy. Shit, he remembered when the damn kid was born. Thinking how uncomfortable that hunk of metal would be crammed in his waist band—he had been putting on a few pounds lately, always did when he tried to slow down on the meth—he left it there on the bottom of the safe, shut the door, and gave the dial a spin.

—

Leaping from his beat-up, white Silverado with a brown-paper bag in hand, Andy shouted, too loudly, "Diesel D, how goes it?" He was dressed entirely in camo: coat, pants, hat, even his boots. His eyes, huge red-rimmed soccer balls, beamed from his face, and he worked his lower jaw, which jutted out from his head, back and forth as he stomped across the gravel.

From the front door, Diesel said, "It goes good, Andy. It goes good." Gesturing to the side entrance, he added, "Wanna meet me over in the kitchen?"

"Sure thing, there, good buddy. Sure thing."

They sat at the kitchen table and Diesel felt good. The Xanax was flowing through his system, taking that terrible edge off his stiff shoulders, and he decided he really liked Andy. He was one of his best customers and always had something nice he wanted to trade, not the trash most of his desperate, tweaked-out customers brought him: stolen car stereos, ancient power tools that weren't worth shit. And he liked the kitchen as a little office to do his business in, a nice, homey atmosphere with a sturdy table to weigh his product on. The police monitor, on twenty-four seven, droned and crackled in the background as Diesel told Andy about DJ and him putting in the new transmission.

"I shit you not, my friend, I seriously thought that damn tranny was going to fall down and crush his head."

"Oh, man."

"Just saw his face all bloody in the gravel."

"Damn."

Diesel laughed. "Anyway, what can I do you for?"

Andy rubbed at the stubble on his chin, jaw going back and forth as he drummed the fingers on the table. He eyed the big bag of meth that sat there between them, his red-rimmed eyes focused on the shards of crystal; beads of perspiration broke out on his sickly, fish-belly-white face. He licked his chapped lips and placed the grocery bag on the kitchen table, glancing from Diesel to the bag of meth, all darting eyes and nervous hands.

Boy's acting funny as hell, Diesel thought. "What you got in the bag, Andy?"

Andy reached in and Diesel saw the unmistakable flash of metal that was a handgun. Fuck, was this asshole going to rob him? He was friends with his fucking father. His mind flashed to the .22 sitting on the bottom of his safe. What the fuck was he thinking doing business unprotected?

But then Andy was offering him the gun, handgrip first. "I was wondering if you had any interest in this thing." Pushing it at him. "Take a look, take a look."

Diesel let out a sigh. Stupid asshole, lucky he didn't get his head blown off. He took the pistol from him.

"It's a .38 special, in real nice shape," Andy said, the beads of sweat on his forehead condensing and running down his face. His ashen lips stretched into a smile to reveal craggy, brown and yellow teeth.

"I see that," Diesel said, admiring the clean sheen of the steel, the dark grain pattern on the wooden grip. "Snub nose." Releasing the cylinder, he held it up and looked through the empty chambers:

unloaded. He gave the cylinder a spin and with the flick of his wrist shut it. "Nice weapon you got there. Got no hammer, that's so you can yank it out your pocket easier."

He put it below the table and drew it on Andy to show his point, chuckling. "Bang. Bang, bang."

Andy laughed along with him, eyes darting left and right, same strange grin.

"How hot is it?"

"Ain't hot at all, Diesel. It's registered to a dead guy."

"Dead how?"

"Natural causes. Natural causes. Guy was old and died. I got it from his daughter, up in Eureka. She's a friend of mine."

"That right?"

"Yeah, man. That's right."

Diesel cast a sidelong glance at Andy, who was staring at the pistol and chewing on his lower lip. Diesel watched his yellow teeth pulling off large, white flakes of skin and the thought quickly passed through his mind that Andy wasn't looking too good lately. And damn if Amber wasn't right about his feet being dirty. Not just his feet but his pants legs, too: the camouflaged-pants legs all covered in mud. He turned his attention back to the pistol.

"This could come in handy. How much you looking to get for it?"

"Well, it's in new condition and totally untraceable. I was thinking, like, three hundred?"

"Yeah, right. How about seventy-five bucks."

"Ah, come on, Diesel. Fuck, man. Give me a hundred for it at least. And I didn't come here empty handed. I got the cash for a couple ounces, too."

"Yeah, all right. Got anything else?"

"I got some OxyContin."

"Just what the doctor ordered."

11.

Black clouds rolled in, darkening the land, and as Rebecca bounced the Outback up the dirt road to check her e-mail and look at Facebook, rain began to patter down against the windshield. She flipped on the stereo: the same live Phish CD Calendula had been playing since they left San Diego. She sighed and turned the stereo off. She couldn't listen to that album again, and had left her iPod back at the cookhouse.

The road rose up and around to a clearing on the summit and her cell began to ding, signaling that she had reception. She pulled over at a spot where the road grew wider, fumbled through her purse for her phone, and, finding it, thumb-swiped the screen.

Nothing from Coyote. Damnit. Why was he not texting her back? She was getting really worried. She still felt irked by how, when she'd tried earlier to talk to Calendula about it, he'd just blown her off. Like he always did.

"Listen," she'd said, "we're almost completely out of cash and the generator only has diesel for another couple days. What are we going to do if Coyote doesn't show up soon?"

"We'll be fine. The pot's just about done. If we run out of diesel we'll just harvest. We've got plenty of supplies. We'll make it."

"We *don't* have that many supplies. What if we run out of propane, how will we cook? Have hot water?"

"We'll cook on the woodstove. Heat our own bathwater. It's called living off the land."

"Calendula, I'm serious."

"So am I. I mean, what are we going to do? Why stress on something you have no power over? When he gets here, he gets here."

"And what if he never shows up?"

"He'll show up. I promise you. Now, relax." And with that he'd kissed her on the head and disappeared back into the grow room.

She checked her email. Ads for organic clothes, vegetable seeds, herbal products, and a message from her mother back in

Bakersfield.

>*Becky,*
>
>*How are you? I wish I could call you. I do not like you out in the middle of nowhere with no phone. It sounds dangerous. Are you sure you're safe? What are you doing for money? Shouldn't you be working? How is Megan? Are you going to be able to put her in some kind of school up there? Please call me.*
>
>>*Love,*
>>*Mom*

Rebecca took off her glasses, rubbed her eyes. No one called her Becky but her mother. It was six-thirty. Her mother would be home from work by now. She should call her, but she decided to just reply to the email instead. She couldn't deal with all the questions and condemning silences. She hit reply with her thumb and went to tapping on the little screen.

>*Mom,*
>
>*We are fine. And no, it is not dangerous. I am working, I'm finally getting my herbal products business together. We are very happy and glad to be out of the rat race. Don't worry, I love you and will call soon.*
>
>>*Becky*

She hit the Facebook app. Pictures of her friends in San Diego, on the beach, in bars, smiling, seemingly without a care in the world. She stared at the blinking cursor—Update your status. What's on your mind?—and then began to type rapidly with both thumbs.

>*Living off the land. So blessed, thank you Mother Earth. Megan and I went mushroom hunting this morning and got a whole basket of oysters and chanterelles which I cooked up for lunch with steamed kale and chard from our garden. Tonight it's wildcrafted redwood sorrel and plantain pesto. Blessed be.*

She sat back and felt like a big fucking liar. Did she say how worried and paranoid she was? How fucking lonely? Already her friends were liking her comment and posting comments of their own.

Yummy. ☺
Send me some. Lol
So lucky, wish I was there

She felt so transparent and fake. Utterly full of shit. She covered her face with her hands and shook her head. She was so unhappy. And no, Megan was not "just fine" either. The more she thought about that weird thing that Megan had done the other night the more it troubled her.

It had been the dead of night, around three. The house was freezing, even in their bedroom, and she had gone to put more wood on the fire. As she was opening the lid on the top loader she heard a rapping sound. It scared the hell out of her, startling her so badly that she almost dropped a log on her foot.

At first she thought it was Coyote. Maybe he was back and had lost his key or something. She was just about to go wake up Calendula when she heard it again and realized it was coming from inside the house, down the hall, by the three back rooms, where Megan's bedroom was.

She crept over to the hall, which they kept lit at night for Megan, and there at the end, knocking on the padlocked door of the room Coyote used for storage, was Megan, her bunny stuffy lying limp under one arm, her image doubled by an old ornate mirror hanging on the wall

"Megan? Honey, what're you doing?"

"Knocking back," she said, the overhead light casting dark shadows below her eyes. "There's a little boy in there and he wants me to play with him." And then she wet herself.

As she'd cleaned Megan up—mopping her legs with a wet towel—and put her into clean jammies, she told herself that these things were normal. They happened. Kids had relapses, peed the bed, peed themselves.

Megan had had imaginary friends before, too, little girls she drank herb tea with. But never a boy.

She talked it over with Calendula the next morning and they decided to stop forcing her to go to the nasty old outhouse at night and just let her pee in the little shower. It seemed to have worked, so far. There hadn't been another incident the past few nights.

Megan's words came back to her and a chill ran down her spine. *Knocking back.*

"There's no such thing as ghosts." She surprised herself by saying the words aloud.

The Galaxy III dinged again. She looked down expecting another Facebook comment but it was a text from Coyote:

I M back. Sorry late. Harvest tomorrow. C U in the morning.

She felt a wave of relief wash over her. Things were fine and she felt foolish for getting so uptight. Coyote would be back in the morning. The pot looked great, and she wasn't a fake: she *had* harvested mushrooms, *had* made a sustainable lunch. She should be proud.

The last of the daylight was gone. With a gust of wind that rocked the car, a heavy rain blew in, pounding against the roof of the Outback. She turned on the headlights. Beams of yellow cut through the inky night, revealing tiny streams of water already starting down the road in muddy tendrils. She put the Outback in drive and turned the car around, heading back toward the compound.

12.

I can't make any money, Coyote thought as the double panes of the McDonalds' take-out window swung open. It's just a stupid cat-and-mouse game of catch up.

He reached up and grasped the cold, dew-laden cardboard cup of his supersized cola, set it into the cup holder of his Lincoln Navigator, speared the lid with a straw, and reached back up to grab the big, warm bag, the comforting smell of meat, grease and sugar filling the SUV.

"Have a nice day, sir," the cashier called out to him with a smile.

Coyote grunted and pulled away, one hand on the steering wheel, the other rummaging in the bag to retrieve his Big Mac and free it from its paper wrapper. He pulled into traffic, taking a big bite, special sauce dribbling off his chin and down his swirling blue-and-red tie-dye T-shirt. Next, he stuffed a fistful of fries into his mouth, then soaked it all with cold soda he sucked greedily up from the straw.

He chomped and gulped the mess down as he steered through the maze-like streets of San Rafael, then turned onto the spiraling onramp and headed north on the 101, away from the Bay area, cranking up the live Band of Gypsies CD he always listened to after a Big Deal, thinking to himself: Bullshit, fucking bullshit. It seemed no matter what he did he couldn't seem to catch up, to get a sizeable chunk of cash. His savings was pathetic.

His Oregon buyer had been so smug at the deal, lowballing the crap out of him.

"It's a changing economy, my friend, and you're going to have to change with it. Now that Washington and Colorado have gone legal, the whole game is changing. Prices just aren't what they used to be. You gotta take what you can get. Just wait till California legalizes. It's bound to happen next year."

"I got all the best strains," Coyote said. "O.G., Girl Scout Cookie.

Everybody wants this shit. And it's dank. Fucking dank bud, man."

"It's not a question of quality or genetics, my man. You've always got the goods. If you didn't, you'd have hit the skids long ago. Like a lot of other people. It's a matter of supply and demand. Turn on the computer, you can get herb delivered to your door at very competitive prices, right over the internet. Why should I come all the way down here to see you?"

"Those stores in Washington and Colorado, all the medical dispensaries everywhere, they're selling this grade of product for twenty bucks a gram, four hundred bucks an ounce. How's that bringing the market price down? Those fuckers are getting rich, I'm barely making a buck."

"It's a buyer's market. You think the C.E.O. of Phillip Morris is thinking about some poor tobacco farmer's family at night?"

"I thought you were some kind of socialist or something."

"Free-market anarchist, bud. I'll give you twelve hundred per, best I can do."

This whole thing was just starting to feel like a loser's game. Hell, with all the expenses and the risk? How many cops had he passed on his way down here? Nine? Ten? And now he barely had enough money to make it for another round. Barely even a hundred grand. He wouldn't be able to pay Diesel the fifty grand he owed him, and he knew that big, crazy fucker was expecting it. He should be able to give him at least ten or twenty, keep him off his back for a while. He'd need enough cash to pay the trimmers when he got back, and he needed enough for fuel and fertilizer for another run. And clones, just the clones were over twelve grand. Christ, could he ever catch up?

—

Seeing his Oregon connect brought back memories of Helen and his little girls—Miriam and Melinda—up there on that hellhole of a commune outside Eugene. The Octagon. He was pretty sure they were there; they always went there, every time she left him. He thought about asking the connect if he'd seen Helen and the girls, but in the end he hadn't even bothered.

The girls would be eight now, what a pain in the ass they must be. Twins. Double your pleasure, yeah right, double your headaches. When he thought of those red-headed girls he always seemed to remember them screaming. Screaming as babies, screaming as toddlers, screaming as children. Always screaming. Screaming in happiness. Screaming in sadness. Screaming in boredom. Screaming and running.

But that wasn't entirely true. He remembered the goofy smiles they'd give him, that utter and complete trust in him that would fill their hazel eyes as they came running up to him.

Sometimes in the loneliness of the night, lying in the darkness, he'd think of how it had been in the early days with Helen and the girls, how they had been a team, a gang, and he'd get that sad, lost feeling and think to himself, maybe I should go find them. Make a go at being a family again. He'd open himself up to that hidden, lonely place that yearned to be needed, loved, and not alone. That sensitive, humane part of himself he tried to obliterate with drugs, sex, and money, that part of him he longed to isolate and sever from the slick, jaded player he saw himself as. Then the arrogant, cynical, savvy, part of himself would say: Forget it. It's over, done. You've both fucked around on each other so much, said such hateful things, spit in each other's faces, you can't go back now. It's over, deal with it.

He remembered the last time he had gone up to Oregon searching for them. That desperate, aching loneliness had grown so heavy in his soul, like a rock in his gut, slowly putting on weight like a kidney stone, growing, layer by layer, until, barely even conscious of what he was doing, he found himself driving north.

He found them at that run-down commune in the wet, rain-drenched Oregon woods. There was only about a dozen people living there at the time, mostly mothers with their children, a couple of recalcitrant, shy, bearded men he didn't recognize who turned their gaze away and wandered off when he came strutting through the door.

They all lived in a huge, eight-sided log cabin with a leaky roof. A gaggle of feral children running around, mattresses and sleeping bags on the floor. A large kitchen and dining area, big stone and brick fireplace for cooking and warmth, blooming up in the middle of the floor. Everyone looked dirty and tired, sulky and angry. The children were wary of him, though he knew all their parents, hell, had fucked half their moms. Little dirty rag-a-muffins who would dart up to him, tap him on the back or mumble something, then run away giggling. But his girls seemed healthy enough, and smart as whips, too, already reading and doing math though they weren't yet five years old. The women prided themselves on their homeschooling skills and their cooking; but he'd always thought that if their teaching skills weren't any better than their cooking skills, the children were doomed to be idiots.

It wasn't hard to convince Helen to leave. She even seemed relieved, happy, especially when he told her he'd just bought a hundred acres with a big house on it—the cookhouse—in the southeastern corner of Humboldt County.

The other women hugged her as she said her goodbyes. Some even wept, but Coyote thought it all seemed subdued and lackluster, a halfhearted ritual they felt obliged to perform. He really couldn't detect all that much love coming from them. He was driving a Toyota 4-runner at the time, and Helen and the kids piled in and they took off south, the girls complaining that they missed their friends before they even reached the highway.

They finally made it to the property, the cookhouse barren and cavernous, a bare mattress for Helen and him, the girls having to sleep in a bundle of blankets on the floor. It was winter and raining, the grow room wasn't in yet, there was nothing for any of them to do, and after only a couple of days he knew he wouldn't be able to take it, wouldn't be able to endure them for much longer. He loved them and missed them when they were gone, thought about them all the time, but having them around him was unbearable. The girls' cyclone of energy, the condemning glances from Helen, that dissatisfied tone she'd get with him: "We *need* more firewood. We *need* a real kitchen table. At the Octagon I had Sarah and Jasmine to help. We always had firewood. Here it's like I'm alone. I *can't* live like this."

He'd get this humming in his head and would wander off to the back cabin and play solitaire in the stillness. He'd sit by himself, smoke joints, sip beer, maybe eat a few valiums, and vegetate in his dingy little cave.

Then Spider showed up. And from that point on, Coyote never wanted to leave.

That ghost became his best friend. Someone he could talk to, who understood.

Finally, as he was skulking back to the house one time, Helen confronted him. "What do you even do back there all day?"

"Nothing. Just drink beer. Puff." What was he going to say? Play cards and trade jokes with a dead man? The ghost of the biker who'd owned the place before him? She'd think he'd gone crazy. She'd be right, too. Spider couldn't be real.

"Why can't you do that here?"

"Dunno."

"Why did you even come and get us if you're not going to be with us?"

Coyote sipped his beer. Shrugged.

"I don't like this place. It's creepy. It's got...bad energy."

"Bad energy?"

"It won't get warm. The girls say they're hearing voices."

"Why don't you burn some sage or something?"

"Actually, I tried that. It didn't work."

The girls were running in circles, chasing each other, screaming at the top of their lungs. He needed some quiet. The buzzing in his ears was unbearable.

"I need help here," Helen said, hands on her hips, mouth an angry line. He just shrugged and headed out the door toward the back cabins.

When he got back she was gone. Hadn't even taken the car. Later he learned she'd just gathered up the girls, walked down the road, and hitchhiked out. She was tough like that; that's one of the reasons he had fallen in love with her to begin with.

He never bothered looking for her or even asking around about her. He had other plans. The neighbor Diesel and his son were going to build a big grow room for him.

He pulled off the highway at the first Petaluma exit, coasted down into the parking lot of the Sheraton. He parked, got out of his SUV and started across the parking lot, a duffle bag over his shoulder and the McDonalds bag clutched in a fist.

"Will that be a smoking room or a non-smoking room, sir?"

"Smoking. Definitely smoking."

The front desk receptionist's fingers quickly beat on the keyboard. "I've got you all set up in room 1603." Her smile never wavered, though her eyes momentarily hung on the sauce smear running down the front of his tie-dye. "Have a wonderful stay." She held the card/key out to him; he grunted and roughly pulled it from her hand.

He strutted through the gleaming marble lobby, sneering at a startled yuppie woman who nearly collided with him, past the wine shop, souvenir stand, and café, to the elevators, strutting like a rock star. This was the beginning of the ritual and he felt like a king, even if he had gotten less than half of what he used to get for his product.

This was his relax time. His come-down time. A ritual he had: After he got rid of a batch of weed he'd spend a couple grand on crack and hookers before heading north and hunkering down to grow another crop, surviving on what he could, mainly Xanax and acid. Coors Light to dull the monotony.

Once in his room he took a towel from the rack and put it in the sink, ran water over it till it was soaked, and laid it along the crack at the base of the door. He flicked on the television, found something mind-numbing, a sitcom about young people in an apartment complex. He opened his duffle bag, took out a balled-up wash rag bound with a rubber band, unrolled it, and removed four blackened glass pipes, placing them in a row on the end table. He pulled out a large Ziploc bag half full of tiny plastic containers with bright red caps and fished one out. He unscrewed the cap, removed a pebble-sized, yellow chunk of crack, put it in the pipe, lit it.

Breathing out a cloud of smoke, he felt his heart begin to race as a chemical-laden euphoria filled the fissures and empty spaces between his skull and brain. That sweet, heady, chemical smell and taste, like a toy store or a new car. Rain began to patter on the sliding glass door that led to his balcony. A bit of poetry he had memorized lifetimes ago, back when he was in high school, slipped into his mind and he said the words aloud.

"Quaff, oh quaff, this kind nepenthe and forget that lost Lenore."

The rush left him like a crashed wave pulling back out to sea and reality returned once more.

He had to get back north, would leave in the morning. He picked up his iPhone, glanced at the messages. Those stupid kids had been calling him incessantly lately, leaving him texts, wondering where he was, what he was doing. Didn't they know he was busy? It was none of their business where the fuck he was. He was trying to make some money. The pot in that grow room better look good, too, or they were getting nothing. Nothing. Fuck them. He owed them nothing. They'd better understand that. He punched in a text:

I M back. Sorry late. Harvest tomorrow. C U in the morning.

He put the phone down, picked up his pipe and hit it. Hit it again. And again, until it was too hot to hold. Then he picked up another one, filled it, hit it, and zoned out on the mindless canned laughter emanating from the television.

There was a knock at the door. He got up and peered in the peephole. There was the girl he had ordered, same one as last time. Tall, black hair, wrinkled, ugly face caked in way too much makeup. He liked her because she didn't mind if he just sat there puffing on his crack pipe while she gave him head. She could go on sucking and sucking all night, and she *never* asked him for a hit. Who cared what her face looked like? She did her job well and that's all that mattered.

He removed the wet towel from the base of the door and let her in.

"Hi, Coyote," she said, slipping in the door as he replaced the towel. The smell of her perfume filled the room, a sweet, jasmine stink.

Coyote grunted, went to the bed and sat down, hit the pipe, rolling it carefully over the flame. He blew out a cloud of smoke, heart pounding like a drum in his chest.

"I'm going to need you all night," he said finally, staring dully at the television, a commercial for a ridiculous game show of some kind. "Is that okay?"

"If you got the money, honey," she said, chomping on a piece of gum. "I got the time."

He set the pipe down and pulled out his wallet, thick with hundred dollar bills. "Here's a grand."

"It's fifteen hundred for the whole night, baby. You know that. Plus a tip."

He grunted and counted out fifteen hundred-dollar bills, fixed her with his glazed eyes, lids hanging halfway down like a wet blanket. "Tip will be based on performance."

"Well, I ain't worried about that, honey." She folded up the cash and slipped it into her purse. "Now let's get those pants off."

—

He woke up to a barrage of banging on the door.

A woman's voice: "Sir? Sir? Housekeeping, sir."

He groaned as he heard the door begin to swing open, sat up, and shouted, "Get out of here. I haven't checked out yet. Get the fuck out of my room."

"So sorry, sir." The door swung back shut.

He pushed himself up, head pounding, white dots dancing in the periphery of his vision, and noticed his wallet lying open on the table.

Guess she helped herself to a tip. Bitch definitely earned it, from what he could remember.

How much had he had left in there? Six, seven hundred bucks? How had he even fallen asleep with all that fucking crack? Then he remembered the fist-full of valium and Xanax he'd chugged down with the Cabernet Sauvignon he'd ordered up from room service. He hadn't even come, never shot his load, at least he didn't think he had. Just sat there puffing on that glass pipe, his money draining away while she knelt between his legs, head bobbing, sucking away at his limp cock. She was a pro, though, never stopped, never complained.

His dick was actually sore.

He got up, went to the bathroom, and fell to his knees before the toilet, sweat breaking out on his scalp and running down his pale, bloated face as he retched, his arms wrapped around the toilet. A mess of wine and McDonalds remnants chundered up and out of him.

Groaning, he stumbled back into the room. To his surprise there was still some crack left. Leftover crack: that was a true fucking rarity. He was surprised the whore hadn't stolen it. Just looking at the little plastic bottles made him gag. He went back to the bathroom, threw them in the toilet, flushed them down. He leaned over the sink and splashed water on his face.

The ritual was done. He was ready to go north.

13.

Rebecca puffed on a joint, leaning back into the filthy faux-velvet sofa as Calendula strummed his guitar. It had been a terrible day. A weird day. But she felt better. So much better. Coyote was coming back. Harvest tomorrow. She could make it through another round. They'd have their land. A little farm. She'd be an herbalist and Calendula a Permaculture Designer. This would work. It was working.

Rain crashed against the chef house, beating on the tin roof and cascading down the windows. A fire roared in the old top loader. Megan, in her pink, piggy pajamas that were starting to fray and grow too small for her, knelt on the ground, bent over the busted-up coffee table, her bunny stuffy beside her, doodling on a pad with crayons: redwood trees and giant mushrooms.

Putting his guitar down, Calendula reached over and took the joint from Rebecca. He hit it a few times and passed it back, then lifted up his mason jar and slurped down the last of his wine. Picking up the bottle, he poured a slug into his jar and emptied the rest into Rebecca's.

Shaking out the last few drops, he said, "Another bottle?"

"I don't know. We only have a couple left."

They'd stopped at an organic winery on the way up and bought two cases of red wine, a pinot noir he picked out and a zinfandel she'd chosen. They had a bottle of each left.

"Come on," he said in his best Jim Morrison voice, cocking his head, giving her his "Lizard King" stare. "Tonight we celebrate, for tomorrow we harvest."

She finished off her glass, her face and belly warm. Another would be so good. "Yeah, I guess so." She gazed over her glasses and smiled at him. He disappeared into the kitchen and returned a moment later with the last bottle of pinot noir, already twisting a corkscrew in. He splashed more wine into their mason jars and then raised his jar up for a toast.

"To the magic and wonder of cannabis," he said merrily. She smiled and they clinked their glasses together. She took a sip while he downed a big, sloppy gulp.

"I'm tasting garden hose and sweat sock, and you?"

Rebecca gave a sly smile. "What did that lady in Mendocino say?"

"Hints of Fireball and Starburst," they said in unison, breaking out in helpless laughter.

"Are you guys getting drunk?" Megan asked.

Rebecca choked. "Megan. Of course not, we're just having a few drinks. Jeeze."

Megan began to slash streaks of black rain over her picture.

Calendula picked up the guitar and launched into the Grateful Dead's "Ripple."

Megan put down her crayon and sang along with him. It was one of her favorites.

Rebecca licked the sweet pinot from her lips, her eyes heavy, the alcohol swirling dizzily up into her mind. She felt content and happy. Things were good. When the song reached its crescendo she joined in.

"La la la la, la laah la lah la." Then Calendula flubbed and hit the wrong chord, the tune suddenly going sour and coming to an abrupt end. Megan frowned.

"Well, fuck a fuck fuck," he said, pausing to grab his mason jar. "That wasn't right, was it?"

Megan's frown turned to a mischievous grin and her big brown eyes sparkled. "Fuck," she said in her sweet, tinny voice, then covered her mouth with her hands and began giggling hysterically.

Sternly, Rebecca said, "Language, you two."

"Oh, baby," Calendula said. "It's just a word. Just a silly, little word. It only has the power *you* put into it. You gotta break down those mental constraints. Free your mind."

"Oh, okay, Charlie Manson," she said, giving him a wry, sarcastic look. Calendula had a weird fascination with the Manson family and Rebecca was always teasing him about it. Every now and then she found him re-reading a dog-eared copy of *Helter Skelter*, and

74

she'd call him on his obsession.

"You like those girls, don't you, you sick fuck?"

"Maybe," he'd answer slyly. "But they're not as hot as you."

"You want me to carve an X in my head? Would that turn you on?"

"Maybe. We could try it out."

A part of her knew this only encouraged him and often she regretted it. She really didn't find his fixation on the Mason Family that amusing. But the wine was going to her head and she couldn't resist the temptation to tease him.

Calendula smirked at her and started strumming a G chord, singing, "Garbage Dump."

Megan asked, "Who's Charlie Manson?"

"Great," Rebecca said, shaking her head.

Calendula put his guitar down. "Hey, that was all you, I didn't bring it up." He leaned toward Megan. "He was a hippie, honey. Like your mom. A famous one."

"Stop it, Calendula. He wasn't a hippie. He was a bad man, a very bad man."

"What'd he do?"

Rebecca sighed. "He killed people, okay, honey?"

Why did she say that? Why was she discussing this with her five-year-old daughter? She hated having Megan ever hear about murder or death. The words just slipped out of her mouth before she realized what was happening. The damn wine was letting her tongue fly. "But don't worry, honey, he's locked up in jail and is never getting out."

"Charlie never killed nobody," Calendula said. "Little Charlie only wanted to play his guitar. It was the girls who done it. Them and Tex."

"Please. How did this conversation start?"

"I think you started it, sweetie."

"Can we talk about something else?"

Megan looked up from her drawing and giggled at them. "You guys are funny."

"Oh, we're funny are we?" Rebecca laughed along with her

now. "Well, I'm glad you're so amused. But now, young lady, it's time to go brush your teeth and get ready for bed."

"But I want to stay up, Mommy."

"Go on and brush your teeth, then we'll see."

Megan got up and went to the big sink in the kitchen to brush her teeth. Rebecca and Calendula looked at each other and burst out laughing.

"What a character," he said.

They could hear her trying to sing as she brushed her teeth, "La la la la la..."

"Brush." Rebecca shouted. "Don't sing."

Calendula poured a splash into her not-quite-empty mason jar.

"Are you trying to get me drunk, mister?"

"Perhaps. It does give me an advantage in certain, shall we say, endeavors."

"You'd best play fair," she said, wagging her finger at him before sipping her wine. She shouldn't drink this much; she was starting to slur her words and was probably going to have a headache in the morning. She usually never got this way in front of Megan, but it was so cozy and warm around the fire. With the harvest looming close it was a time to celebrate. She took another sip, her glasses slipping down her nose, and caught Calendula staring at her with a sardonic grin. She gave him a playful snarl and pushed her glasses back up.

14.

Rebecca was suddenly awake and sitting bolt upright in her bed, naked and covered in sweat. She was still drunk and the room tilted and swayed slightly. She must have passed out: she couldn't remember going to bed.

Had she taken her own clothes off?

It was stifling hot. The grow room hummed, emitting a dull glowing light through the cracks of the door even though they had draped two layers of black plastic over the doorway. Her mouth was dry and tasted of stale wine and pot smoke. The room wobbled and spun slowly. She reached out her hands and braced herself. Jesus. This wasn't just the wine. She'd been having crazy dreams. Weird, insane, sex dreams. She closed her eyes and tried to remember.

She was stumbling through the woods. It was dark and she was lost. And she didn't have her ticket. She kept searching her pockets, looking for it, but it wasn't there.

But then she was on the beach and none of that mattered. None of that mattered at all.

It was a beautiful night. The moon full and high, its light shimmering across the crashing ocean waves. There were people there, their forms gleaming in the pale-blue light of the moon. They were naked and entwined. Fucking. They were all fucking and it was beautiful. So beautiful. The most beautiful people she'd ever seen.

And she was horny.

So fucking horny. A literal heat ripping up through her and making her head spin.

There were girls around her now. Helping her undress. Pulling silky garments up over her head. Gorgeous hippie girls with long, dark hair. And they were kissing her and giggling. So pretty and soft. And she was kissing them back and it felt good. It felt wonderful.

She found herself shuddering at their touch, on the brink of orgasm.

And a man was watching them, smiling. A little man with a beard. And she wanted to come, wanted to come so badly as the girl with the razor blade approached her and said, "Don't be afraid: in love there is no wrong," and she realized they all had it, that bloody X carved into their foreheads. And she leaned back quivering. And she wasn't afraid, wasn't afraid at all. She wanted it. Wanted to feel that sharp metal sink into her skin, wanted to be one with them, all of them, wanted the mark. Wanted it as surely and deeply as she wanted to come. And when the blade pierced her she gasped in pleasure, the blood warm and sticky as it ran down her face, salty and sweet in her mouth, and she was going to come. She was going to come, and suddenly she was awake.

She shook her head, and almost instantly the dream began slipping away from her, disappearing faster than she could recall it. She was drunk and felt sick, but was so worked up and turned on. She couldn't remember the last time she felt this charged up. Her body ached.

She looked over at Calendula. She could just make him out in the dim glow. He was asleep on his back, naked, his mouth hanging open, the sheets in a knot at his feet.

She felt moisture slipping down from between her legs. She told herself to just go back to sleep, but before she even knew what she was doing she was reaching out and taking him in her hand, stroking him till he stiffened, bowing her head down and pressing him against her lips, taking him in her mouth, feeling him harden against the back of her throat.

Calendula moaned, awoke, and looked down at her. "Rebecca, *what are you doing?*"

She gazed up at him, still feeling drunk, bashfully turning her head and shrugging before climbing on top, straddling him. He grasped her hips as she arched her back, fell forward on top of him and clamped her lips on his, filling his mouth with her tongue.

She pulled her lips from his face, moaned, and threw her head back, her long dreadlocks cascading behind her as she rose up and fell down, grinding herself against him. She trembled, a torrent of warmth washing over her as she orgasmed. She was panting, shaking, her mouth hung open, fingers pressed into the slick flesh of Calendula's chest, and that's when she felt the eyes on her.

She didn't see or hear anything, just knew she was being watched. A scary, preternatural feeling. All the sweat cascading down her body suddenly turned to ice and the skin on the back of her neck pimpled as the tiny hairs there rose.

Yes, something was in the doorway, staring at them. She was certain of it. Positive. She could feel it, sense it. She turned her head, looked over her shoulder, and saw it. There it was, a tiny figure silhouetted in the open doorway: *the ghost.*

It was the ghost of the little boy, that's who it was. It had to be him, and she gasped loudly and stifled a scream with her hand.

Calendula shot up. "What? What is it?"

And then the tiny figure spoke.

"Mommy," Megan said as a cascade of urine spilled down her leg. "I'm cold."

15.

DJ picked up a coin from the big bag of nickels he'd gotten from the bank, looked at it, put it aside, picked up another, looked at it, put it aside. It was four-thirty in the morning and he'd been kneeling on the ground, hunched over the chipped-up old coffee table, looking at nickels, for over six hours now.

Rain crashed down outside and a gust of wind rocked the little trailer on its cinder block foundation. He had three hundred dollars in nickels. It was a big bag, a lot of work. He rubbed his face, picked up another nickel, looked at it.

Katie was in the tiny kitchenette, a mere square of linoleum, scrubbing with some new type of mop that squirted cleanser out of its head. She had four mops, testing them all on the little piece of linoleum. Ever since she'd gotten pregnant all she ever did was clean. Clean and talk.

"You know this swifter really gives a nice shine, and it smells *so* good, too. That other one just smells like bleach. So much it even makes my eyes water. But bleach *is* the cleanest and we need it clean for the baby. Right, hon?"

"Yeah, whatever you say."

Katie put down the mop and spread herself out on the sofa. She picked up the iPad Diesel had given earlier that afternoon and began swiping her finger across it. DJ picked up a lighter and used it to crush a pile of meth shards that lay on a Kid Rock Mirror with a cheap wooden frame. He rolled the lighter back and forth over the crystals, trying to get a nice fine powder. Kid Rock, dressed like pimp in a purple velvet hat, smiled up from under the glistening pile.

He had won that Kid Rock mirror at the county fair up in Ferndale last year. It had been his first real date with Katie. A magical night—the spinning lights, the taste of cotton candy on her lips. They held hands as they wandered the fairgrounds, the stars shimmering in the sky and the moon rising up fat and full. Later that evening, in the backseat of his old Mustang, she had given in and let him press himself between her legs. The next day he had tried to clean the upholstery, but to no avail. The blood was still there now, an irritating, faded-brown patch.

"Can I have another bump?" Katie asked as he took a straw and snorted a small pile.

"You're pregnant and you've been at it all night. You sure that's a good idea?"

"I know. I know. I'm going to stop after tonight. It's just so cozy in here. You know? With the rain outside and all?" She gave him her sweet little girl smile and he cut her out a small pile with a razor blade.

She took one of the brightly-colored children's straws they'd been using and snorted her small bump, then sat back with a satisfied look on her face and began to talk rapidly.

"That sure was sweet of Diesel. He's just the best. I can't believe he wants me to call him Pops. That's so sweet. Who else calls him Pops?"

"Nobody." DJ picked up a nickel and looked at it, then put it aside and picked up another. "Nobody fucking calls him Pops. He's just high."

"Don't be mean, DJ. He's so sweet."

"He ain't fucking sweet, trust me. And he's a fucking idiot for letting people walk all over him. I set up that whole fucking grow room. That chef house and all that land should be ours, that fucker Coyote owes us, and Spider before him. I'm gonna get that fucking land, watch me."

Katie draped her hand over his head, caressing his scalp. "Oh, DJ."

DJ was pissed. He felt he had missed out on his birthright.

When he had been living with his mother up in Eureka he'd seen his old friends down here quickly get pot rich. Suddenly they had new pickup trucks with custom bumpers and headache racks, land, houses. Pot was going for four to five thousand dollars a pound and you couldn't grow enough. He was determined to get down here and get in on the scene. He scraped up enough to buy these forty acres from his uncle and put a trailer on it. It was happening. But suddenly everyone was doing it, and with the Medical 215 law it was even quasi-legal, and now the price of pot had dropped to a thousand bucks a pound, sometimes even less. After you paid to get it trimmed, what did that leave you? With fertilizer and soil prices going through the roof?

And it was hard to unload. The market was flooded. In order to get anywhere near a decent price the stuff had to be this year's trendy shit: Headband, O.G., Sour Diesel. He couldn't keep up with it, didn't know where to get the designer clones. He was still growing the Purple Urkle and nobody wanted that shit anymore. His last batch of outdoor had turned yellow before he was able to sell it. He ended up making the whole crop into hash. Now he was getting by selling meth and pills. Doing what he had to and trying to get up a nut.

His old man had some nerve telling him to lay off the meth. That fucking old tweaker? Fuck him. He'd never been there for him, never gave him shit as a kid, was always in fucking jail. Now he wants to get all buddy-buddy? All high and mighty with his cranked-out biker-momma girlfriend, always telling him to go to school, be a diesel mechanic like him, like that ever helped him, like he'd ever used it for anything. Who had time for that bullshit? He needed to get his nut up now.

He picked up a nickel, put it in the pile, picked up another nickel, looked at it: BINGO.

"Got one," he shouted to Katie.

"Yeah." She lit a cigarette. "Good job, hon."

He smiled. That's right, he would get his nut. He would get what was coming to him. One way or another, he would get his.

TWO

"We remembered not the dank tarn of Auber,
Nor the ghoul-haunted woodland of Weir."
—E. A. Poe. *Ulalume*

"Sing a song of sixpence, a pocket full of rye,
Four and twenty black birds baked in a pie."
—English nursery rhyme

1.

Rebecca started down the long hallway to her little office, unable to look away from the glint of the padlock on the door to the storage room. Rain poured down outside and the black clouds had grown opaque, the darkness nearly complete and all encompassing: a wet, rain-drenched heaviness that hung in the rooms of the cookhouse, clinging to the shadows, giving the weird orange light of the overhead incandescent bulbs that lit the hallway a garish nightmare-horror-movie pall. At the end of the hall, her reflection stared back at her from the dusty old mirror.

Coyote was back and he and Calendula were in the grow room, harvesting the pot. Coyote had been ordering Calendula around, grunting out commands and motioning with a Coors light. She hated the obsequious manner Calendula adopted around him: slavishly following behind like a dog, waiting for his orders and jumping at them. And Coyote was such an asshole; the first thing he'd said after he pulled up in his gleaming black Lincoln Navigator was, "Where's all the fucking firewood? We need the fire going to dry the pot."

Calendula just stared at him, mouth going up and down but no words coming out. Rebecca stepped forward. "We burned it. It's freezing in there."

"Even with all those grow lights?"

"In Megan's room, yes. So cold you can see your breath."

He just stomped inside. "Well, let's check out the grow room." Calendula followed behind him, head down, ever obedient, while Megan quietly watched with her big baleful eyes, her bunny stuffy clutched to her chest.

Rebecca followed them, anxious to see what Coyote thought of the pot, ready to defend Calendula if Coyote dared say anything negative. The nerve of him. To leave all this responsibility on them and then just storm back in with his customary bad attitude. They went through the bedroom and past the big steel door and into the bright

84

light and humidity of the grow room. The unnaturally large space assaulted her senses: the loud hum of the lights, the whir of the fans, the stink of the flowering marijuana: skunky, pungent and musky. Dank.

Coyote's attitude immediately improved when he saw the weed. He even began lightly chuckling to himself. Calendula had been very attentive and the reefer looked amazing: thick, dense nuggets of tight flower clusters, coated in crystals, hairs shriveled to rust, gleaming under the bright industrial lights. Coyote smiled and knelt down to a plant, squeezed it, pressing his face against it.

"Did you flush them?" Looking up to Calendula.

"Oh, yeah. First with floral flush and then with plain water for the last week."

A clown-like grin seeped across Coyote's face, spreading from ear to ear, and Rebecca thought that the only things that made this man smile were pot and money. Coyote rose up and clapped his hands together, vigorously rubbing them against each other. "All right, looks like the Girl Scout Cookie and Green Crack are ready to harvest. We'll give the O.G. and Sour Diesel another couple days." Then his eyes hardened. "But you're going to have to clear out those back rooms. We need them to dry the weed in. Megan can sleep in your room till we're finished with the trimming. And we're going to have to get more firewood."

So now she had to pack up the spare room she'd been using as an office for her herbal business. She'd already emptied Megan's room, her clothes and all the stuffed animals she liked to sleep with, covering the little bed with a tarp so it wouldn't get filthy when they hung all their pot in there. She pushed open the door to her office and stepped in.

It was sparse inside: a card table with her laptop on it (though without internet the thing was practically useless to her), a small printer she used to make labels, pamphlets and business cards. Jars filled with lotions, packets of immune sprinkle, and sachets of tea. She sat down in the wooden chair she had dragged here from the kitchen, sighed, and began packing up her stuff: stowing the laptop back into its case, putting all her products in a large cardboard box.

She tucked the last bottle of lotion in and closed the lid, heaved it up and started out, thinking about last night, how Calendula had finally convinced her to stay for another run.

—

He'd begged her to stay, literally getting down on his hands and knees and pleading with her not to leave.

She'd sat on the edge of the bed, that same bed Megan had seen them fucking on, feeling something within her begin to divide.

"I just don't know if I can stay here."

The wind outside moaned and the old house creaked. The only light in the room seeped in from the cracks of the door to the grow room. Shadows loomed everywhere. She took off her glasses and, in a quick and caustic gesture, squeezed her eyes, trying to ignore Calendula as he paced the small bedroom, a silhouette emerging from and sinking back into darkness.

"It's only two and half more months, and we'll get half this time. *Half!* Think of all we can do with the money. Get our own land, have an organic homestead. No indoor grows, no generators, no diesel. We'll get some solar panels and find a place near a town with a farmers' market and a community center. Some place like Briceland or Harris. Somewhere with a good school for Megan."

"I don't know. I just don't know if I *can* stay. I—I don't feel happy here, *or safe.*" Was he making her decide between him and this place? Would he do that to her?

He stepped out of the darkness, knelt down before her, reached out and tucked a long dread that was hanging in her face behind her ear.

"I love you. Please, don't leave me here alone."

And there it was: He was staying with or without her. And so she made her decision. In the end, it wasn't the mother in her that responded to his pleas, though she felt that tug, it was her fear of being alone. She had given everything to be with him, invested so much in this relationship. And there was nothing to go back to: Everyone at the co-op either hated her or thought she was crazy. What were her options? Go back to her mother's house in Bakersfield? Find some new town and try to start over again? She couldn't bear the thought. She couldn't do it again: be alone in that desultory existence. He was all she and Megan had, her only hope, so she finally relented.

"Fine," she'd said, shaking her head and gnawing on her lower lip, tapping her foot and refusing to look at him. "I'll stay."

—

She stepped out of the room, arms filled with boxes, laptop hanging from her shoulder, just as Coyote came down the hallway, pulling a ring of keys from his pocket. Calendula followed behind, dragging a blue tarp piled with a mound of freshly cut weed. She stepped back into the room to let them pass, watching as Coyote grasped the padlock and slipped a key into it.

"What's in there?" she asked.

He paused, the lock grasped in his fingers, his veiled eyes regarding her suspiciously. "Nothing. Why?"

She thought of Megan standing in front of it, knocking, standing in a puddle of piss, saying how a little boy lived in there. "I... I was just wondering why you keep it locked."

"I keep it locked to keep it from getting all junked up. I need this space to dry herb." He squinted at her. "Why?"

"Just wondering."

He pulled the lock from the hasp, pocketed it, and as he swung the door open—creaking on its rusty hinges—a frigid rush of cold air blew out. She turned to the doorway, craning forward to tentatively peer in. It was just a large, dark, bare room: the walls fake wood paneling, the three windows at the far end covered in black plastic sheeting. String lines for drying herb ran across it and three large, blue, industrial dehumidifiers sat parked in the back corner.

She nodded and gulped, staring into the vacant room, noting the fetid, musty odor that emanated from it.

Coyote gazed at her with a vaguely questioning look in his hooded eyes, as if asking, *satisfied?* Then he strolled in, giving his keys a quick twirl on his finger and jamming them in his pocket. Calendula shuffled along behind and gave Rebecca a hopeful smile as he dragged the pot-laden tarp into the dark room.

She watched them in there, Coyote mumbling to Calendula as they hung the marijuana on lines to dry, and she had a fearful sense that she had crossed an invisible boundary, had wandered off the map, and was now in a strange territory she didn't know how to navigate.

2.

Calendula couldn't believe what a scammer Coyote was. When he'd told him they'd put in a thousand bucks of their own on diesel, the last of their money, he'd looked back dully, eyelids hanging at half mast, and asked, "You got the receipts?"

"Well, no."

Coyote had already paid them the thousand bucks a week he'd promised, and the money lay on the table between them: a stack of newly-minted hundred-dollar bills. He motioned towards it, curled his upper lip in a sneer. "You're getting paid, ain't that good enough?"

Calendula could feel Rebecca getting ready to blow, he quickly reached out and put his hand on Coyote's. "Hey, come on, brother. Fair's fair."

Coyote grinned as if the little people amused him: a court jester who had asked the king for a raise, wasn't it cute? "I tease, I tease. Of course I'll reimburse you for your expenses." He chuckled and counted out another thousand, this one not crisp hundreds but a pile of twenties, fives and tens, dirty and worn. "But seriously, next time save the receipts."

Calendula fingered the bulge of cash in his pants, caressing it and licking his lips before he pulled it out and stuck it in a sock, pushing it deep in the back corner of the drawer. It wasn't much, eleven grand. But it was something. He could do this— *they* could do this. He could get his land, put his permaculture design certification to use and live his alternative life style: creating energy patterns, stacking functions, being organic and sustainable.

He thought of his father's reaction when he had gotten his permaculture design certificate. He'd saved up the sixteen-hundred bucks to take the course, gone up to Occidental and for three weeks been drilled on alternative energy, organic gardening, water conservation, and how they all played together, how to stack their functions and learn to see pathways of energy in nature, to harvest the wastes of entropy.

"You are certified in *what*, exactly?" his father had asked. They were on the large back deck of his father's sprawling suburban home, the smell of fresh cut grass in the air. His stepmother had hired caterers, and an elaborate brunch was spread out on the glass-covered wrought-iron deck tables: croissants, crepes, elegant bowls brimming with sliced fruits, bottles of champagne, carafes of fresh-squeezed orange juice. Expensive vodka and tomato juice.

"Permaculture design. Developing forms of a permanent agriculture that are self-regulating and sustainable."

"Well, Mark—"

"Calendula. Please, Dad, call me Calendula."

"Calendula. I'm sorry, what *is* a 'Calendula', exactly?"

"It's a medicinal herb. A flower. It has the power to heal."

"Yes. Well...okay." His father stared at him, cocking his head as he dropped a strawberry in his mouth. "As I was saying... Calendula...you know, this permaculture thing you're talking about, it sounds more like a hobby. You need to think about a career."

"It's not a hobby. It's my life. Do you even know the concept of Gaia? That the earth is a living, breathing organism? Understand how precious our soil is?."

"I'm talking about your future and you're talking about playing in the mud."

His dad was a corporate lawyer who commuted to Chicago every day in his BMW and lived in a suit and tie.

"Maybe I don't want a future of defending corporate greed and getting rich off the destruction of the planet."

"Son, I don't think you understand what I do. Lawyers help people, we don't hurt people."

"You help the rich."

"I can't talk to him. I can't," his father said, rising from the ornate wrought-iron chair and marching away, the ice clinking in his empty glass of Bloody Mary. Then his step-mother, a woman he barely knew but who was always sweet to him (he assumed because of her inimical relationship with his notoriously difficult sister, Bethany, whom he noticed strutting his way right now) followed after his father and said, obviously for Calendula's benefit: "Don't get so upset. Everyone is different and there's nothing wrong with that."

Bethany strode up, eyes like ice as she looked him up and down, taking in his patchwork pants, the hole in his Phish T-shirt.

"Hello, Mark." Her mouth curved into its customary half-smile perma-smirk. "Wait, no, it's, it's...Don't tell me...Ca-len-du-la. Am I right?" She spoke in that nasal tone all her upper-crust, socialite friends used when speaking with someone below them: waiters, caddies, caterers.

"Hello, Bethany. Yes, I'm going by Calendula. It's my forest name."

"Your...wait, *what?*"

"My forest name."

She was dressed in a pink, Prada suit-dress with a matching headband. She clacked her long, perfectly manicured fingernails (painted the same soft shade of pink as her outfit) against her champagne flute.

"What's up with the hair?" She took a sip of her mimosa, eyebrows furrowing into a deep-set V, which gave her the look of a predatory bird. "Those aren't...dreadlocks?"

He ground his teeth and nodded, meeting her gaze dead on.

"I suppose this means you're over the 'Yo, dog, what's up' stage?"

He just stared at her.

"And I hear you work in a *super market* now?"

"It's a co-op."

"Like a health food store?"

"It's a cooperative market, which means as an employee I'm a co-owner and on the board, having voting privileges. It's an experiment in socialist capitalism."

"Gotcha." She tossed her hair back with a quick shake of her head. "You know, Rodger and I are eating all organic now. I don't want poison on *my* food." Rodger was her fiancé who had recently passed the bar on his third attempt. "It's terribly expensive, though. Honestly, I don't know how you can afford it." She laughed in that awful, fake way that always grated against his bones.

She didn't get it, didn't get it at all. None of them did. It wasn't about keeping the poison from yourself, it wasn't about *you*. It was about keeping the poison out of the rivers, out of the mice who got eaten by the owls and hawks and eagles. It was about realizing that humanity was a parasite using up all the resources of this tiny finite planet.

They made him feel alone, like a freak—worse, like an abysmal loser—even his overly sweet stepmother, who obviously wanted him in her corner of the ring. She came up behind him and put her arm around his shoulder, declaring, "Well, I for one, am proud of Mark, er, Calendula. The world needs more free spirits who do what they believe in."

Later, she slipped him a few hundred dollar bills, told him she didn't want him to go hungry. He took the money. But taking it made him feel even worse.

He just wanted to run, get as far away as possible. Which is what he always did. Running west to until the ocean met the land in San Diego and there was nowhere further west to go.

And now he was here, in these dark, wet, back hills: as far away from them as possible, in every conceivable way.

—

The headaches and buzzing in Calendula's ears had grown worse since he'd started cleaning out the grow room and getting it ready for another run. He thought maybe it was the bleach fumes, or the pesticide, the same damn pesticide that'd caused that awful fight with Rebecca.

The pot was harvested and hanging, industrial dehumidifiers whirring and sucking the moisture from the air in the back rooms, and the grow room was almost ready for the clones, the baby plants, Coyote had gone to get.

It had taken days to clean out the little plastic baskets, stripping out the roots and separating the marble sized balls of rust-colored lava rock. Cleaning them in a bleach solution that burned his hands, singed his cuticles, and stripped the color from his fingers. Bent over the big laundry sink in the back corner of the grow room, hour after hour: rinsing and draining, rinsing and draining. Then the buckets, scrubbing, mopping, till he was soaked through with water, his nasal passages burning with bleach fumes and his eyes stinging and raw.

When Coyote had pulled the metal canisters of industrial pesticide fogger out of the plain, brown paper bag, he'd grinned. "This stuff is illegal in California. I had to have my buddy in Oregon drive it down to me. It'll kill every bug in here. Every motherfucking one of them."

"But won't that kill the, ah, beneficial insects, too?"

Coyote gave him a look like he was the dumbest motherfucker he had ever met. "Come on, three in each row. Let's try to get out of here before the room's full of gas."

They set off the foggers and darted out of the room. Calendula grabbed some duct tape and tried to seal up the door after they shut it, but the noxious chemical smell, like melted plastic, leaked through the cracks of the doors, the reek permeating their bedroom.

Coyote left to go get clones, and when Rebecca came back in the bedroom and smelled the pesticide she went berserk.

"In our bedroom? Where we sleep? Calendula, how could you?" Her hands clenched into fists that she put to either side of her head.

Calendula just looked away, thinking, If she knew how dangerous this shit really was she'd absolutely lose it. Coyote's words echoing in his head: *This stuff is illegal in California.*

She flung open a window, wind and rain blowing in, then turned back to him. "What is *wrong* with you, Calendula?"

"Hey, I didn't do it. Talk to Coyote."

"I feel like I don't even know you anymore. Who *are* you?"

"It wasn't me."

"Stop it. You were there. You could have stopped it." She gave him an insanely angry look—eyes bulging from their sockets, teeth bared—and he actually thought she might attack him.

Megan came to the doorway. "What's wrong, Mommy? Are you fighting?"

"No, Megan, we're just talking. Now go in the kitchen and work on your puzzle. It's not safe for you to be in here now."

"Come on," Calendula said. "It's perfectly safe. The smell will go away in a minute."

Rebecca's eyes glinted like razor blades; her hands were trembling. She looked down at Megan, panting in her effort to remain calm. "Go on, honey. I'll be there in a minute."

After Megan had gone out the door and the sound of her shuffling feet disappeared down the hall, Rebecca spun toward Calendula and got in his face, virtually nose to nose. "Know what I think? Coyote owns you. You're nothing but his little bitch. And you're becoming everything I hate."

Suddenly he wanted to hit her. The ringing in his ears went up a notch, his headache flared and pounded, and he almost took his fist and cracked her across the face. But as suddenly as the violent urge came upon him it disappeared, leaving him slightly startled.

He stared at her, silent.

He was so tired; he didn't know how to defend himself. She turned and started pulling at her hair, where her thick dreadlocks met her temples. She kicked the bedframe so hard he could hear the wood crack.

She was right, of course. But what could he do? He was only taking orders, and Coyote did have a point, they couldn't take a chance with bugs. If spider mites got a foothold in there they'd be impossible to stop, even with the nastiest of pesticides.

She sat down on the edge of the bed. "I'm trapped," she said. "Fucking trapped." And she started to cry.

He couldn't take it, he was so tired, so spent, so spun. There was that terrible ringing in his ears and he wasn't used to her crying. She had never cried before like this, had always been so tough. Even during that whole Starbucks fiasco back in San Diego she had never wept. She would get angry, curse, pout, grown sullen and silent, but never cry. He had always admired her strength. He turned and walked away from her, down the hallway, past Megan at the kitchen table wading through puzzle pieces, and out to the screened-in porch.

He lowered himself on to a battered old chair, the enclosure damp and musty, rotten holes in the floor, moss growing in the corners. He stared at the falling rain. He felt funny. As if a part of him wasn't here at all. When he tilted his head just right, the grumble of the generator sounded like laughter. The kind you'd hear at a fair, by the fun house, coming out of some robot clown with a giant head and a menacing smile that ate up half its face.

3.

Rebecca eased the big Ram pickup beside the diesel pump at the Last Chance Market and put it in park. Coyote was out doing whatever the hell it was he did, and Calendula was still working on the grow room, so she had taken Megan on a fuel run. She'd needed to get out. She sighed and looked over at her little girl gnawing on an apple. So small and frail in the big bench seat with the thick, blue seatbelt strapping her in.

After the fight with Calendula, Rebecca felt as overwrought as ever, like she hadn't slept in days or was coming down off some hallucinatory-drug trip, her spirit a dishrag that'd been wrung out. Last night she'd taken her last bottle of wine, sat out on the dirty porch and drank it. The whole thing. Straight from the bottle, without a cup. And strangely enough, she didn't dwell on being stuck on Coyote's land or that her little girl was obsessed with ghosts; instead she just kept thinking about how badly she wanted a cigarette. She hadn't had one in nearly six years, when she'd made the decision to keep her baby and live a healthy, righteous life. But God how she had wanted a smoke.

Now, walking across the gravel parking lot and towards the little store, holding Megan's little hand in hers—sticky from the apple—that urge came over her again.

A few locals sat beside the door, sucking beers down from brown bottles and guffawing, the one with the frizzy hair and overalls exclaiming, "And when I saw that snakebite on him, I just whipped out my dick and pissed all over it. Didn't tell him I was going to or nothing."

"Does that really work on rattler bites?"

"Hell, I don't know."

They burst out in fit of laughter, and as Rebecca and Megan approached the door, an older guy with a bushy salt-and-pepper mustache and mutton chops, a cowboy hat perched atop his head, stepped up and opened the door for her. He was huge, a giant of a man, and he loomed over them, googly eyes bulging out from a simian face

"Thank you," Megan said in the polite way Rebecca had taught her.

"Sure thing, missy." He grinned a wet, toothless smile that chilled Rebecca, though she managed to smile back at him and give a polite nod of her head as she stepped in.

The wood-walled, dimly-lit little store had a musty smell of hardware, dirt and industrial soap, like a garage. She picked up a plastic basket and wandered down the dingy aisles. Such crappy food: cans of pork and beans, boxes of sugary breakfast cereal, sardines, crackers, two-liter bottles of soda. She still had a few packages of tofu at the house, a big strip of tempeh, and all the greens from the garden, but she was going to need something to stretch it out until they could make another run up north to the health-food store in Eureka.

She finally settled on a couple cans of diced tomatoes and black beans. They weren't organic but they would have to do. There was a small produce section on the refrigerated shelves at the back of the store, but it looked like the same soft tomatoes and browning broccoli as the last time she was here, slowly rotting beside plastic-wrapped steaks and ground beef, pink and glistening in the fluorescent light. There were some nice-looking apples and bananas, though, and she put those in her basket.

Turning to the next aisle and heading back up towards the cashier, she came to the wine section. A few cheap boxes on the bottom shelf beside a couple dusty, gallon-bottles of Carlos Rossi burgundy, and on the top shelf some good local stuff. She recognized the Briceland zinfandel right away. The two red stripes meant it was organic. It was expensive, nearly thirty bucks a bottle, and they were really trying to save money. Oh screw it, she thought, grabbing a bottle and putting it in her basket, and then, on an impulse, grabbing another as well. For a laugh, she even tossed in a couple bottles of really cheap champagne. *You never know when you might want to celebrate.*

"Can I have an ice cream cone, Mommy?" Megan pulled a brightly colored triangle from the freezer and waved it back and forth. Rebecca sighed.

"But, honey, it's not organic."

"Please. Just this once?"

She really shouldn't. She knew the thing was full of high fructose corn syrup and artificial flavors and preservatives. Who knew what types of hormones and anti-biotics were in the milk? But Megan had been through so much lately, with the move and this weird place and everything else, and the wanting smile on her face was breaking Rebecca's heart. "Okay, honey. But understand we can't get them all the time. This is a special treat."

"Yay," Megan said, skipping around in a quick circle.

The bell on the door jangled and Rebecca noticed the toothless guy in the cowboy hat slinking in. When he saw her he nodded and she turned away, walking to the register.

Rebecca laid out her groceries on the wooden counter. An elderly woman with white hair and incredibly thin wrists began to ring up her items as the giant in the cowboy hat stepped up behind her with a six pack of beer clutched in his hand. She cast a glance over her shoulder at him and his face lit up and he started nodding at her again, the gray fur around his mouth parting in a grin that exposed his glistening-pink gums. Rebecca quickly turned back to the counter as the old woman opened a brown-paper shopping bag.

"Oh, I brought my own bags," Rebecca said, holding out her cloth bags.

"You say you brought your own bags?"

"Yeah. Here you go, ma'am."

"Why? We got bags."

"Mine are reusable."

"Reusable?"

"Reusable."

"Suit yourself," the old woman said, taking the bags

"And three-hundred and fifty dollars in diesel, please," Rebecca said.

"What's that?" the woman asked, her lips pressed so tight they went white, her wet, leaky eyes—yellow and pink rimmed—darting from Rebecca's long dreadlocks to Megan and back again. Rebecca thought she could smell her, sour like turning milk.

"Three-hundred and fifty dollars in diesel."

"You want three hundred and fifty dollar dollars in diesel fuel?"

"Yes, ma'am. Please."

"Huh, well, okay-dokey, if that's what you want." The woman shook her head in a slightly bewildered way and punched the keys of the ancient register. How many times had Rebecca and Calendula bought large amounts of diesel here? Eight? Nine? And the old witch acted surprised every time, eyeing her like she was some space alien asking for directions to the White House. Rebecca could feel the eyes of the over-friendly redneck in the cowboy hat on her, checking out her hair, her ass.

She eyed the cartons of cigarettes behind the old crone's head.

"Do you have American Spirit?"

"What did you just ask me?"

"American Spirit cigarettes? Do you have American Spirit cigarettes? The organic kind?"

The old woman eyed her with pursed lips. "No. Got Camels. Got Marlboros and Winstons. Dip and chew. No organic cigarettes."

"Just give me a pack of Camels."

—

It took forever for the damn tank to fill, the diesel slowly gurgling into the rusted tank welded into the bed of the decrepit truck. Megan sat in the cab with her ice-cream cone, waiting for Rebecca to be done. Cowboy hat was back outside, staring at them. Finally the tank was full and Rebecca pulled the nozzle from it and set it back in the pump. It came to three dollars less than she had paid, but she wasn't going back in that store. She swung herself up into the truck and started it up.

"Ready, kiddo?"

Megan nodded, melted ice cream running from the corners of her mouth and dripping off her chin.

Rebecca put the truck in gear and started forward as a white pickup came tearing into the lot, screeching to a stop in front of her. She hit the brakes and lurched to a stop inches away from it. The guy in the truck eyed her from beneath a baseball hat cocked all sideways. She could see a glimmer of gold chains around his neck.

She gestured with her hands for him to move out of her way. He just sat there, never taking his eyes from her. Slowly, he lifted a hand and pointed at her.

Shaking her head in disbelief she gave the horn a quick blast. He squinted, then inched the truck forward, out of her way. She pulled out, glancing over her shoulder to see his finger still extended, now turned sideways with his thumb held up, like a pistol, jerking his arm up and down as if he was firing.

"Fucking rednecks," she said under her breath, hitting the gas, the tires spinning in the gravel lot and then chirping as she swung out onto the asphalt road.

4.

Calendula gaped at the clones Coyote had brought back, rubbing his wart with his thumb in quick, tiny circles. They were beautiful. Trays and trays of little marijuana starts in rock-wool cubes, their roots creeping out in white, mycelium-like tendrils. Twelve hundred of them, covered in clear-plastic humidity domes, like little alien embryos, incubating, taking root, getting ready to colonize. Take over.

"Plant the best and toss the worst two hundred," Coyote said. He gave Calendula a wink, then added, singing: *"That's the way you do it."* This prompted a cough. "By the way—the, ah, expenses? They come out of your half. At, you know, market value."

It took Calendula all day to set the tiny plants in the lava-rock-filled baskets, get the pumps going, the nutrient solution slurping through the elaborate maze of tubes, pulsing, flowing, circulating.

Now, he lay in bed, exhausted, the humming in his head slowly giving way to sleep, and behind his aching eyes all his vacuous mind could envision was those tiny green plants perched in circulating waters.

—

There had to be mice in the house. Calendula could hear them at night, when he wandered out to the living room to put more wood on the fire: scurrying about inside the walls, scratching and gnawing. But he never caught one. The traps he set, baiting them with peanut butter and bits of cheese, were a mystery—if they weren't set off they were just plain gone. But there was never any sign of rodents: no droppings or chewed up food. No nests.

Lately he'd begun to dream of mice. Large, furry black ones with wet-pink noses, climbing over him in a swarm, their tiny claws scratching at his face as they fought their way into his open, screaming mouth. He would beat and flail at them, pulling them away in handfuls, but it was always too much, and they would fill his mouth so that he couldn't breathe and, suffocating and gagging, flailing his head back and forth, he would be conscious of the awful feel of their whiskers tickling the back of his throat before he woke in a terrible panic, his heart pounding.

But it had to be something much larger than mice dragging the traps away. It was the only thing that made sense.

He checked the traps behind the woodstove. Gone. He went to the kitchen and checked the ones in the back corner, behind the porch door. Gone as well. He got down on his hands and knees and opened the bottom kitchen cupboard and peered inside.

There, to his utter amazement, was a huge pile of traps. All the missing traps, stacked intricately into an elaborate pyramid, like a house of cards.

As his eyes adjusted, he saw in the darkened corner of the cupboard what could only be a pair of glowing eyes.

A terrible, terrifying shudder went through him, sucking the breath from his lungs. Crammed into the shadows, folded up upon himself in the tight, cramped space, was a little boy—he couldn't have been more than seven—wearing nothing but a pair of cut-off jeans. The slick, waxy skin of his chest was a gleaming white and his eyes were playful in their dark sockets, twinkling with a malignant, obstinate gleam. His pale lips twitched into a smile and suddenly laughter was everywhere.

Calendula leapt back in shock. Sweat poured from him and his hands shook uncontrollably. That's not real, he thought. It can't be real.

He caught his breath and turned back to the dark cupboard and peered in once more. Yes, there in the corner were those eyes again, but they were different this time. Closer together, smaller and yellow, and he realized with a start that it wasn't laughter he was hearing but the low murmur of a growl, followed by a hiss. And then he made out the face. It wasn't human. It was an awful mess of fur and rotten skin, with a long fang-filled snout.

Before he could react, the beast sprung at him: a possum—big as an alley cat—trailing a scaly, pink tail as thick as his thumb.

The creature crashed through the pyramid of traps as Calendula threw himself away from the cabinet. He landed sprawled on his back, traps scattering everywhere, and then the thing was on top of him. It scrambled up his chest and went for his face with its sharp yellow teeth.

He managed to get his hands around its neck and hold it back as it thrashed and scratched at him with its black claws, but it was deteriorating, falling apart in bloody clumps of flesh and fur, slipping through his hands, and he couldn't hold on to it. He watched helplessly as it melted through his fingers and descended upon him in a fury of fangs and claws while whirlwinds of echoing laughter swirled all about him.

Suddenly he was in bed, howling, and Rebecca was there, rubbing his shoulders and back and telling him it was all right. It was a nightmare, just a nightmare.

He fell back, breathing so hard he was on the verge of hyperventilating, and realized he couldn't remember how he'd gotten there. In bed. Couldn't remember coming in or getting undressed or anything else about the day. Nothing made any sense anymore, and he lay there in the dark, panting, wondering what day it was, what hour it was, trying to figure out what was real, what wasn't.

5.

The mannequin—a pale, bald and curvaceous female figure with rosy-red lips and heavily made-up eyes—dangled by one leg from a rope hung on a giant Doug fir, lazily spiraling in the cool winter breeze. Diesel carefully centered the crosshairs on its face, took in a breath through his nose, held it, and gently squeezed the trigger.

The shot rang out, echoing through the hills, obliterating a chunk of the mannequin's head and sending it dancing up and down on its tether. He brought a hand up, rotated the bolt and pulled open the breech—ejecting the casing—then closed the bolt back. Holding the rifle out in front of him, he took a moment to admire it: a thing of beauty, well-polished, the steel and wood gleaming.

"Merry Christmas, son." He handed the 30.06 over to DJ. "A Winchester Model 70, the 'Rifleman's Rifle.' Belonged to my father, and his father before that. Now it's yours."

DJ took the rifle into his hands, chewing loudly on a piece of gum. "Thanks, Pops." He seemed distracted and far away. Diesel suspected he was high on meth. Real high, and that he'd been that way for days.

"It's a classic, pre-64, with cut checkering, Mauser-type extractor. An all-around superior firearm to the ones manufactured after '65. What do you think?"

"Awesome. Love it." DJ was barely looking at the rifle, his eyes instead constantly returning to the .38 snub-nose pistol which lay on the truck's hood with several other weapons from Diesel's armament: his beloved Beretta submachine gun, and a scary-looking, matte-black SR5 with a big banana clip.

The storm had passed, and the sun was gleaming down from a white, winter sky, the earth releasing a fresh scent of soil and sod that mixed pleasantly with the stink of gunpowder smoke and hot metal.

"A lot of deer been taken down with that rifle. A lot of meat. Hunting season don't begin for a while now, but when it comes I was hoping we could take ourselves a trip. Go camping. Come back with some venison for the girls to cook up. Fill both our freezers. Whaddaya say?"

"Sure thing, Pops."

"Course, just cause it ain't hunting season don't mean we can't take down a few hillside trout sometime. No one's going to miss any of them pesky black tail, that's for sure. Just have to butcher 'em ourselves."

DJ nodded silently, eyes glazed, looking at nothing, just chomping on his gum. Diesel sighed. "Yup, hoping we can pass this tradition down to that son of yours. Once he's born and grownup enough to fire a rifle, that is. Well, go on and try her out."

DJ put the rifle to his shoulder, squeezed his left eye shut, put his right to the site, and pulled the trigger. The report rang out—a loud *crack*— and the mannequin's crotch exploded.

"Damn, son. You mean to shoot out that thing's pussy?"

"Thought it'd be more realistic if it had a hole to fuck."

"Christ. Ain't you a character."

DJ grinned, then gestured to the .38. "S'up with that one there?"

"Just a little thing I picked up the other day." Diesel lifted the pistol from the hood of the truck, his big hand swallowing it and making it look tiny, like a deadly little toy. He flipped open the cylinder, and pressed six bullets into the dark, empty holes. Spreading his legs and aiming with both hands he fired off all six rounds in quick succession. The first two missed but the last four sent the mannequin spinning wildly. "Ain't too accurate at a distance, but it'd come in mighty handy in a up-close situation. You wanna try?"

"Yeah, man. Please."

Diesel emptied the spent shells onto the ground and reloaded the weapon, then handed it to DJ who—gripping the stock—turned it over in his hands. "No hammer, huh?"

"That's right."

DJ held the gun out at arm's length and fired once. Then again, and again, each shot missing the swaying mannequin while Diesel laughed, finishing off his beer and lighting a cigarette.

"Told you, ain't too accurate. You might wanna try with two

hands next time."

"How much you want for it?"

"Wasn't looking to sell it."

"Yo, come on, Pops."

"Nope. Don't want to do it."

"*Every man has his price.* You told me that, Pops, those are your words."

"Ha. Well, I guess I did. And if that ain't true I don't know what is. Shit, I don't know. I paid three hundred for it."

"Give you three fifty."

"You are good. That's for sure. I'll give you that. Okay it's yours."

"For real?"

"Sure. Just don't do anything stupid with it."

"Naw. I won't," DJ said, releasing the cylinder and giving it a spin.

"You got the three fifty?"

"Not on me."

Diesel spit. "Typical. Now, you wanna shoot the Beretta or what?"

THREE

"You gotta jump down, spin around, trim a bale of ganja.
Jump down, spin around, trim a bale a day . . .
Boss man gets a big old stash. All we get is finger hash."
—Judi Bari and Darryl Cherney
"Trim a Bale of Ganja"

"Eeny, meeny, miny, moe, catch a tiger by the toe,
If he hollers let him go . . .
O-U-T spells out, pig snout, you are out . . .
Not because you're dirty,
Not because you're clean,
Because you kissed a girl behind the magazine."
—Children's counting rhyme

1.

It was Christmas when the beat-up black van splashed down the muddy driveway and pulled to a stop in front of the chef house, the screeching guitar of black metal music blasting from their stereo.

Immediately, Rebecca didn't like them.

It had stopped raining. Megan—her dark hair pulled into pigtails with an uneven part down the middle—was eating a grilled cheese and Rebecca had just opened a bottle of champagne. She sipped it—satisfyingly ice cold, from a chipped coffee mug—and watched them from the kitchen window.

The driver was a short girl with stringy hair, bleached a gleaming platinum white. Rebecca could just make out a line of black marks tattooed beneath her eyes. She leapt down from the van, landing squarely on both feet, and slammed the door shut behind her. She scanned the area, her head bobbing slightly to the music, both thumbs tucked into the belt loops of her jeans.

Then the side door slid open and the other two stepped out, both men with beards and long hair. One wore a floppy felt hat like an old-time preacher might wear, the other a leather vest with patches sewn all over it. They whispered amongst themselves, then the girl came strutting up to the chef house. Preacher hat leaned against the van, rolling a smoke, while leather vest kicked at a muddy clump of dirt.

"You must be Coyote's new worker," the white-haired girl said when Rebecca opened the door.

"Uh, yeah. Who are you?"

"I'm Tatum." The girl slipped a cigarette into her mouth, lit it, and, squinting, peered around Rebecca into the house. Megan, sitting at the kitchen table eating her sandwich, ketchup running from the corners of her mouth, looked up and gave a friendly wave. "You got a kid in there? Pretty fucked up place to bring a kid."

Rebecca stared down at the smug little woman blowing smoke

from her nostrils: narrow eyes above an ugly slash of tattooed symbols, a frayed shirt that read Cannibal Corpse, tall boots reaching nearly to her knees with bright red laces. Rebecca pushed her glasses up her nose, shrugged back her dreads and tilted her head, feeling her eyes and lips clench, her fingers beginning to shake. But before she could get a word out, Coyote was suddenly there, sucking on a Coors Light.

"Tatum! About fucking time you showed up. You and your crew ready to get to work?"

"That's why we're here. Let's get to it."

"All right. Good attitude. Rebecca will get you some scissors and trays."

"No. I won't. I've got to go."

"Where you going?"

"It's Christmas. I've got to call my mother."

Tatum and Coyote glanced at each other and grinned. "Okay," Coyote said, taking a gulp of his beer. "Go call your mother."

—

Phone pressed lightly to her ear, Rebecca tried to focus on her mother's words.

"I'm so glad that you called, and didn't just send me some text or email. So impersonal."

"Well, I call when I can. It's a long drive to get service and by the time you're off work it's usually late, so—"

A blast of gunfire echoed out from the hills. The shots were clearer up here, parked atop the ridge. Megan, oblivious, stared stone faced at her bunny stuffy, holding it stretched out by either arm and making it do a little dance. Christ if it didn't remind Rebecca of her playing with dead birds. A shudder went through her. Why hadn't she brought a glass of wine with her? She should have known she'd need one to talk to her mother.

She gazed out the dirty windshield. From this high vantage point, the snow-capped Trinity alps could be seen, slinking along above the tree line, hazy and distant.

"It's just so nice to hear your voice," her mother was saying. "You know, I'm all alone here. It can be terribly lonely during the holidays. At least when you were in San Diego you were close enough to visit on Christmas, so I could see Megan—"

"Next year, Mom. We'll be there next year for Christmas. Promise."

"Now I'm lucky to even hear a voice on the phone."

Rebecca watched as a turkey vulture floated by, hanging languid in the air, it's wings stretched wide and stiff, caught on a thermal and slowly drifting down into the valley below.

"I'm glad you called, Becky, because there are some things we need to discuss."

God how she hated it when her mother called her Becky. "What is it?"

"I want you to come home."

"Mom, we've been through this a million times."

"Come back to Bakersfield. This living in the woods with no phone thing is crazy."

"Mom, I—"

"Listen to me, Becky. Megan needs a good school. And she needs to see her father."

"Her *father?*"

"I saw him the other day."

"You *what?*"

"Just bumped into him. Completely random."

"I can't. I can't have this conversation now."

"Why, Becky? Why? He wants to see you. Wants to see his daughter. What did he ever do that was so bad? Did he beat you? Hurt Megan?"

Something cold inside her clicked. She clenched her eyes shut. Unbelievable. *What did he ever do that was so bad?* No, he hadn't beaten her. He hadn't done anything. Nothing. Except tell her he didn't want kids. Try and get her to have an abortion. He wasn't there for her during the pregnancy, or the birth. Never gave her one dime for child support. Not that she'd asked. He didn't have one to give anyway. He was everything she hated: a jock in high school and a redneck drunk as a man. All her ideals and values, the things that meant something to her, that had guided her life, that she had sacrificed for, meant nothing to him. He made fun of the fact that she was a vegetarian, that she wanted to grow her own food. And after Megan was born he was a non-entity. Not there for a single birthday, holiday, never called. Nothing. When she had moved to San Diego he hadn't said a word. To hell with him.

"He's changed," her mother said. "He wants to see Megan. He wants to see you. He's got a better job now and says he is ready to make child support payments."

"He's not changing oil at the Quick Lube anymore?"

"Well, he is. But he's the manager now and the pay increase was, apparently, significant."

"Christ. Give me a break."

"Look, Becky, you could have a life down here. A family."

She pressed her thumb and finger into her eyes. Back in high school her mother had always hated Brett. *What was she talking about now?*

"I have a life and family here."

"He said he'd come get you. Take you home with him."

"What makes you think I'd ever go with him?"

"He's Megan's father—"

"I can't talk about this, Mom. Please. It's not the time or place."

"Well, just think about what I said at least."

"Here, Megan wants to talk to you." Rebecca handed the phone to Megan who grabbed it excitedly, eyes going wide and a huge smile blooming across her face.

"Merry Christmas, Nona!"

—

The kitchen table was piled high with weed. Around it sat the trimmers—Tatum, preacher hat and leather vest—scissors clacking away. She could smell them. Even over the scent of all that weed. A greasy, musky scent. Like the meat of an exotic animal.

They glanced up at her as she walked in, then looked back

down at their trays.

"Go brush your teeth and put your jammies on," Rebecca said to Megan. "We're going to bed early tonight."

"But, Mommy, it's Christmas."

"Megan, do as I say. Go on."

"But, Mommy."

"*Megan.*"

With a pout Megan stomped away. Rebecca immediately went and opened a bottle of wine, taking a big swig off of it before pouring a few fingers' worth into a mason jar. Then she remembered the unopened pack of cigarettes in her purse. Suddenly the urge to smoke was overwhelming and she grabbed her purse and headed out, off the porch, and sat down on an old tire on the front lawn.

The days were crazy short and the sun was nearly down. Slapping the cigarettes against her palm she thought about her mother. *How could she?* How could her mother be in touch with that man that had done nothing for them? Nothing for her, nothing for Megan, for all these years?

She ripped the cellophane off, and pulled a cigarette out, her hands shaking slightly. She thought about how her mother said that Brett would come get her. Take her back to Bakersfield. Was that an option? If things just got too crazy? No. No, it wasn't. She'd never go back like that. Defeated. She'd sooner go back to San Diego and beg one of her old friends to let Megan and her crash on their couch while she got her shit together. Sadie, Leslie. They'd do it. Let her and Megan stay with them until she could find her own place.

But she was being rash. Things would work out. They'd get their own land. That's all that mattered. Getting their own land. Having a farm. A homestead. A place of her own where she could dig her hands into the dirt, work the soil.

She lit the cigarette and took a long pull on it. Her mind went light and dizzy. Her first cigarette in nearly six years. Since she'd discovered she was pregnant with Megan. She took a gulp of wine.

—

A voice called out from the dusk. "Rebecca? Rebecca?" It was Calendula, poking his head out the screen door to the porch. She didn't answer but knew he had noticed her there, dreads hanging down in her face, pulling on the smoke so that the ember burned brightly.

"*What* are you doing?" he asked, sidling up to her, hands on his hips. "Are you smoking?"

"Look, don't give me any shit. All right? If I want to hear what a failure I am, I'll just call my mother back." And she found herself laughing, though she didn't know why.

"I'm not here to judge you, baby," he said, sitting down beside her. "Do what you gotta do."

She took a sip of her wine, then held the jar out for him. "Want some?"

"Yeah. I'd love some actually. So, I take it the conversation didn't go too well."

"You could say that." She blew out a jet of smoke. "Look, I don't want to even get into it now. Okay?"

"Sure, sure."

They sat in silence for a while, passing the wine back and forth as the air grew cold, the last of the daylight slinking back behind the trees.

"What about those trimmers?" he asked. "What a bunch, huh?"

"They seem nice."

"You really think so?"

"No."

Calendula laughed. "How do they get into those tight jeans?"

"Maybe they sew them onto themselves."

"I'm going with the lube theory. They oil them up and force their legs in. That's why they're so greasy. I know they don't take them off once they're on. I can smell it."

Rebecca laughed, snubbed out her cigarette and wrapped an arm around his waist, sank her head into his shoulder.

The sound of distant gunshots drifted from the trees and an unkindness of ravens beat their black wings and took to the air.

2.

The trimmers kept to themselves. They slept, cooked and ate in their van, went to the van to smoke and talk, went there to listen to music. Sometimes Rebecca could hear their voices out there as she cooked dinner, above the screech of their metal music, talking among themselves.

A routine developed.

At night, after Megan was safely tucked into bed, Rebecca would trim with them. They were a sullen and quiet crew, but, driven by the tedious boredom, they'd get to talking. Preacher hat's name was Boris. Leather vest was Theo. They were brothers, their parents German immigrants who'd moved to California when Boris and Theo were boys. They still had mild accents, a slightly stilted way of speaking. They'd gather up big balls of hash by scraping all the resin off their scissors and fingers, then smoke it in a corncob pipe.

Passing the pipe back and forth they'd get to giggling hysterically, then recount how, when they met Tatum at Fortuna High, she'd been trying to fight the entire cheerleading squad at once.

"They might have gotten the better of you, Tatum, but at least you gave Shelly Holverstein a bloody nose."

"Bloody?" Theo said. "She crushed that thing. Had to get plastic surgery. Didn't her parents try and sue you?"

Tatum made an exasperated face at Rebecca, then said over her shoulder, "Why don't you guys shut the fuck up?" She rolled her eyes and shook her head. "Jeeze. You always got to be talking?" Which caused another eruption of laughter from the brothers.

It had been a quiet night. The rain was back, slashing down against the windows and peppering the roof. Rebecca sat at the table with the trimmers, manicuring, manicuring, manicuring, till she was nearly in a trance, seeing tiny leaves and calyxes when she blinked or shut her eyes.

Then Coyote threw the whole scene into chaos by crashing into

114

the kitchen with a couple of hippie girls he'd picked up at the bar, one on each arm.

"Rebecca," he said, his voice a slurred, boisterous bark. "Get my friends here some trays and scissors. They wanna work. Right girls? You ready to make some money?"

"Damnit, Coyote, keep it down," Rebecca said. "Megan's sleeping."

She stared at the rain-drenched trio swaying in the doorway, wasted and drunkenly holding each other up. The girls looked pretty sleazy, in that nasty hippie way Coyote always seemed to attract. The blonde was wearing a tie-dyed halter top with a Grateful Dead steal-your-face skull printed on it. It was nothing but strings and a tiny, wet piece of fabric that clung to her small breasts. The other, a brunette with dark eyes, was barefoot with a strand of tiny bells wrapped around her right ankle, a miniscule denim skirt, sewn together from jean scraps.

"Right, right," Coyote said, his voice now a harsh whisper. "My bad."

"Hey, sister," the blonde said, extending a slinky arm in some sort of drunken greeting. "Blessed be."

"Yeah," Rebecca said. "Hi."

"Wow, you're beautiful." The brunette, stepping forward, tried to wrap her arms around Rebecca, the bells on her ankle jangling.

Rebecca made a disgusted face and stepped away from her. "Coyote, maybe you ought to come back in the morning. It's late."

"Hey, these girls are here to work. You wanna get this shit finished or what?"

Rebecca stewed inside. She didn't need to deal with this. Where was Calendula?

She stormed down the hall to get them their trays. When she got back the two girls were slumped at the kitchen table, completely passed out. Tatum had stopped trimming and was staring at them, her sharp eyes and tiny mouth clenched in contempt. Coyote was rummaging through the refrigerator, cramming a hunk of leftover tofu into his mouth.

Tatum pushed herself away from the table, stood up, and

slammed the refrigerator shut.

"Hey, I wasn't done in there."

"What the fuck?" Tatum said. "You said we'd be the only trimmers."

"Figured you might want a little company."

Tatum gestured at the two girls, one face down on the table, the other with her head thrown back and her mouth hanging open, already beginning to snore. "You call this company?"

"Come on, Tatum. Ivy's just here for the night. And you'll love Sunbeam."

"Really? She seems utterly useless. Look at her."

"You'll be surprised. She cleans up nice. You might even get to really like her. She's got a thing for girls."

"What the fuck's that supposed to mean?"

"You know what it means."

"Fuck you, Coyote. We had a deal."

"I'm sorry, but I'm just not getting what the problem is."

"For one there's no room for them. It's already crowded as it is."

"We'll make room."

"For another, *the job is supposed to be ours.*"

"Don't be that way. There's plenty to go around."

"No. This is bullshit. You broke the deal."

"What are you going to do? Leave? You got somewhere else to go?"

"How about I just slit their fucking throats right now? Let you clean up the mess."

Theo and Boris looked at each other and smiled.

"Oh, you are a nasty little girl. I've always liked that about you."

Rebecca had had enough. She threw the trays down on the table and stormed off down the hall and to bed.

—

Morning. When Rebecca came into the kitchen, Megan shuffling along beside her, Sunbeam and Ivy were sitting at the kitchen table,

116

scissors clacking furiously. From the window, Rebecca could see Tatum out in the yard, milling around her van, Theo making coffee on a portable camp stove. Boris smoking, his face hidden in the shadows of his black-felt hat.

Sunbeam smiled at Rebecca. "Sorry about last night. Ivy and I really tied one on."

"Don't worry about it," Rebecca said, filling a kettle for tea.

"We had some catching up to do," Ivy said. She laughed and winked at Rebecca. "You know how it is when you see old girlfriends. This your little girl?"

Megan creeped around to the side of Rebecca and hid behind her legs.

"Don't be shy, little one," Sunbeam said with a smile and a wave.

"You want some pancakes, sweetie?" Rebecca asked, stroking Megan's dark curls.

Megan nodded, clutching her skirt and peering around her legs at Sunbeam who continued to wave at her, now bent over so that she was eyelevel with the little girl.

"Okay, go wait in the living room. I'll bring them to you there."

Megan darted away, her bare feet pattering against the floor in quick thumps.

As Rebecca mixed the batter and poured it into a hot skillet, Calendula came strolling in, looking disorientated and lost, scratching at his dreadlocks.

Sunbeam smiled up at him, "So, you must be the new partner Coyote was telling us about."

"Uh, yeah. That's me." He pulled out a chair and dropped down into it. Ran a hand down his face.

"Heard you got a real green thumb."

"Sure. Plants really dig me." He laughed. "Actually, I'm a permaculture designer. I'm thinking of making a couple positive changes around here. Develop a few more symbiotic relationships."

"Cool. I've always been fascinated with permaculture. Where'd you get your certification?"

"Occidental."

"Nice. I hear that's a really enlightened place."

"Enlightened, yeah. Magical too."

Rebecca flipped the pancake and glanced over her shoulder. Calendula, with a pathetic, lopsided smile, was blatantly eyeing Sunbeam's skimpy halter. And Sunbeam was encouraging it. Tossing her hair as she talked, moving her bare shoulders with a shimmying twist.

Taking a plate from the dishrack, Rebecca slammed it down on the counter, then caught a whiff of smoke on the air. The damn pancake was starting to burn. She quickly scooped it up with the spatula and lay it on the plate.

"Everything all right?" Calendula asked.

"Great. Everything's just great." Rebecca turned her back to him and strode into the living room.

Megan was in the corner, sitting cross-legged on the dirty green shag carpet, mumbling to herself and playing some kind of game.

"What you doing, kiddo?"

The little girl jumped, startled, her eyes wide. "Nothing."

"Come sit down and eat your pancake."

Megan unfolded her legs and got up slowly, glancing back at the corner once before sitting down on the sofa.

Rebecca sat the plate on Megan's lap, then sunk down into the couch beside her and closed her eyes. She could hear them talking in the kitchen, Ivy getting ready to go and asking Sunbeam if she was sure she wanted to stay, if she was going to be all right. Calendula assuring them that Sunbeam would be fine.

Hearing Calendula talk to her like that, protective and compassionate, sent a shiver of jealousy through her, immediately followed by a sense of foolishness. Calendula was just being Calendula. He hadn't done anything to be angry about.

She let out a deep sigh and tried to imagine the little farm they'd soon be able to buy. A cozy cabin tucked deep into the woods, with a big kitchen garden right outside the door. She pictured her and Megan canning together, making preserves and fruit leather. Starting trays of seeds: heirloom tomatoes, squashes, cucumbers for pickling. She just had to focus on the dream. Focus on the dream.

3.

Rebecca never expected to become friends with Sunbeam. Didn't want to become friends with her. Nevertheless, in the days that followed, that's what happened.

The first-time Sunbeam had tried to ingratiate herself, sidling up next to Rebecca as she scrubbed burnt beans from the bottom of a pot, asking her if she needed help, Rebecca had rebuffed her.

"No. Thanks. I've got it."

"You know, I just love your daughter." Sunbeam leaned against the counter languidly. "She seems like such a sweetie."

Rebecca rinsed the pot and put it on the dishrack. Sunbeam handed her Megan's plate.

"So, you're a vegetarian?"

"Yup."

"Me, too. Have been all my life. My mom was some kind of super-hippie. Sunbeam's my real name. Right there on my birth certificate. She did it all. Communes, Buddhism. Was even a Hare Krishna for a hot second."

Rebecca glanced at Sunbeam. She was wearing one of Coyote's thick flannel shirts. It was much too big for her, hanging off her shoulders. She looked like a little girl dressing up in her father's work clothes.

"Huh," Rebecca said. "That's pretty interesting." She looked into the sink, decided the rest of the dishes could wait, and poured some wine into a mason jar. "What's your mom do now?"

Sunbeam let out a choked laugh. "She works at a gas station. Swear to God. But she's happy. And I wouldn't trade the way she raised me for anything."

Rebecca offered her a glass of wine and she took it. That's how it began.

The next day Sunbeam insisted on cooking for them. She made a vegan lasagna, using nutritional yeast as cheese, kale and chard from the garden, and mushrooms Rebecca and Megan had harvested from the woods. It was delicious. After dinner, the four of them sat around the table—Calendula, Megan, Rebecca and Sunbeam—and talked.

"Where'd you guys meet?" Sunbeam asked.

"At the co-op in Ocean Beach," Calendula said, rolling a joint.

"San Diego?"

"Yup."

"I know that place."

Calendula lit the joint, puffed on it and passed it to Rebecca. Megan doodled on a piece of torn paper. "Look Sunbeam," Megan said, holding up the drawing. "Sunflowers!"

"They're beautiful!"

Rebecca took a hit and passed it to Sunbeam, who took the joint with a gleaming smile, her eyes glittering. Rebecca saw that Sunbeam hadn't been flirting with Calendula at all. It was just her nature. She was extremely friendly and didn't even seem aware of the sexual vibe she threw off. She was a sweet girl, and Rebecca smiled back at her as she passed her the joint. She liked her. She couldn't help it.

But what really made Rebecca warm up to Sunbeam was Megan. The two just hit it off. Megan would pull her by the hand into the garden—"Come on, come on, Sunbeam, see how tall the favas have gotten!"—and the two would romp around. Sunbeam would pin two huge chard leaves—their stems and veins a fluorescent red—to Megan's back and tell her they were fairy wings, and they would hold hands and spin in circles, pretending to fly off to some enchanted land.

Leaning against the doorway to the porch, Rebecca would watch them run around the garden and the yard. Fairy princesses on an adventure. Seeing them play warmed some inner part of her. It felt so good to see Megan playing again. Happy and grinning, her tiny white teeth gleaming. She'd grown so odd and morose since they'd moved to the compound, and Sunbeam brought out the child in her again.

And Rebecca realized *she'd* needed a friend as well. They'd make runs to the Last Chance Market together. When the weird local rednecks would try to flirt and stalk Sunbeam, she'd laugh right in there faces. "Back off, mister. Didn't your mother teach you any manners?" They'd pick out wines and go through the shitty produce, plan that night's vegetarian feast.

In the evening, after Megan was tucked into bed and Calendula was off in the grow room, they'd sit on the porch and smoke and drink. Talking.

"I'm glad you're here," Rebecca told her.

Sunbeam laughed. "I bet. I can't imagine being stuck with those freaks." She gestured with her head into the kitchen, where Tatum, Boris and Theo sat around the table trimming. "Do you think they're, like, together?"

"Together?"

"Yeah. Like are they fucking in that van at night?"

"I don't think so. Boris and Theo are brothers."

"I can't see that stopping them weirdos."

Rebecca laughed, choking on wine.

The ensuing silence, not unpleasant, lingered. Finally, though, Rebecca asked, "So, what's your plan?"

"Hawaii."

"Hawaii?"

"Yeah. Ivy and I are moving to Hawaii. Fuck Humboldt. So over the rain and cold. We're out of here. What about you?"

"We want to get a little homestead. Just a piece of land where we can grow our own food. Someplace I can get my herbal business going."

"The hippie dream."

Rebecca chuckled. "Yeah. But, I don't know. It's only a couple of months till the next harvest, but sometimes I wonder if I'm going to make it. This place, it's just freaking me out."

"You'll make it. Don't worry. And it will all be worth it."

"Jesus, how I needed to hear that. Thank you."

Sunbeam grinned and lit a cigarette. "Of course."

—

Night. Megan was sleeping. Calendula was off somewhere with Coyote, and Rebecca was sitting at the kitchen table with Sunbeam, Tatum, Theo and Boris, making a half-hearted attempt at trimming. It was difficult, because she was halfway to sloshed and starting to see double, the scissors either missing their target altogether or gouging huge chunks out of the buds. She squinted at a thumb-sized hole she had taken out of a large cola and sighed, put down the nugget, and took another sip of wine.

Out of the blue, Tatum asked, "Ever see any ghosts around here?"

Rebecca pushed her glasses up her nose. "Please. I've had enough of that nonsense to last me a lifetime."

Tatum looked up from her tray, the dim light catching the hard angles of her face and casting the hollows of her cheeks and eyes into shadow. The strange markings tattooed across her cheeks seemed to shift and dance as her eyes turned to slits. "Don't tell me you don't know the history of this place."

"Okay, what history?"

"This place has always been fucked. From the start." Tatum put a manicured bud in her bag and reached for another stalk from the pile of weed on the table. "Back in the day, before white men came and chopped them all down, this whole valley was an ancient redwood forest. The Indians, the Weott and Hoopa and Yurok, wouldn't live in 'em. Said they were full of evil spirits and only the mad and insane would live in such a place."

"Are you saying redwoods are evil?"

"I'm just telling you like it is. Ever notice there's barely any animals in the redwoods? No birds. No deer. Only thing you see there is banana slugs. Some say it's the tannins in the duff. Redwoods release shit-tons of tannins to ward off insects and other plants. Even after the white man came, they didn't live in the redwoods. Only outlaws and tramps made camp in 'em."

Rebecca thought about the lack of any animals around here. No mice, no squirrels or chipmunks. Only ravens. And so many of them dead and lying scattered in the woods.

"I think the redwoods are sacred and beautiful," Sunbeam said. Boris and Theo cast a quick glance at each other and giggled. Sunbeam shot a look at Rebecca, and motioned towards the other three, mouthing the words: *What the fuck?*

"So, that's it?" Rebecca said. "Evil spirits from the redwoods?"

"Naw, that ain't it. They say these woods are lonely and looking for souls to keep."

"Give me a break." Rebecca took a branch and began stripping off the sticky, lime green buds, her fingers black and caked in resin.

Tatum said, "That's why them hippies abandoned the commune. Things kept going wrong. Weird accidents. Then that little boy drowned. They were all high out of their minds on acid. Left the next day."

Rebecca tossed the bare branch onto a pile on the floor. "Is that story even true?"

"Oh, yeah. It's true. My Uncle lives in Zenia and used to work for Spider."

At the mention of that name Rebecca nearly dropped her scissors.

The room was quiet except for the clacking of metal against metal. Tatum looked around, her mouth a cruel smirk. "You do know about Spider, right?"

"The guy who lived here before Coyote?"

"That's right. He's the one got this place named Homicide Hill. They say he buried over a dozen bodies back there before a posse of locals took him down."

"More bullshit," Sunbeam said, working the tips of her scissor into a nug.

"Naw. That's true as true can be. Look it up. Google it on your little phone."

Sunbeam gave Rebecca a look again. Rebecca could see that Sunbeam was getting seriously pissed.

Tatum rapidly clipped the large fan leaves off a stalk, talking all the while. "Craziest thing, I once went back to Coyote's shack, and heard him talking to him."

Sunbeam slammed down her scissors. "Are you really going to sit here and tell me you heard Coyote talking to a dead guy?"

"That's the question, I guess."

Sunbeam let out an exasperated sigh. "Why don't you just quit it with the bullshit. You don't scare me."

"I'm not trying to scare you."

"Yeah? Then why were you following me around in the woods?"

"Following you in the woods? You're delusional, girl. I never followed you nowhere."

"And you weren't throwing rocks at the outhouse this afternoon? While I was trying to take a shit? Whispering all kinds of bullshit about the river?"

"Bitch, I don't know what the fuck you are talking about."

"The fuck you don't."

"Are you calling me a liar?"

"What if I am?"

Tatum leapt to her feet, her tray somersaulting off her lap, spraying a shower of clipped leaves into the air. Crouched, brandishing her scissors: "Go ahead and call me a fucking liar. I dare you."

Rebecca was up before she knew what she was doing, holding her hands out placatingly. "Tatum? Chill!"

Boris and Theo were up, too. Whispering to Tatum, getting her to sit back down again.

Rebecca turned back to Sunbeam, who just stared open-mouthed across the table. "You're fucking crazy."

"Maybe so," Tatum said. "But I ain't no liar."

Rebecca closed her eyes and took a deep breath. "Okay. Let's call it a night. We've all been working nonstop."

"Ya, ya," Boris was saying, tying off his bag of finished buds. "We just need some sleep."

Theo put his hand on Tatum's shoulder. She violently shrugged it off. "Yeah," she said. "It's getting late. Let's go crash."

Tatum turned and strutted out the door, Theo right behind her, while Boris gathered up their trays and stacked them neatly atop each other. He turned his attention to Rebecca and Sunbeam.

"Sorry about that, guys. Tatum's got a quick fuse, but she doesn't mean anything by it. She's had a tough life." He nodded, his eyebrows lifted placatingly beneath his floppy felt hat, then focused on

Sunbeam. "And she wasn't fucking with you. Following you or anything. Trust me. I've been with her all day."

"Whatever," Sunbeam said.

Rebecca nodded appreciatively. "Thanks, Boris."

He gave her a grin and touched his fingers to the edge of his hat, like he was a cowboy in some western movie, and was out the door.

Sunbeam got up and brushed the trim off herself. "Fuck them."

"Wine?" Rebecca asked, pouring a slug into a mason jar.

"Sure." Sunbeam took the jar and gulped it down, then handed the empty jar back, started off down the hall.

Rebecca followed her into the living room, watching her as she gathered up a pile of blankets she had folded up in the corner, then sat down heavily on the sofa, pulling a fraying quilt up around her neck.

"That was fucking nuts."

"Yeah," Rebecca said, sitting down beside her.

Sunbeam dipped her head down and began massaging her temples with the tips of her fingers. "And I've been having fucked-up dreams. Nightmares."

A chill went through Rebecca. So had she. And Calendula. Remembering how Megan had told her she had dreamed about Spider.

"Like what?"

"I don't know. I can't remember. But I'll wake up in the middle of the night. It's like I'm trying to scream, but I can't get it out. And then I'm awake. All amped up. And I'll just lie there. Listening to the generator. Imagining all kinds of weird shit. Does that generator ever sound like laughter to you?"

"No. But I've had nightmares, too."

Sunbeam lay back on the sofa, her head on the armrest. "I'll tell you one thing. I'm not going to be scared off by that bitch's stupid stories. Fuck her. I'm not going anywhere." She turned on her side, pulled her blankets up under her chin and shut her eyes. "I'm so tired. All I can see is weed."

Rebecca let out a weary laugh. "Yeah. I know the feeling."

"Will you lie down next to me for a minute? I just need a friend to hold me."

"Yeah," Rebecca said. "Okay. Sure."

She lay down on the sofa and squeezed in next to Sunbeam. She had a musky, slightly dirty smell, but beneath that was a fruity, sweet scent, that reminded Rebecca of the lip-gloss she'd worn as a teenager.

Sunbeam turned herself around so she was facing Rebecca. Wrapped her arms around her, stroking her dreadlocks. Then she was kissing her, gently placing her lips against hers and running her tongue softly over them.

Rebecca pulled back. "What are you doing?"

"Nothing. I just figured we'd have some girl time. Don't you like it?"

A part of her did like it. She'd never done anything like this before. But then she thought of Calendula or Coyote walking in on them. Megan. "I can't," she said. "I'm sorry."

"It's all right."

Rebecca stood up. "I really like you. I do. I just...I can't."

"Don't worry about it," Sunbeam said. "I really shouldn't have. Ivy would be pissed if she ever found out. I just felt lonely. Friends?"

—

Rebecca leaned against the doorway of the grow room, watching Calendula work, squinting against the bright light and humidity. She took a sip of her wine, though her head was already spinning. Kissing Sunbeam, just for that one moment, had electrified her body, more than she'd even admit. She was actually trembling.

"You know, I saw you staring at her tits when she first got here," she said, the words slurring, barely decipherable.

"What?" Calendula asked, distracted, carefully pouring blue liquid into a beaker.

"Sunbeam. I saw you ogling her tits."

Calendula sighed and put down the gallon of micro-nutrients. "Rebecca, what the hell are you talking about?"

"You were flirting with her. It's okay."

"Christ, you're fucking losing your mind. You know that?"

"No, I'm not."

"Dude, I was not flirting with her. I was just talking to her. She's into permaculture."

"That's not all she's into."

"What are you going on about?"

"Me."

"What? What about you?"

"She's into me."

"Why am I not getting what you are talking about?"

"Girls, Calendula. She likes girls. I just wanted you to know that you're not her type. She's into girls. She's into me."

"How do you know this?"

"She kissed me."

"Really?"

"Yup."

"Well, that's interesting." Calendula walked up to her. She eyed him drunkenly with half-closed lids. The room spun slightly and she tried to focus on him.

"Did you like it?"

"Not really."

"Not really?"

"Maybe a little bit."

Rebecca wondered at this weird feeling of victory she felt. That Sunbeam had wanted her and wasn't interested in Calendula. Wondered why she wanted him to know. It just made her feel special in some strange way.

Calendula took the wine from her and took a long drink, set it down on the floor, and wrapped his arms around her.

"That's pretty hot."

"I knew you'd say that. But you can forget about that."

"Forget about what?" He kissed her, gently at first, then harder as her mouth opened and their tongues met.

Then they were all over each other, his hand sliding up her shirt as she fumbled with his belt. He was pulling her skirt up, and she was sliding out of her panties, knocking the wine over as she stepped out of them. His jeans were around his ankles and he had her pressed against the wall, her legs wrapped around his waist, and he was inside her as she whispered in his ear: "Fuck me. Yeah. Come on. Fuck me," her glasses slipping down, off her nose and clattering to the floor.

And she was trembling, digging her nails into his neck with one hand and grasping his short dreadlocks in the other as she orgasmed, her eyes clenched tight, the scent of pot overwhelming in the humid air as she gasped in quick, short breaths. All the while thinking about Sunbeam.

How soft her lips had been.

4.

The next day Sunbeam was gone. The blankets she had been using lay folded up in the corner of the living room. Out in the kitchen, her bag of trimmed pot rested beside her tray and scissors, but her usual chair at the table sat empty. Rebecca had been hoping the two of them might share a breakfast glass of wine and a cigarette.

Tatum, Theo and Boris were all clipping away, heads bent down in concentration.

"Anybody seen Sunbeam?"

"No," Tatum said.

Theo and Boris shook their heads.

Maybe she was in the outhouse. Or taking a hike.

Rebecca cooked Megan breakfast, then took her for a nature hike, half thinking they might run into Sunbeam out in the woods. But they didn't, and when they got back she was still nowhere to be found.

Rebecca decided to go to the back cabins and talk to Coyote.

—

She knocked on the door to his cabin and stepped inside. He was lying on a ratty sofa listening to Stevie Ray Vaughn, eyes shut, puffing on a huge joint. A string of Christmas lights gleamed above him, tiny bulbs of green and red cutting through the shadows.

"Have you talked to Sunbeam?"

"No. Why?"

"She's gone."

"Gone?"

"Yeah, gone." Rebecca crossed her arm and glanced about the little shack. It looked disgusting. Empty beer cans everywhere. Molding posters falling off the walls. A table with a game of solitaire laid out, half finished.

"Huh," Coyote said, staring at the tip of his burning joint.

129

"Well?"

"Well, what?"

"Where'd she go?"

"How the fuck am I supposed to know?" He stubbed out his joint and sat up.

"Don't you care that she just disappeared?"

He ran a hand through his hair. Burped. "Yeah. She should've finished the job before she bailed."

"How would she even get out?"

"Probably walked out and started hitchhiking. Wouldn't be the first. I thought she might cruise. Seemed like that type."

"You don't think it's weird? You're not worried at all?"

"Naw. Probably just missed her girlfriend. She'll be back."

"She will?"

"Yeah."

"How do you know?"

"I didn't pay her. She'll be back to get paid. Trust me. They always come back when they wanna get paid."

"Sweetie," Calendula said when Rebecca told him how upset she was that Sunbeam had just vanished, "you're always getting yourself all worked up about things. I'm sure she's fine. It's like Coyote said, she probably just hitchhiked."

"The dirt road is ten miles out. Would she just walk that?"

"I don't know. Maybe the neighbor gave her a ride."

"The gun freak with the barking dog? That's scary right there."

"Look, you yourself said she didn't like it here. That the other trimmers were fucking with her."

"I know, but, we were friends. She wouldn't leave without telling me."

"Maybe she was pissed you didn't reciprocate her, you know."

That thought had occurred to Rebecca. But no, she wouldn't be like that. Would she?

Calendula put his hands on her shoulders, stared into her eyes. "She's fine. I promise. It's like Coyote said, she'll be back when she wants to get paid. I'm sure she'll end up helping trim the next harvest.

Just relax and forget about it." He kissed her on the forehead. "Okay?"

No, it wasn't okay.

5.

Coyote threw an armful of weed down on the table, stepped back, and slapped his hands together. "That's it. The last of it."

"Thank God," Tatum said. "I'm so ready to get out of here."

"What?" Coyote belched, his fat belly sticking out from his filthy tie-dye T-shirt. "You didn't have a good time?"

Tatum winced and spit out a sigh. Shook her head.

"I had a great time," Theo said. "Thank you for having us."

"See?" Coyote said to Tatum. "Why can't you be more like your friends?"

Theo and Boris grinned and shot each other a quick glance.

The next morning Coyote was sitting at the kitchen table with a notebook and a pen, a pair of reading glasses perched on his nose, tapping away at the calculator function of his iPhone.

"And the winner is, Theo! With thirty-two pounds trimmed."

"Yah!" Theo said, holding his arms up in the air like he'd just won a marathon.

"Bullshit," Tatum said, grabbing the notebook. "No way he trimmed more than me."

"Check out the numbers, sweetheart. You actually came in third. Even Boris trimmed more."

The brothers high-fived.

Then Coyote was slapping greasy bills down onto the table. "Weigh plus pay means go away," he said, dishing out a stack to each of them.

"What about Sunbeam?" Rebecca asked.

"What about her?"

"Isn't she going to get paid?"

"I don't see her sitting here."

"But all the work she did. That's not right."

"Hey! I've got her numbers. She's covered. Trust me, she'll be back. Like I said, they always come back when they wanna get paid.

And Rebecca?"

"Yeah?"

"I'm sorry, but I'm not going to be able to pay you until I sell a little weed."

"You're not serious."

"'Fraid so."

"No, Coyote. No."

"Can't get water from a rock. I'll be back with cash."

"As in when?"

"Soon."

Outside, Tatum strutted up to the van and opened the driver's side door, turning and giving a nod of her head to Calendula and Rebecca before she swung herself inside, shoulders set stiff and straight, lank white hair churning with her movements. The van started up with a spattering cough and the shriek of black metal. Theo and Boris piled in through the side door with grins and friendly waves, Theo clutching at his preacher's hat, and they were gone, up the dirt road, disappearing into the hills. A few minutes later, Coyote followed them out, honking the horn and waving as he passed.

Megan ran around in the front yard, singing her song: "The leaves are all brown. The leaves are all brown." Rebecca felt a pang in her heart. Gnawing on her thumbnail, she wondered if Sunbeam really would have just left like that, without saying goodbye. A raven swept down, its shadow moving swiftly over the earth before it perched in a tree and stared down at them.

Rebecca realized they were all alone again, and a chill ran down her spine.

FOUR

"Whom the Gods would destroy . . . they first drive mad."
—Euripides

"Red rover, red rover,
Send that one over."
—Line from a popular children's game

1.

Calendula was eating Rebecca's pussy, working his tongue through the wet folds, lapping at her juices, her ass gently cradled in his hands, her legs wrapped around his neck, the softness of her inner thigh pressed against his cheek.

He slipped a finger into her. She moaned and grabbed him by the hair, taking a clump into her fist and rubbing herself against him. He took his free hand from her ass and slid it up over her hip and to her left breast, caressing it, feeling her nipple harden beneath his fingers. She arched her back, one arm bent behind her head, the other gripping his hair tighter in her fingers until it pained him. But the pain was nothing, he was so enthralled by her coming orgasm.

She smelled of earth and fruit: a salty, slightly sea-tinged taste, and pot. She smelled and tasted a lot like pot. Reeked of it actually. He extended his tongue fully into her, burrowing his face between her thighs, the taste and smell of weed overpowering now as she began to writhe and moan, her legs suddenly tightening around his neck, her grip on his hair like a vice. And now he was fucking her with his tongue, stretching it as far as it would go.

Then he panicked, for something inside her had clamped onto his tongue with what felt like tiny teeth. Fangs. And it would not let go. It began to tug on his tongue, yanking it painfully. He struggled, pulling backwards as whatever was inside her stretched his tongue out to an impossible length.

She bucked like a horse, both hands now gripping his hair, his tongue swelling with the trauma. As his mouth filled with blood and he felt his tongue beginning to tear, he opened his eyes and saw it wasn't Rebecca at all.

It was something hardly human, though definitely female. A demon of some sort, mewling and cackling, half-woman, half-plant, green with glowing-red eyes, sharp teeth, and great curved horns.

Branches extended from it, swaying like the tentacles of an octopus, with Venus-fly-trap-like pinchers on the ends, snapping open and closed. He struggled and was just able to crane his head up high enough to see huge, bat-like wings blooming out of her back. Black and leathery, they began to beat, then another vicious tug sent his face slamming against her pubic bone.

His tongue was ripping now, torn at the edges and affixed only by the thick center muscle. And there was another scent, behind the reek of pot, something putrid and rotten, like garbage or death, and a thick, viscous slime was oozing from her, coating his face and burning his eyes. Her lips went black and expanded into a great maw, chomping, slurping, her cunt growing bigger and bigger, till it swallowed his face, pulling him into her.

As his tongue was ripped free from his mouth, his head was consumed, her pussy lips gobbling at his neck and working on his shoulders. And he could feel her rising up, sense her great wings flapping and lifting her up airborne as he hung down below, flailing and kicking his feet, screaming tongue-less within her.

Calendula awoke on the grow room floor, surrounded by plants, the musky, dank miasma of weed coating his mouth and throat. How had he gotten here? The last thing he remembered was going to the back shacks.

Yeah, he'd been going to the back shacks.

There was a break in the rain and he'd decided to take a walk, shuffling along the worn path without purpose, meandering slowly, head hazy, pausing to run his fingers over a rusted Harley frame, the metal soft with patches of moss, and then kicking at an old baby-doll head.

And when he looked up the path, to where he was heading, there was Coyote's cabin: a claptrap of weathered boards that seemed to be somehow beckoning him.

He passed the generator and stepped up to the door of bolted-together redwood slabs, placed his fingertips against its rough-hewn surface. His heart fluttered quick in his chest like the wings of a baby sparrow. He pressed softly, a rock in his throat, and the door slowly swung open.

A musty smell permeated the place, but not a bad one necessarily. The sweet, slow rot of a grandparent's house, a basement,

KIND NEPENTHE

den, or ancient library. Over the windows hung tapestries festooned with paisley and mandalas which gave a crimson tint to the light.

He glanced around: plywood floor, a single bed in the corner, sofa, a counter with a portable cook stove atop it, small sink, and a table with two chairs on either end, playing cards spread out in an unfinished game of solitaire.

His eye twitched savagely and he ran his thumb over the rough surface of the wart. On the walls hung old concert posters: Jimi Hendrix at the Fillmore 1968: a flying eyeball gripping a skull, a snake-like tail slinking behind it; The Grateful Dead, New Year's at Winterland with the Blues Brothers, 1978: a blue rose and the sun dawning over snowy mountains.

Jesus, he thought, these things must be worth a fortune, and here they were, thumbtacked to the wall, no frames, the damp and rot slowly eating away at them, their corners yellowing and curling. He caressed one, running his finger over the psychedelic font that spelled out Grateful Dead. The paper was thick and soft. What a shame. More than a shame, it was a fucking crime to leave these works of art hanging here unprotected like this. His finger went up to one of the tacks that secured it to the wall. He wondered if he should pull it free, when a deep voice bellowed from the corner.

"I wouldn't do that if I was you, Hoss."

He turned, his heart leaping, his body going cold all over.

Had he really heard that?

His eye twitched, the buzzing in his ears rising a decibel. Nothing. There was nothing there. He was losing his fucking shit, is what it was. This place was driving him fucking mad.

What the hell was he doing back here anyway? It was spooky as hell, the rot and decay, the trash, the way the forest loomed and it was always dark. He turned to leave, quickly stepping to the door and that voice—a grumbling, scratchy baritone—came again.

"That's right, run away. And what type of faggot name is Calendula anyway? What are you, a pretty little flower?"

And then he was running, fear flowing slippery and cold through his veins. Bolting away from the cabin, down the road. And then . . . and then he was with Rebecca. Kissing her, fondling her

137

breasts, pressing his lips to her belly, her thighs, as she spread her legs and his head fell down between them.

But that hadn't happened. That was a dream.

He pushed himself up from the damp floor and stumbled out of the stiflingly hot room, past the plants, iridescent green and trembling slightly in the breeze of the fans. He wandered into the kitchen where Rebecca and Megan sat at the table, a large jigsaw puzzle half put together in front of them.

"There you are," Rebecca said. "I thought I saw you out on the trail."

"No. I was...in the grow room."

"Are you all right? You don't look so hot. You're all pale and clammy."

"I'm fine. Fine."

"Well, we've got a problem."

"A problem?"

"Yeah, no water."

"No water?"

"No water."

She went to the sink, full of dirty dishes, and turned the knob to demonstrate her point. Nothing came out. He stared at the puzzle on the table, tried to decipher what the picture was, but there were too many missing pieces.

"Hello? Calendula?"

"Yeah?"

"Do you think you can fix it?"

"Huh?"

"The water. Do you think you can figure out what's wrong and fix the water?"

"The water. Yeah, I can fix the water. I'm sorry. I fell asleep and just woke up. I, ah, had a nightmare."

"Mice again?"

"No. It was something else. It can't...I don't really remember."

"Okay." She seemed wary, dubious, but there was a hint of concern in her voice as well. They'd all been having wicked dreams. Then, playfully, she said, "Well, snap out of it, big fella. All right? We need water."

"Sure. Sure. Probably just an air bubble in the line. Or maybe it froze somewhere and burst. I'll follow it up to the tank."

2.

Calendula made his way to the back of the chef house, a foggy drizzle pissing down on him. He pulled the hood of his sweatshirt up over his head and cursed himself for never having bought a decent rain jacket. The yard was flooded and his shoes were squelching water by the time he found where the black polypipe waterline connected to the house and then snaked up the hill to the spring-fed tank: an ancient, five-thousand-gallon beast of a barrel made out of redwood.

The hillside was banked in by clouds. As he climbed upward, following the waterline along, looking for where it could have sprung a leak or somehow gotten clogged, he found himself swallowed in mist. He found a spot where the line had been repaired, spliced back together with a three-quarter-inch connector. He knelt down in the wet leaves and worked the line apart to see if there was any water getting to this point.

Nothing. Just a thin trickle.

Could just be air in the lines, he thought, and sucked on the tube, hoping to get some flow going. He got a solitary mouthful of foul-tasting water, but that was it. Whatever was going on, it was further up the hill.

The slope began to grow steeper as he followed the line and soon he was climbing on all fours, clawing his way up through a dense blanket of fog. He came to another splice in the line and pulled it apart. Still no water. He put the line to his mouth and pulled on it. A flood of foul, brackish water filled his mouth and shot down his throat before he pulled the line away.

He grew excited for a moment, seeing water gurgle out and thinking he had gotten it going, but then watched with disappointment as the flow slowed to a trickle. He took a deep breath and sucked on the line again. Nasty tasting water was filling his mouth but he could feel something start to give so he swallowed it and continued sucking. Another sudden rush of water, and then nothing.

Not even a trickle now. Damn it. Something was clogging the line. He put the polypipe down. The taste in his mouth was awful, putrid, and then he realized his tongue was covered in tiny hairs. He spat and scraped his tongue with his fingers, put the line back together, and started back uphill.

He pulled himself up to the plateau where the tank sat, already feeling queasy from the bellyful of stale water, covered in dirt, with heavy clumps of mud hanging off his knees and elbows. As he lumbered toward the tank, out of breath and exhausted, he caught the ominous smell of something dead and wrinkled his nose. He grasped the line with both hands where it attached to the tank and heaved on it, pulling it free, and was hit in the face with the most godawful stench he had ever smelled in his life.

Gagging, he stared in horror at what hung out of the pipe

There, limply dangling from the nipple, was a rat carcass. Just a skeleton really, with ribbons of slimy-gray flesh slinking along the yellow bones and dripping off it. The sight, smell, and taste in his mouth, the feel of all those tiny hairs, overwhelmed him and he leaned over and began vomiting.

Wiping the tears from his eyes and the puke from his chin, he turned his attention back to the tank.

He had to unclog the line. He *had* to do it; so, he took hold of the rat's neck to pull it free, its rotten skin cold and wet in his hand, and—struggling not to gag, his eyes watering and his guts churning— he gave it a hard yank. His fingers slipped into the soft skin and the skull pulled free from the body, releasing even more of that rank smell. He stumbled backwards and fell down. He rolled onto his side heaving up mouthfuls of foamy yellow bile.

How had the thing even gotten in the tank? It was the only other animal besides ravens that he'd even seen at the compound. It didn't make sense.

He lay there for what felt like a long time, the rain peppering his face, sticky-wet oak leaves slick beneath his cheek. He could hear the neighbor's dog barking far in the distance, then gunshots. And fuck if the pattering rain didn't seem to sound like laughter. His teeth chattered and he pulled himself up into a sitting position and concentrated on breathing. He felt around in the leaves and mud and found a thick, straight stick.

He turned back to the tank, stepped forward, and, gritting his teeth with resolve, jammed the stick into the rat's soft carcass, easing it back and forth, feeling the pressure from the water exerting its mass on the other side of the body. Suddenly—with a *whoosh* of water—the rat's skeletal remains jetted out of the tank and washed down the hillside.

He let the entire tank drain. It would fill again; he could hear water from the spring gurgling in already. He could never tell Rebecca about this, he thought, fighting back waves of nausea as he connected the line back to the tank. If she knew, she'd never have anything to do with the water again. One more little secret. Like the pesticide. His nightmare. He thought he heard someone laugh and he looked around quickly. Nothing but forest and fog, the soft patter of pissing rain.

And then he was stumbling down the steep hillside, engulfed in cloud, trying to keep up with his legs, but they were all tangled up beneath him and he was tumbling. Tumbling and falling and falling and falling through the mist.

3.

He was in a world of shit and puke, thrashing in it. He wretched, spitting up bile, acrid and hot on his tongue.

And now the mice were within him. He could feel them burrowing under his skin like slithering parasites, sliding around inside him as he fought to dig them out with his fingers, ripping into this flesh with his nails, reaching in and pulling out one blood-slick creature after another, flinging them away by their moist, pink tails. But there were so many. Too many to ever be free. It felt like he was made of them, composed of them. That he was simply an empty pouch of skin filled with nothing but horrible, squirming, black vermin.

—

"Calendula? Calendula? Can you hear me? *You had a seizure.* We have to get you to the hospital." Rebecca was there, wiping his face with a rag, her face so twisted up with worry that she looked like a different person. He looked around the room, dazed and blinking.

"How'd I get here?"

"I found you. In the rain out back. Having a seizure."

"How long have I been asleep?"

"Since yesterday. I was so worried."

He rubbed his eyes. He felt...different. Not bad. But definitely different. Rested.

He yawned.

"Did you hear me? You had a *seizure*. We have to get you to the hospital."

"No. I'm good. I feel fine."

"But you have to see a doctor. Please, I was so scared. I didn't know what to do."

"Have you checked the fuel tank?"

"No, I haven't checked the fuel tank. Are you listening to me?

143

You had a goddamn seizure. You were flailing all around, foaming at the mouth. I was scared, Calendula. Scared."

"You didn't check the fuel tank?" He sprung out of bed, surprised to find himself naked. "Jesus, Rebecca, you remember what Coyote said. 'Don't ever let the generator run out of diesel.' It's our job. Fuck."

He pulled on a pair of pants and a T-shirt, Rebecca screaming behind him, "This is crazy. You're acting insane, Calendula. You have to go to the hospital."

"Look, sweetie, chill. Okay? I'm fine. I just, I dunno, I think I hit my head. Okay? But I'm fine now. I promise. I just gotta check the fuel tank." He kissed the top of her head. "I love you, okay? Thanks for taking care of me, but I gotta get to work."

4.

DJ watched the gate swing slowly open, an uneasy feeling stirring in his gut. He had never asked his father to front him crystal before. Had never asked the old man for shit. Had prided himself on it. But an old friend had called asking for serious weight. Two pounds. If he could make this deal happen then he would seriously come up. And if it became a steady thing, he'd be fucking set. He hated the idea of having to ask his father to front him, but the old man was the only one he knew who had that kind of weight. As well as the quality he knew his friend wanted.

He put the truck in gear and steered it down the gravel drive, the gate swinging shut behind him. The sky was a slate gray, the land devoid of shadow. He tapped the steering wheel with the palm of his hand and ran possible scenarios through his mind.

He knew the old man wasn't going to hook him up without a fight. The fucking hypocrite. He loved to rant and rave about what a horrible poison meth was, while at the same time making no secret that he was the biggest dealer on the mountain, with the highest quality merchandise, who had no problem sampling his own supply. It was just a matter of convincing him to hand it over.

The thick bed of gravel crunched beneath his wheels as DJ eased the truck to a stop in front of the house and pulled the hand brake. He took a deep breath and swung himself out of the truck. As usual, his father's ugly ass dog was barking its head off and straining against its tether. Knowing how the old man hated it when he let his pants ride down low exposing his boxers, DJ hitched his fingers in his belt loops and pulled them up as he strolled towards the house.

He entered through the kitchen and found his dad at the kitchen table polishing the bolt head of the Beretta M12 laid out in pieces on a towel in front of him,

"S'up, Pops?"

"Keeping my parts lubed. It's important when you get my age."

145

He let out a long chuckle and shook his head. DJ forced himself to laugh along with him. The old man looked good. Not so wild eyed and strung out. Even his thick mop of orange hair and Grizzly Adams beard cut back and tamed. The police scanner on the counter grumbled with a low hiss of static.

"You need any pills?" DJ asked, pulling a prescription bottle from his jacket pocket and shaking it so that the pills rattled inside.

"The old Southern Humboldt mating call. Naw, I'm good, been sleeping like a baby." He paused, laid down the bolt, squirted a bit of gun oil onto a rag. "Amber might want some, though. If you're feeling generous."

"Sure," DJ said, sliding into a chair across from him and shaking out a few pills onto the table. "You get a haircut?"

"Yeah, I let Amber have at me with the scissors."

"Looks good."

His father scrubbed his face with hands, then cracked open a Budweiser and leaned back in his chair so that it creaked beneath his weight. "Well, I know you didn't come here just to talk about my hair and give away Xanax. What do you want, kid?"

"Well, Pops, I need to ask a favor of you."

"Shoot."

"I need you to front me some crystal."

The old man just sat there, staring straight ahead for what felt like the longest time, then put down his beer, picked up a long black spring, slipped it into the receiver, and slowly screwed the rear cap back on.

"What makes you think I'd have any of that crap?"

"Come on, Pops. I'm not fucking stupid."

"I thought you were playing the weed game. What do you want to mess around with that shit for?"

"Need the money."

"So grow some plants."

"There ain't no money in growing no more."

"That ain't true. You just got to put the time and effort into it now. Ain't easy like the old days. It's work, but there's still a lot of money to be made in the pot business."

"Even so, I'm going to need me some money for dirt and plants. Fertilizer. Shit, need at least five, six hundred plants. That's a lot of cash to get them going."

"You want me to loan you some cash?"

"No, Pops, I want to earn it. Come on, front me two pounds."

"*Two pounds?* What makes you even think I'd have that much tweak?"

"Look around! You don't seem to be doing so bad. I know you're up to something."

"I'm a certified diesel mechanic."

"Don't give me that, Pops. Shit, when was the last time you worked on an engine?"

"Yeah, yeah, point taken. I was just hoping you wouldn't get yourself wrapped up in that. Specially now that you got a kid on the way."

"An old friend asked a favor. And I stand to make some good money."

DJ silently watched his father finish reassembling the machinegun, sliding the barrel into the bolt and screwing on the front cap, the only sound the hum of the refrigerator and the clink of metal against metal.

"How well you know this guy?"

"Known him nearly all my life, Pops. Big T was my best friend all through Middle School. Stand up dude. Great fucking guy."

"It's safe?"

"Yeah, it's safe."

"Cause that's a lot of money. I really don't want you owing me a lot of money. It can make a relationship go...sour."

"Ha, don't I know it. Don't worry. S'all good. S'all good."

"Fuck. I don't know. Your mother would kill me."

"Come on, Pops. I'm a man now. Treat me like one."

"Fuck. I guess. Just stay the hell off the crap."

"I will. I will."

5.

The rains came, pattering the tin roof, streaking the windows so that what tepid light came in was warped and strange. Even when the rain stopped, Rebecca found little comfort in the sky, which seemed perpetually dark and menacing as the days turned into weeks, the weeks into a blur.

Now that the pot was in full bud, Calendula never seemed to leave the grow room. The points of the serrated, fang-like leaves grew from three to five to seven, and he switched the light cycle from eighteen hours to twelve to initiate flowering. Then the calyxes and hairs began to appear and stack, forming dense clusters of white female flowers.

The pot wasn't the only thing changing. Ever since his seizure, despite his first insistence that he was fine, Calendula seemed increasingly sullen and morose. Even when he was around, eating dinner or strumming his guitar, he wasn't fully present. His mind invariably returned to that hot, humid room full of plants, as though that was where he truly belonged. The grow room had become his home, the plants his family.

Rebecca began drinking herself to sleep every night. No more organic bottles of pinot noir from biodynamic vineyards: now it was cheap box wines of burgundy and table red.

Some nights the wine would run out and she'd remove the inner bag from the cardboard box, cutting it open to drain the last few precious drops. And some mornings she would awake, mouth a dirty carpet, a head full of helium, to see a bag cutup and bleeding on the counter and not remember having butchered it.

She'd take Megan to the little store for supplies and diesel and it seemed the eyes of the clerks and customers at the Last Chance Market began to grow kinder, their suspicious gazes lessening. They knew Rebecca and her little girl now. Maybe they even sympathized, knowing what she was going through. Now they smiled at her, called her *dear* and *hon.*

She was becoming one of them.

She gave up on eating only organic, non-GMO foods. Now she shopped for whatever was easiest: Pop Tarts, Spaghetti O's, cans of tuna and peanut butter. She couldn't seem to find the energy to cook big meals anymore.

She even thought about cutting off her dreadlocks. They felt fake. Wrong. She didn't deserve them.

She found an old tube television in a back closet, a small thing, its screen no bigger than fourteen inches, and a VCR with several boxes of video tapes. She set it on the counter in the kitchen and began watching the tapes: home-recorded sitcoms and soap operas from the early nineties—*Friends, Roseanne, Days of Our Lives*—complete with ancient commercials for laundry detergents and soaps: smart, sassy moms with mouths of gleaming white teeth. The shows' theme songs became a source of escape, the old melodies providing a vessel to drift away on as she sipped her wine, Megan beside her clapping her hands and giggling at the nonsense on the screen.

She thought of the story Megan had told her that long-ago day, the story of the little girl who lived on a boat in the bathtub.

No, she's not a princess, Mommy. She's just a normal little girl.

A normal little girl whose mother had accidentally set out to sea by pulling the drain plug—was that how it had gone?

At some point she found herself blearily drunk and trying to concentrate on *The Bold and The Beautiful*, a bowl of greasy potato chips in front of her. Megan was going bat-shit crazy from being cooped up inside for so long. Screaming at the top of her lungs, racing around the living room, then down the hall, back into the kitchen where Rebecca was trying to watch the little television.

Megan bounded into the kitchen, screeching and giggling, leaped up and down several times, pointed under the table, and started singing, "The leaves are all brown! The leaves are all brown!"

"Megan! Will you please stop?"

"What, Mommy?"

"Just stop."

"Don't you like that song?"

149

Rebecca returned her focus to the grainy image of a blonde hunk confronting his cheating wife. "I do, sweetie. I do. It's just..."

"What?"

"Well, for one you've got the lyrics wrong."

"That's the way he taught it to me."

"Who taught it to you that way?"

"Nobody."

"See?" Rebecca's voice suddenly rose. She was almost screaming. "This is what I'm talking about. Who? Who taught it to you that way? Huh? You're not making any goddamn sense!"

Megan stared at Rebecca. Her mouth turned downward and her lower lip began to tremble. Then her entire face crumbled, she began to cry, then turned and ran into the living room.

Rebecca, feeling her heart crack open, pushed herself from the table and went after her. Scooped her up into her arms.

"I'm sorry," she said. "So sorry. Are you hungry? Want something to eat?"

Megan nodded and Rebecca carried her back into the kitchen, sat her down at the table and poured her a bowl of Fruit Loops, splashed some milk into it.

Megan lapped it up, fluorescent-purple lines of milk spilling from either side of her mouth. "This is yummy, Mommy. How come we never ate this before?"

Rebecca remembered loving the sweet, crunchy cereal as a child. Watching the commercials for it on Saturday mornings.

She looked around with a terrible, dawning realization. The gaudy orange of the walls and the 1970s style of the counter and cupboards, the bile-yellow of the linoleum on the floor. The sound of soap opera theme songs coming from the little television. She was a single mother, struggling to survive, her boyfriend gone, weird and absent, her patience for her strange little girl growing tissue thin.

She had become her mother.

She dropped her head into her hands, shook it back and forth so that her long dreadlocks fell across her face and shoulders.

Megan left her cereal, came around and wrapped her thin arms around her. Rubbed her back. "What's wrong, Mommy? Don't cry."

Rebecca couldn't find words. She just kept shaking her head.

6.

It was after his seizure that Calendula began seeing the ghosts.

At first it was just the little boy. When the rain stopped, Megan would run outside to play in the trash-strewn yard, and he would see him, sometimes sitting there on an old tire rim, watching her with an amused face, other times running along beside her while she shrieked and leapt. Other times he saw them huddled close, whispering to each other.

Then he met the other one.

He couldn't resist the strange urge to return to Coyote's cabin. It pulled at him, until one day he just found himself standing there before it. The door hung ajar, open from the last time he had been here. So, it wasn't a dream after all.

Before he stepped inside, on a weird instinct, he cranked the key to the generator, not knowing if it would start or not. It roared to life and electricity coursed into the tiny cabin.

A stereo came on, spitting out music: The Mommas and the Poppas. "California Dreamin'."

Multi-colored Christmas tree lights were draped over the walls and ceiling, and they gleamed and glittered, giving shape to the darkness. And now the room didn't feel so dank and lonely, so confined, ugly or sinister. It felt festive.

He told himself he wasn't afraid. That he wanted to hear the voice he had heard before. Confront it. But the sound of shuffling cards startled him so badly that he jumped, and when he spun around, the hairs on the nape of his neck stood erect like porcupine quills.

There at the table, shuffling cards, was a skinny, gnarled looking old man with a long, graying beard, and an orange Harley bandana wrapped pirate-style around his head. And despite himself, Calendula was afraid, very afraid.

"Relax, kid. I ain't gonna hurt 'cha."

The man split the deck and let the cards flutter back together between his boney hands, a tangle of pale scar tissue on his knuckles and long fingers gleaming red and green in the glare of the Christmas-tree lights. "Care for a game of Texas Hold 'Em?"

Calendula stared, frozen, his breath caught in his throat, too afraid to even exhale.

"What's up?" the man asked. "Cat got your tongue?"

"Who...?" Calendula could barely get the word past the bird's nest in his throat. "Who are you?"

"Why, I'm your Uncle Spider, kid."

7.

The truck went up, over the sidewalk, careening past the cars lined up outside Sears, then crashed off the curb and back onto the asphalt, the back tires of the pickup screeching and fishtailing as DJ cranked the steering wheel left and whipped past the DO NOT ENTER ONE WAY sign, barreling the wrong direction down Bayshore Way and out of the mall parking lot.

"Oh my God," Katie said. "You're bleeding. What happened? Where are you hurt?"

DJ gritted his teeth. "It's not my blood."

He could hear the sirens already. Fuck. He should have known something like this was going to happen. Should have known. He steered the pickup around the thin backroad, barely dodging a Subaru coming the opposite direction, horn blaring. When he hit the 101 he slowed down, swung right onto the highway, merging with the traffic and hoping he blended in, that none of the shoppers he had roared past had taken down his license plate.

It had originally seemed like a good idea to do the deal in the mall parking lot. A wide open, public place, familiar to them all. But when he realized it was a back corner, in an empty, unused part of the lot that backed up to the homeless encampment known as the Devil's Playground, he got a queasy feeling in his gut.

When he'd pulled up to Big T's Camaro and saw Jimmy Cankerly in the passenger seat and Clint Cankerly in the back seat, his gut went from queasy to straight nauseous.

Jimmy and Clint Cankerly, two brothers less than a year apart in age, did not have the best history with him.

"This don't look good." He opened the console and grabbed the snub-nosed .38 his father had given him.

"What's wrong?" Katie asked, stubbing her cigarette out in the overflowing ashtray and blowing out a cloud of smoke.

"Big T fucking brought the Cankerly brothers with him. I don't get along with those fools."

"What are you going to do?"

"I don't know. Feel it out, I guess." He slipped the pistol into the waist of his jeans and draped his shirt over the bulge.

"S'up, DJ?" Big T shouted, rolling out of the Camaro.

Christ, the fat fuck had actually gained weight and was now enormous, easily a good two-eighty, maybe even heavier. He wore a baggy T-shirt, dripping with gold chains and bling. His eyes were tiny black dots in a mound of doughy flesh.

DJ stepped down from the truck, nervously eyeing the two brothers. Jimmy came strutting over with a predatory, pimp-like gait: one hand clutching his crotch, the other swinging back and forth. He was wearing a gold-colored vinyl hoodie covered in hot-pink dollar signs and pink faux-fur trim. Clint hung back by the car and crossed his thick arms over his wife-beater. His head was shaved and he had SS lightning bolts tattooed on the side of his muscular, long neck.

DJ knew their routine: Jimmy the mouthpiece and deal maker, Clint the silent muscle.

"DJ, DJ." Jimmy pulled off his Elvis-style aviator sunglasses. The sun glinted off the gems in the gold grill that filled his mouth and he sucked spit as he spoke. "You looking good, dog. Healthy. Yeah, yeah, I see you doing all right."

DJ nodded at him. "Hey."

Big T held out a palm for a soul shake. When their hands slapped together he pulled DJ in for an embrace, swallowing him up into his enormous bulk as he patted him on the back. "Why so tense, bro? Relax, my man."

DJ brought his face up to Big T's ear and whispered, "Why did you bring them here?"

"Relax. Relax. I'm just here to broker this deal. Nothing more. S'all good. S'all good."

Jimmy sauntered closer and amiably held out a closed fist for a bump. DJ lightly tapped his knuckles against his.

Jimmy finally broke the silence. "So, you got the goods, or what? We hear you'se got the bomb shit. Icicles. Is it really as good as all that?"

"Yeah. It's good."

"Sweet. Two elbows, right?"

"You got the money?"

"Course I do, my man. Think I'd show up without my paperwork together? I ain't fucking around. Yo, Clint, toss me that paper, dog."

Clint reached into the side pocket of his cargo pants, never taking his eyes off DJ, and pulled out a brick-sized bundle of cash, secured with numerous rubber bands, tossed it to his brother.

"All hundreds, too. Three-hundred and twenty of 'em: thirty-two large." He held the bundle out to DJ. As DJ reached for it he quickly pulled it back. "Uh, uh, uh," he said waving a finger. "Not till we see the product. And for that price it better be as good as we was told."

Jimmy slipped the cash into the side pocket of his cargo pants, crossed his arms, cocked his head and stared at DJ while sucking obnoxiously on his grill.

DJ lit a cigarette. Blowing out a jet of smoke, he gazed out at the empty corner of the parking lot, then back to Jimmy and his brother, and finally over to Big T, who smiled and nodded his head to get on with it.

"All right," he said. "All right."

He turned and opened the door to his pickup, reached across Katie who smiled dumbly, and felt around under the seat.

"Everything okay?" Katie asked.

DJ grasped the brown paper bag with the meth in it. "Yeah, seems legit enough."

Katie made a kissing face at him, puckering her lips like a fish. DJ rolled his eyes and slammed the door shut. He handed the bag to Jimmy, who opened it, pulled out the freezer-bag full of crystal—the shards clattering with the sound of ice in a glass—and examined it for a moment before stuffing it back in.

"Looking good, looking good," Jimmy said. "Yo, Clint, weigh this shit for me," tossing the bag to his brother.

"Now let's see the cash," DJ said, nervously watching the product as it whipped through the air and landed in Clint's hands.

"Hold on, hold on. We got a little incident to discuss. You owe me. Don't you?"

"What the fuck you talking about?"

"A little incident a few years ago involving a lot of trim and a very, very little bit of hash."

"Shit, man, you know that wasn't me. That was Dave Patterson."

"You best check yourself right now and own up. Be a man. Cause I know you was in on it and if you try to make me out to be a liar I'm not going to be too kind."

"I swear, man. I wasn't in on that shit. And it was only, like, three-thousand bucks' worth of hash."

"Three thousand, plus interest. *Plus*," he said, spittle spraying from his mouth, "you humiliated me. Made me look like a fucking idiot. Now it's time to pay the piper."

As if on cue Clint took off running with the bag of speed, sprinting across the parking lot and into the woods. DJ made a move to follow and Jimmy quickly stepped up, arms spread wide, and slammed into him with his chest, knocking him onto his ass.

Big T stepped up, giving Jimmy a pleading look. "The fuck, man?"

"Stay out of it Todd, you fat ass. This is between me and DJ." Then, turning his attention back to DJ: " So, what you gonna do about it, bitch?"

DJ scrambled up, stepped back, and pulled the gun from his waist band, watching Jimmy's eyes go wide and his mouth fall open. "Give me the fucking money."

Instantly, with jack-rabbit grace, Jimmy ducked behind Big T, slunk around the Camaro, and took off across the parking lot in the same direction as his brother.

"Dude," Big T said, throwing up his hands defensively, "I had nothing to do with that shit. You gotta believe—"

"Get the fuck out of my way," DJ said, pushing past him.

As his feet beat against the cracked asphalt, DJ watched Jimmy disappear into a tangle of vegetation where the parking lot ended. His heart hammering in his chest, a trail of sweat beginning to leak down his face, DJ was leaping over the curb and tearing through the woods, down the path after him.

There was the bay to the left, a massive black expanse of water. The path widened and suddenly he was in the middle of a huge homeless encampment.

He stopped, his breath coming in short, jagged pants, and cut his eyes across the maze of tents and make-shift shelters. A dog was barking somewhere. The stink of the bay was strong in his nostrils.

Then he spotted him: darting around a group of men huddled around a fire. Tearing after him, DJ negotiated badly around a rusted shopping cart full of recyclables, clipping it with his hip. It bit painfully into his side, tearing his shirt, and sending him tumbling. His face hit the ground and he tasted dirt. The cart came crashing down behind him, showering him with beer bottles and soda cans. Angry screams and threats rang out as he pushed himself up off the ground.

A dirty, bearded man in a ripped parka was shouting and storming towards him. "You gonna pick that shit up, motherfucker?"

DJ flashed the revolver at him. "Back the fuck up."

The guy held up his filthy hands, palms outward, and slowly backed away. "It's cool, man. It's cool."

DJ caught sight of Jimmy, just a streak of gold and pink, rounding a tilted flagpole topped with a tattered Confederate flag, and was after him. Then they were out of the camp, racing through pampas grass and sand dunes.

He was gaining on him.

Jimmy cast a furtive look over his shoulder and darted right, towards the beach, disappearing behind a bank of sand.

DJ leapt off a small incline and landed on the beach, the bay lapping at his feet. Sea gulls circled, squalling. In the distance, fishing boats were returning to Woodley Island. He frantically looked either way down the beach. Nothing. Not a sign of him, when—*crack*— Jimmy's fist slammed into the left side of his mouth. He saw darkness, then a flash of light, then he was falling backwards, the revolver slipping from his fingers.

When he could see again he was lying on his back, half in the surf, and Jimmy was on top of him, his knees pressing DJ's shoulders into the sand so that the water washed up over his face. Coughing and sputtering, DJ flailed with his hands as he watched Jimmy pull his arm back and cock his fist. Then, by some miracle, DJ's hand fell onto the .38. He pulled the gun up and his finger found the trigger just as Jimmy's arm shot forward, and DJ squeezed, aiming blindly.

The bullet ripped through Jimmy's knuckles, just as his fist was falling. Splinters of bone and blood showered down on DJ. Jimmy howled and tumbled off of him, clutching his wrist. His hand was a tangled mess of muscles and tendons.

DJ leapt up, pointing the .38 down at him. He was shaking badly. His mouth filled with blood. He struggled to control his rapid breaths. "Gimme the money."

Jimmy rolled back and forth in the surf, screaming in agony.

"I said give me the money," DJ yelled, squeezing off a round into the water by Jimmy's head.

Jimmy flinched spasmodically in the tide, squirming like a hooked fish. Then, with his good hand, he reached into the side pocket of his cargo pants and pulled out the big brick of cash. "Take it."

DJ took the bundle from him and clasped it to his chest like a football. "Lucky I don't cap you, motherfucker."

He bolted away down the beach.

8.

Spider dealt out seven cards in front of him, talking calmly to Calendula. "That's right, I'm the reason they call this place Homicide Hill, and I ain't got no regrets. You gotta do what you gotta do. Yep, you could say I planted a few seeds out there in them hills. Dug a few holes and filled 'em, if you catch what I'm saying." He looked up at Calendula, his face haggard and ghastly, like some kind of leprous pirate, and winked.

Calendula started to laugh and then caught himself. Be cool, he told himself. It's cool. But it wasn't cool. Things were funny. Real funny. Weird. Time was not acting right. Events were not following each other correctly. Sometimes he would get déjà vu so terribly— everything mimicking itself in crazy patterns—that he wondered if he wasn't caught in some kind of time loop.

He was in the back cabin again, with Spider, listening to his stories and bravado. He couldn't remember how he had gotten here. He nodded, trying not to appear too disconcerted as the bearded old man rambled on. "You get a skunk in your wood pile you take care of it. Simple as that. You gotta ask yourself: *Am I a man or an ant?* See? There's the question right there. Are you a fucking man, or a goddamn insect to be stomped on? A piss-ant. You know what a fucking piss-ant is?"

Calendula shook his head.

"A piss-ant is a little bug trying to crawl its way out your toilet. Something you piss on to wash it back down to the gutter where it belongs. So, are you a man or are you a piss-ant to be flushed down the fucking drain?"

Calendula stared at the scary old man, unsure whether he was asking him a question or making a philosophical statement, relieved when the grizzled biker started back up again.

"Motherfuckers come here and shoot me, sneak up on my ass and fill me full of holes, kill me. But jokes on them. Fuck you. I ain't leaving. I ain't going nowhere. Get where I'm coming from, kid?"

Calendula nodded. This couldn't be real. He had lost his shit, his cookies got spilled somewhere and smashed to bits. Only explanation.

"That's why me and Coyote get along so well. He never minded me being here none. Matter of fact, that good old feller done liked me, the lonely cuss. So we got along real nice like. Famously you might say. You hear what I'm saying?"

"Sure," Calendula said, wondering if maybe he was dreaming. Maybe this whole thing was a dream, all of it, a dream within a dream. Where had he heard that before? His mind raced back to a paper he had written in a high school English class on the nature of dreams in literature. Was that Poe? Or Conrad? No, Conrad was, "We live as we dream—alone." It had to be Poe.

"But I got a good feeling about you, kid. We're going to be pals. That's for sure. You want you some instant coffee? A little wake-up powder?"

"Ah, sure. You want me to put some water on to boil, Spider?" Trying out his name for the first time, seeing how it felt on his tongue, coming out of his mouth—Calendula was trembling. But the name felt natural enough.

Spider laughed again, this time so hard he began to cough and choke, slapping his knees with the palms of his hands. "Ha ha. Ain't no need for water with this get-go powder." He wagged a tiny baggy of white splinters at Calendula. "Devil's dandruff."

Spider reached behind him and took a dusty Pabst Blue Ribbon mirror off the wall. He began to vigorously clean the surface with his sleeve, smiling up at Calendula with a mouth full of rotten teeth. "Stole this thing off the wall of a bar in Reno back in eighty-two." He laughed a deep guffaw and placed the mirror in front of him and then emptied the bag on it. Rolling up a greasy bill, he inserted one end in his nose and snorted a mound of powder.

"Whoa-we. That'll get you going. Here, give you a try of it."

He scooted the mirror forward and handed Calendula the rolled bill, which Calendula noticed was an ancient twenty. Reluctantly, Calendula put the bill to his nose and took a snort.

Applause rang out and then there was laughter. There were others here now, bearded bikers, a tall man that looked like a cowboy, a bunch of hippies, even a dog. It was a party and Calendula sat back in the warm sound of chattering voices, hands slapping his back, the Eagles crooning over the stereo how they were living it up at the Hotel California.

And when Calendula looked up, out the window, he could see the little boy looking in at all of them. Smiling.

9.

Once they were safely out on the backroads, DJ grabbed up the bundle of cash and tossed it over to Katie. "Ever see thirty-two grand before?"

"No." She lifted the bundle. "It's so heavy."

"Yeah, it is."

Then she gasped and cried out. "Oh, DJ. It's not real."

DJ slammed down on the brakes with both feet, the tires screeching and the big truck lurching dangerously to the right for a moment before it skid to a stop on the side of the road.

No, no, no, he thought as he grabbed the bundle of cash from Katie.

He frantically pulled the rubber bands off and ripped the bundle apart. It was nothing but cutup newspaper with a few hundreds on either side. He let the paper rectangles roll off his hands and scatter. Inside, something broke. He felt his face crumble and began to shake uncontrollably as tears welled in his eyes. He couldn't fucking help it, he was whimpering like a baby. And she was taking him in her arms, holding him and rocking him as his head slipped down onto her lap. He couldn't speak. In his belly was a heaviness he had never felt before—enormous, crushing—threatening to heave itself up his throat and choke him.

"What am I going to do? My daddy's gonna want his money."

"I never heard you call him your daddy before."

And suddenly the sadness was gone.

"Shut the fuck up."

The heaviness turned to something else. He sat up, wiped the tears from his eyes and felt stupid. His mind began to churn, scrabbling for some way out of this.

"Fuck, fuck, fuck!" He pounded the steering wheel with his palms.

"You're going to have to just be honest with him. He'll understand."

"No, he won't. It's you who doesn't understand. I've gotta come up with the money. Gotta pay him back."

"But how, DJ?"

"Fucking Coyote. That scumbag's been ripping my family off for years. I'll take it from him."

"DJ—"

"That weed at the chef house should be nearly done."

"DJ—"

"Get in there, get the weed and a few grow lights."

"No, DJ. It's only going to get worse if you do something like that."

"Yo, Katie, why can't you support me, huh? Why you always got to shoot down every idea I have?"

"I do support you, baby. I do. But we've just got to be honest with Pops. It's the only way—"

That's when he hit her. Square in the left eye. Striking so fast it surprised both of them.

"See what you made me do, you stupid bitch? Now keep your fucking mouth shut."

"Fuck you. *Fuck you!*" And then she was slapping him. Hitting *him*. Swinging blindly, and he had had enough.

Enough of it all.

And that thing inside him, that heaviness, turned red as he clenched his hands into fists and, grinding his teeth, eyes burning in their sockets, he decided to teach this bitch a lesson.

10.

Rebecca had the dream again last night. It seemed like every night the same awful dream returned. She was on a hillside, looking down at the river, and Megan and a little black-haired boy were walking hand-in-hand along the shore. She could see the little boy was dead: his skin cyanotic blue, his elbows and knees rotted away.

She wanted to call out, to get up and run, but she was frozen, paralyzed. She struggled to move, to scream, anything, but could not. And then she would awake, gasping, with an ache of despair in her chest so powerful that she would have to literally tell herself over and over: *It's just a dream. It's not real. It's just a dream.*

To forget the dream, she drank. She'd drank nearly an entire box of wine when the idea of a sacrifice came to her. The notion that she had to give something up.

And scissors wouldn't work. She'd have to use a knife.

She went to the big mirror in the hall. She barely recognized herself. Her face seemed distorted and strange, a pale remnant of who she used to be. Even her lips looked white, the year-round, San Diego tan long gone. She lifted up the butcher knife and gazed at it.

She could hear Megan in the kitchen, laughing at some old sitcom that had gone off the air years and years ago.

She cringed, then lifted up a long, knot of hair, a snickering voice within her head saying, *Do it, do it.* Taking the knife, she cut into the base of the dreadlock, sawing back and forth until it was free of her head and dangling in her hand. She dropped it to the floor, lifted another, and began to cut, nicking her scalp.

A rivulet of blood trickled over her forehead and down her face. So red, so impossibly red. A deep scarlet against the ivory white of her skin.

When she was finished, every thick tangle of hair gone, she looked at herself and laughed.

Uneven clumps of hair stood up on her head; streaks of blood smeared her face. She looked like a lunatic. An escapee from the local mental hospital. She wrapped both hands around her nearly full, quart mason jar of wine, fingers interlocked, knuckle upon knuckle. Then she lifted her vessel upwards, and bringing the glass to her lips, she began to drink.

Slowly at first, delicately, but then chugging it down. A trickle began to spill down the right side of her mouth, then the left, but she kept on gulping, lifting the glass up and pouring it down her throat, hot and ugly in her belly, letting it all spill out till there was nothing left. Then she put arms down, barely noticing the empty jar slipping from her grasp and tumbling to the floor, her laughter waning as her reflection began to tilt and rock.

For there in the mirror, directly behind her, she saw the black-haired little boy. Smiling, eyes twinkling delightedly. She knew then that he was real, had always been real, had always been here.

11.

Katie wandered down the road, holding her belly, past copses of oak and cedar and pastures full of heifer, cattle guards and rusted-barbwire fences held aloft with rotten boards. The asphalt was cracked and broken, barely wide enough for two cars to pass. When the occasional pickup or dirt bike came whipping past, she turned to the forest, ashamed to show her broken face.

Already her left eye was swollen shut. Her lip a shredded piece of meat.

But that was nothing. This was the worst of it. This. The abandonment. Walking alone. She could take the hitting. When it had started she just curled up against the door as he wailed on her, protectively guarding the baby inside her, thinking somewhere deep within that she probably deserved it as his fists rained down. But when he leaned over, grasped the handle, and swung the door open, kicking her out onto the road, that's when the real pain started. Watching him tear away in a cloud of diesel exhaust, wheels kicking up dust and grit, while she lay there on the hard pavement all alone.

And now what was she going to do? She had no one. No friends. No family. Her life just one long string of abandonments. The only one she could think of was Pops. He'd put his number on the iPad he'd given her and told her to call him anytime. But now the iPad was gone. What was that number? If she could just remember his number. As she stumbled forward, the Last Chance Market coming into view around the bend, she concentrated, trying to remember.

12.

Rebecca turned from the mirror. Her long dreadlocks, which she'd been growing for nearly a decade, lay in a jumbled mess about her feet. She shambled forward down the hall, drunkenly falling into the wall and then leaning heavily against it. Feeling the eyes of the ghost upon her, she pulled herself along, scraping against the cheap wood paneling, the floor bucking like a ship in a storm. She slid around the corner and into the kitchen. Megan sat at the table eating Jiffy peanut butter with a spoon straight from the jar and watching *Thunder Cats*.

Megan's eyes left the TV, and grew wide. The spoon paused.

"Mommy, what's wrong?"

She was gripping the wall, fighting to stay up. "Nothing, baby. Just watch your show. Mommy's fine."

"But your hair, Mommy. What happened to your hair?" Megan began to whimper, tears spilling down her face, the spoon still hanging there before her mouth.

Rebecca fumbled over her words, fighting to push herself from the wall and navigate the room which spun about her grotesquely. "It's okay. Mommy needed...a change. Mommy just needed a change."

She took a deep breath and shut her eyes. She was going to puke, the tumult in her belly causing her mouth to water and her skin to prickle in cold sweat. She was distinctly aware of her teeth—they felt mildly electric, pulsing in her jaw.

I have to get outside quickly, she thought, but instead she fell to her knees and unleashed a torrent of deep-red vomit onto the kitchen floor. She watched the puddle of puked-up wine spill out across the linoleum, thinking how much it looked like blood. She could hear Megan screaming, leaping up from the table and running from the room—yelling "Help!"—but was unable to do anything beyond comprehend it. And then even that was too much and she sank down onto the floor and curled herself up into a ball, clutching her knees to her chest and shivering, the acidic stink of her sick heavy on her face.

—

Calendula was working on clipping back the large fan leaves that were blocking light to the lower branches, trying to find patterns in the foliage, crowded places that needed thinning, when Megan started pounding on the big metal door, hollering.

"What?" He eased himself up, his spine stiff and his numb feet stinging.

"Mommy's hurt and has no hair."

No hair? He couldn't be hearing her right. He deftly guided himself through the maze of tubes and buckets, careful not to brush too hard against any plants and break any branches.

"Help. Help. Hurry."

Jesus. "I'm coming. I'm coming."

Finally, he reached the door, swung it open. There was Megan, hysterical and babbling, reaching in to grab him by the hand and pull him out of the grow room, tugging him through the bedroom, down the long, dark hall, and into the kitchen where Rebecca lay curled in a ball on the floor. And, yes, all of her hair was hacked off.

"Oh my god, Rebecca." He knelt down beside her. "Are you all right? Can you hear me?"

"Go away," she moaned.

"What happened to your hair?"

"I needed a change."

"Come on, baby. Let's get you up. We've got to get you cleaned up."

"I said, *Go away*! I hate you."

"Aw, baby. You don't know what you're saying. Look how drunk you are."

"You knew. Knew all along and did nothing."

"Knew what?"

"Knew. Knew that this place is haunted. Dangerous. Knew all along."

"I don't know what you're talking about."

"Ghosts."

"There is no such thing as ghosts and this place is not dangerous. It's perfectly safe."

He looked at Megan, who sat in the doorway staring at them, big eyes bulging from her mop of curly hair, gripping her bunny stuffy to her chest. Calendula gave her his best reassuring smile. "We're almost done, anyway, and then we can leave. I promise."

"Liar. You'll never let us leave." Her ragged mess of hair gave her a diseased look, like a sick animal losing patches of fur. Her eyes narrowed to fierce slits and she locked them with his. "What about Sunbeam? If this place is so safe, then what happened to Sunbeam?"

Calendula bent down so that his face was inches from Rebecca's, looked into her eyes, and whispered low so that Megan couldn't hear. "Who the fuck cares what happened to that stupid dyke cunt, anyway?"

Then he burst out laughing.

13.

Coyote was in a strip club in LA, working some new customers—a crew of surfers who were wearing sunglasses even though the place was dark as a mineshaft at midnight—when he got the call from Sunbeam. He was immediately sorry he took it.

"What do you mean you want to get paid?" He set down his scotch and soda and signaled with his free hand that he'd be right back as he pushed away from the table. Head honcho gave him a nod. "You left on your own. The job wasn't even finished."

Nine Inch Nails's "Closer" blared from the speakers as a girl in leopard-skin lingerie pranced across the black plywood stage and threw herself onto a gleaming silver pole, spinning round it, one leg clamped tight around the shiny, floor-to-ceiling cylinder, the other lifted high above her head.

The noise—screeching music and jeering crowd—was deafening, and he ducked into a dark hall that led to the private rooms. The bass boomed right through the walls and he clamped the phone to one ear and covered the other with his hand.

"Whatever, dude," Sunbeam said. "You had your crew there to finish it. I did the work. You better pay up."

A naked blonde slinked by, leading a guy in a business suit by the hand. The guy's shoulder knocked into Coyote as he passed. Coyote shot him an angry glance and watched as they disappeared into a curtained doorway framed in hazy red light.

"Yeah, well, even so. I don't know about no four grand. No one pays two hundred bucks a pound anymore."

"Fuck you, Coyote. That was the deal."

"Fuck me? Whoa, little lady, kiss your mother with that mouth?"

"Let's just leave my mouth out of it. I need that money. I've got some plans."

"Whoa, big plans. What'cha up to?"

171

"Just you never mind about that."

"You know I've always felt protective toward you, baby. Fatherly even."

"Fatherly? I distinctly remember you trying to fuck me before you realized I wasn't into guys."

"Well, let's just say a deep concern."

"I thought you'd be ecstatic at having one less trimmer to pay. Except, you know, you're gonna pay."

"Sunbeam, honey, do I really come off that callous to you?" He eyed the ass of a redhead strolling by—fishnets, garter belt, G-string he wanted to reach out and pluck. "Anyway, I'm not in the area."

"You're coming back when?"

"Couple of days." The redhead looked over her shoulder and caught him eyeing her. She turned around slowly, and slipped up beside him, gently placing her hand on his shoulder as she swayed and rocked to the music. Coyote couldn't take his eyes off her. She was drop-dead gorgeous: angular face, cat-like eyes, tits to die for. "Look, I gotta go. Call me back later."

"I want my money, Coyote."

"Yeah, yeah. You'll get paid. Don't worry." Coyote thumbed the end call icon.

"You want a lap dance, mister?" The redhead dropped her chin and tilted her head to look at him coyly. Her heavily made-up lips gleamed black in the dim light. Her eyes fluttered and she danced closer so that her left breast brushed briefly against his arm.

Coyote looked at her and smiled.

14.

The binoculars DJ was using to peer down at the compound kept fogging up from his breath and the heat of his face. Not that they would've been much help anyway. Fog was rolling in heavy from the river and it was dusk on a dismal day, so all there was to see down there in the gray abyss of the valley were the squares of light from the windows of the chef house and shadows.

He lay flat on his stomach in a patch of tall, wet grass between two boulders. A gust of wind howled through the valley, bending trees and flattening the tall grass around him for a moment, then it was gone.

He squinted, spat, and squinted again, and thought he could just make out the generator shack and the fuel tank poking out of the fog. Beneath the moan of wind and the patter of tiny rain drops, he could just discern the hum of the generator if he concentrated.

He'd been casing the place since early morning. From his calculations, based on what intel he'd been able to ascertain, the grow should be nearly over. Now was the time to strike. Coyote was nowhere to be seen. With him out of the picture the place would be easy to hit.

About forty minutes ago he'd crept down to the generator shack and loosened the nut on the fuel tank's drain so that diesel trickled out. Any minute now and the generator should come shuddering to a halt.

It wouldn't start again very easily. The lift pump wouldn't be able to cycle fast enough to overcome the air in the lines. There'd be no vacuum, even if they filled the fuel filter with diesel, and DJ doubted those dumb hippies would have enough mechanical know-how to get even that far.

Naw, they'd be plunged into darkness and panic. Most likely run off somewhere to start calling for help. He doubted they'd stay the night there with no power. When they left he'd hit. If they came back while he was in the middle of taking down the grow, well, he'd just have to cross that bridge when he came to it.

He thought about Katie. He didn't even know where she was. Probably at his old man's place. He hadn't wanted to hurt her, and felt a lingering sense of sorrow over it. But she'd asked for it. Getting all in his face like that. Teach her a lesson at least. Bet she'd think twice before pulling that shit again.

There it was: the sputter of the engine dying. He heard it distinctly even over the squawk of ravens fighting in the trees above him. He watched with a grin as the lights flickered and went dark. The valley below him was now just a pit of darkness, quiet but for the sound of wind whipping the trees and the occasional patter of rain as a storm cloud blew over.

He felt a lopsided grin come on as he heard voices, scared and panicky. Trying not to laugh he struggled to hear what they were saying, but couldn't really make out any words. He recognized the roar of the old Dodge Ram starting up. They must be trying to pump more diesel into the fuel tank. He laughed. That would only send the air pockets deeper into the engine. He could make out the grinding of the starter and shouting. Fucking idiots. Screaming, crying, the whimpering of a little kid. Then darkness and silence.

Here was the moment of certainty. What were they going to do? Dig in and wait until morning in the darkness, or run away like frightened little rabbits?

15.

Calendula was in the grow room. The first red hairs were beginning to appear on the buds, as well as a thin sheen of crystals. The pH had been starting to climb in the nutrient solution, so he was adding liquid-down to the vats, doing the math on a calendar on the wall with a stubby pencil and then carefully measuring out the correct amount into a large beaker.

He was checking the led indicators on the digital pH meter when the lights began to flicker. For a moment the ballasts and fans all went quiet, then hummed again loudly, then went silent. Only the buzzing in his head remained.

At first the orange glow of the incandescent bulbs left the plants cast in amber shadows. But then, as they cooled, the glow faded leaving darkness, complete and absolute.

"Fuck." He used his hands to guide himself along the wall, knocking into jugs of fertilizer, banging into the CO_2 tanks, terrified he was going to trip and fall, crashing into plants and destroying them. But then he was to the far side, feeling along until he found the knob to the heavy, industrial door. He thought he heard laughter, high pitched and bright, but it seemed like he was always hearing someone laughing. It had grown as prevalent as the humming in his skull.

—

Megan was in the kitchen watching episodes of *Full House* while Rebecca sat on the porch going through the trash, looking for boxes of wine with a splash still left in the bag. She had just found a heavy box at the bottom of the heap. She ripped it open and pulled the clear plastic bag free, tore open the corner with her teeth, and was sucking the sweet, purple juice from it when she heard the generator begin to sputter. She sat for a moment, stunned, the beginning of a serious drunk just coming on, surrounded by trash and unable to comprehend

175

what was happening, what this meant, when suddenly Calendula came rushing by.

"What's going on? What's happening?" She looked at him with a myopic squint, glasses dangling lopsided from her face, as he bolted past her and towards the door.

"The fucking generator turned off."

"Why?"

He cast a cursory glance back at her, tinged in disgust and impatience, and went out the door without answering her.

—

Just let it be the low oil shut-off, he thought, an easy fix. But when he saw the puddle of diesel spreading out from the generator shack, he knew that it was something far worse.

The spill glimmered with incandescent rainbows as it leaked across the wet clay ground, through the scattered trash, Bermuda grass and thistle sprouts.

Throwing open the door to the shack, he desperately glanced around, squinting for light in the evening's murky glare. Then he saw it, up on the ceiling where the fuel tank lay, oily fuel still streaming from a loosened bolt on the fuel tank's drain.

Could the vibrations of the motor have loosened it? That's what must have happened.

He fumbled about for a wrench, climbed up onto the generator, and with some serious stretching managed to tighten the nut with his hand.

He had fucked up. This was his job. To make sure things like this didn't happen.

Then he thought of the ghost of the little boy. Could that motherfucker have done this? No, no, he couldn't have. Crazy just thinking like that.

He tightened the crescent wrench around the bolt, wincing as his knuckles scraped across the fuel tank and fire-like pain danced through his hand. He gave it another push till it would turn no more and the bolt was tight. Maybe if he could get the motor cranked up quickly everything would be all right.

He leapt down and hurried out of the shack, Coyote's words from his first day there swarming his mind like angry bats: Never, *ever* let the generator run out of diesel.

"Calendula," Rebecca called as he passed her, "help me."

"What? What is it?"

"The diesel, we have to stop it from leaking into the river."

She was on her knees, digging a trench with her hands, trying to damn up the gigantic puddle of fuel.

"It's going to go where it's going to go. We can't stop it now. It's too late." Leaping into the old Ram pickup and cranking it up he hoped upon hope there was still some fuel in the transport tank.

"But, Calendula, the river. We can't let it all go into the river. It will poison the river."

"Fuck the river. What about the plants? We need to get this generator started."

Throwing himself from the cab he scampered up into the bed of the truck, grabbed the nozzle from the transport tank, and pulled himself atop the generator's fuel tank. He unscrewed the cap, stuck in the nozzle, and squeezed the handle. The sound of fuel gurgling out and splashing into the tank gave him hope. Maybe it would be all right. Maybe it would start back up. Please, let it start back up.

He climbed back down, ignoring Rebecca, who inched along on her hands and knees trying to divert the stream of diesel, covered in mud and fuel, weeping quietly, dusk deepening into darkness around her.

Licking his lips, his eye twitch going batshit crazy, Calendula cranked the ignition key. The starter churned and the giant generator shuttered and hiccupped but nothing more.

Again—that grinding churning and nothing. Again. And again.

"Fuck," he hollered. "Fuck, fuck, fuck."

He searched for the choke, hoping that might help—though he could feel that the generator was still hot and knew deep down that it was a useless gesture—found it, engaged it, and cranked the ignition again. Churning, churning, churning. He disengaged the choke. Tried again, panting, the smell of the wooden shack— diesel, oil, mold and rot—filling his lungs and face.

He paused and wiped the sweat from his brow with the back of his forearm, waiting, thinking maybe he had flooded the engine, the only sound now his own heavy breathing and the sobs of Rebecca outside in the mud. He thumbed his wart, sweat gathering and dripping down from his hairline and into his eyes. He scrubbed his face with his hand then put his fingers on the ignition key, pulled his lower lip into his teeth.

Again he cranked the ignition, again the starter grumbled but the engine did not catch. "Come on, you motherfucker," he said, now keeping the key cranked to the right, the starter churning and churning till it started to grumble and slow.

He released the key and closed his eyes. He tried again and the starter churned even slower. When he tried again there was only the click-click-click sound signaling that the battery had grown too weak to power the starter. Coyote had mentioned the battery was weak and needed replacing. Mentioned it several times in fact.

Calendula stumbled from the shack. He could hear the river. The trees in the distance were black skeletons in the mist. He turned back toward the shack and began to slowly and rhythmically beat his head against it as the world turned away from the sun and darkness grew about him.

—

Whispering to herself as she scurried through the muck on all fours, shoveling up clumps of diesel-soaked earth and clay with her hands, Rebecca felt a presence before her, eyes peering down, and she looked up, startled to see Megan standing there, bunny stuffy clutched to her chest. She was nothing more than a shadow, a tiny figure of darkness.

"Megan, honey, you all right?"

"It's dark in there. I don't like it."

"I know, honey. We're trying to get the lights back on now."

Rebecca rose from the muddy puddle of diesel, her face and hair streaked in dirt.

Megan said, "What happened?"

"It's just a little accident. Everything is going to be all right. Just wait on the porch, okay? Mommy's dirty and has to get cleaned up. I'll meet you there in two minutes. Kay, kiddo?" She forced a smile, trying hard not to sound as deranged and lost as she felt.

"Okay, Mommy."

Watching Megan shuffle away, Rebecca was suddenly very sober. She looked down at herself, caked in filth. What'd become of them? They had definitely crossed some line, gone far over it. She closed her eyes and focused on breathing. She had to be rational, had to get them out of here. She had to convince Calendula to leave.

—

Calendula thumped his head against the side of the generator shack, slower now, and softer, but steady still. Rebecca stepped up to him and began talking.

"Calendula, we've got to get out of here. Get a hotel. It's dark. I'm covered in diesel and need a shower. We have to get in touch with Coyote. He'll know what to do."

Yes, Coyote. They *did* have to get in touch with Coyote. It was true. Only Calendula needed to think of a way to make this seem like it wasn't his fault. He had to think.

"Let's get a hotel room, make some calls. Google diesel engines. Think about this. Coyote will know what to do."

Calendula said nothing. He felt spent, defeated. He rested his aching head on the plywood wall of the generator shack, unable to muster the motivation to move, to acknowledge her, though he knew she was right.

The sound of distant wind and the river. The night was upon them and the distance between them grew very dark.

Finally, Rebecca took him by the hand and gently pulled him away.

16.

Night had fallen and the whole place was simply darkness now. Shit, DJ thought, maybe they were more tenacious than he had thought. But then he caught the muffled sound of their shitty little Subaru station wagon starting up and the twin glow of headlights.

He watched as the lights ascended up the driveway, paused, so someone could open and close the gate, started off again and began to slink back and forth up the cutbacks and out of the valley. As they grew smaller and finally disappeared into the far-off hills, he began to laugh. Ha. Just like clockwork. Perfect fucking plan.

He pushed himself up from the ground, his legs numb and full of stabbing needles. He flicked on his headlamp, ran in place for a moment to get his circulation going, slapping his hands together, and then started down the thin deer path that cut through the thick tangle of whitethorn and manzanita.

Coming to a clearing, he sauntered over the crest of a grass-covered hill bordering a stand of live oaks. He stopped and took out a small prescription bottle, twisted off the lid and poured a small bump of meth onto his palm, snorted it up. Whoa, it was a beautiful night, the fog and the trees. An owl hooted. Yeah, one beautiful motherfucking night.

He jogged the last quarter of a mile through the woods and back to his truck.

Swinging himself into the cab, he turned over the engine, put her in gear, and made his way around the hills and down to Coyote's gate. He parked, got out, and unlocked the gate, remembering Coyote's old combination that hadn't changed in years: 6969. Stupid, dirty old man. Leaving the gate open behind him, he drove down into the valley, towards the compound.

Pulling up in front of the chef house, he killed the engine and waited a moment in the darkness, looking for signs of life. Nothing stirred.

He slipped the elastic band of his headlamp over his baseball cap, pressed it on, and got out of the pickup, ambling across the yard and up to the screened-in porch. He glanced quickly left and right, opened the screen door, and ducked inside. He stepped up to the front door, hammered his knuckles against it.

"Hello? Anybody home? Avon calling."

He wondered what he'd say if the door swung open and someone asked him what he wanted. *S'up? Just thought I'd stop by, being in the neighborhood and all. Spider still live here?*

He jiggled the doorknob, gave it a push, just out of curiosity. Locked tight. He was getting ready to kick in the door when he thought he heard a squeal of laughter to his left, outside the porch.

He glanced over and for a moment thought he saw, poking around the corner of the house, the smiling face of a little boy, snickering at him. He blinked and it was gone.

"Hello?"

He looked around the side of the house, his headlight beam scouring the grounds. Nothing. Just his imagination.

It was easy for your mind to play tricks on you in the darkness. The speed didn't help.

Truth was, this old, falling-down shithole always was spooky as hell. Everyone said it was haunted. Whatever, time for business.

He went back to the front door, heaved in a breath, lifted his right leg, and brought his boot slamming down against the door. It was sturdy and didn't budge but he thought he heard a mild cracking sound.

He repeated the action. *Crack.* Yeah, this time, it definitely made a crunching noise and he could feel the door begin to give. One more time, he lifted his foot, slammed it home, and—*BAM*—the door flew open.

Ha ha. Easy-peasy.

"Honey," he shouted, sticking his head into the darkness and peering about, the headlamp casting its light about the kitchen, "I'm home."

FIVE

"It was written I should be loyal to the nightmare of my choice."
— Joseph Conrad, *Heart of Darkness*

"You've made your bed. Now lay in it."
—Common folk saying

1.

Calendula straddled him and raised the shovel up, gripping it tightly by the shank with both hands.

"Fucking thief!"

He slammed the blade down into his neck—blood spurting up into his face as the body writhed—then jackhammered it up and down again and again in a savage frenzy.

Tearing into the neck, he worked his way through the windpipe, which quickly shattered and crumpled, and then into the tendons and muscles, hacking past them until he found the spine, digging the rusty edge of the shovel in until he felt it slip between the vertebras.

He leveraged the handle back, and with a grunt, snapped the head free. It rolled about a foot or so away and came to a stop, facing him, eyes staring wildly as if incredulous of this indignity, mouth slowly opening very wide before beginning to close again.

The body was still twitching as Calendula rolled off and collapsed to the ground, all of the adrenaline in his system suddenly spent and gone, leaving a dark emptiness in its wake.

The rain had abated and the wind blew the black clouds from the sky exposing stars and a dirty sliver of moon. He lay on his side, breathing heavily, his nose and lungs filled with the strange scent of death: metallic, sweet, and already somehow putrid though the body was still warm. The cold, rain-drenched earth grew warm as the puddle of blood seeped into the ground and bellied out around him, blooming like a hot, liquid flower.

How? How had he gotten to this point? He'd done it for Rebecca, for Megan, for the dream. They'd worked too hard, given up too much, to see their reward vanish like that. Spider had been right, he needed to stand up. Be a man. It was the only way to make the dream a reality. The only way to get their own land.

A flash of distant light and then the low murmur of thunder. He was now a murderer. Somewhere deep inside him this truth acknowledged itself and a part of him cracked and gave. He felt his belly drop within him, that sensation you get in a plane when going through turbulence, and he began to shiver uncontrollably.

Again he wondered: how had he gotten to this point?

He supposed that dark part of himself had always been evident, lurking in the background like the shadows of winter which never seemed to leave the chef house.

But it wasn't until the generator shut down, all that diesel spilling out like blood from a gutted animal, that he felt himself tumbling over some precipice, desperately reaching for a handhold and finding none, everything foggy and in slow motion. They were just so close. So fucking close...

—

After Rebecca had convinced him to leave, taken him by the hand and led him to the Subaru, forced him to put the key in the ignition and drive them away, it had taken forever to find a hotel that would take cash. Driving up and down the 101 in Eureka going from one seedy place to the next while desperately calling Coyote over and over again, leaving messages and texts, letting him know they had an emergency on their hands.

Of course Coyote didn't answer the phone and Calendula, panicked and desperate, left him message after message. "Bro, there's been a problem, we gotta talk. Call me."

He texted him: "911- call me- 911."

Finally, after how many excruciating hours, Coyote called back.

"What the fuck—"

"The generator ran out of diesel."

"Yeah, and?"

"It won't start back up."

"Try the choke?"

"Yeah."

"Well, is anyone dead?"

"Uh, no. No."

"Are the cops there?"

"No."

"Then it's not a real fucking emergency, is it? Look, kid, relax. You sound like you're going to fucking cry. You're not going to cry, are you?"

"No, I'm not going to cry." He looked to Rebecca, who flashed a strange look back at him.

"Good, I hate that shit. All right, first thing first: Weed just about done?"

"Two more weeks."

"Well, we can harvest early if we have to. Tell you what, I'm on my way back right now. I'll meet you there tomorrow. We'll assess the situation. I know some tricks with a diesel generator. Okay? We'll figure it out. Don't have a fucking aneurism, kid."

And he believed that. That everything would be all right. He really did believe it.

2.

Coyote was in a great mood before being inundated with all the goddamn phone calls. He was halfway back from L.A. and ecstatic. He had a new buyer and a duffel bag full of cash. He knew Don—his Oregon buyer—had been full of shit, telling him that supply had eclipsed demand, that the price had dropped to nothing.

That low-balling, player-hating, lying sack of shit.

Coyote had gotten the lead on a guy who owned a whole conglomerate of medical dispensaries in L.A. Young kid, maybe twenty-two, twenty-three, with an army of players at his command. They weren't potheads as much as cannabis enthusiasts who embraced the marijuana world as part of their uber-hip lives, weed-chic. Fucking surfers who only took off their sunglasses and brand-new baseball caps when they got in the ocean. They dragged him along to strip clubs and weird parties in warehouses with bass-heavy music that sounded like noise and girls who looked impossibly young. They were all about the dabbing, smoking this concentrated honey oil shit with fancy machinery, torches and glass pipes. More complicated looking than freebasing cocaine. It wasn't really his scene at all. He felt old and very uncool. But the guy loved the weed. Bought it all for twenty-two a pound.

So now Coyote had over two-hundred grand in cash, packed into a duffel bag in the back of his Navigator. Enough to pay off Diesel, even kick some interest his way, cause—hey—fair's fair. Maybe even do some repairs to the old homestead and still have plenty to stow away.

He was so happy he didn't even want any crack or whores. Maybe he'd go up to Oregon and visit Helen and the girls, bring a whole mess of presents. Fuck his wife for a change instead of the skanky hookers he paid to suck his dick all night. He wanted to see her, could finally admit how much he missed her cute face and tough little stance, the good strong Irish woman in her. He felt like he was turning over a new leaf. He was going to get healthy. Shit, maybe he'd go all hippie again, do some yoga, eat right.

Some tantric sex definitely sounded good.

Then the phone calls from that dimwit Calendula started.

Panicked voicemails full of distraught whining. That stupid fuck. Now the high of a deal gone good—the rush of money in hand—gone. Suddenly two-hundred thousand bucks didn't seem like that much, especially now that the next crop could be ruined, and Coyote was back to his usual, inescapable, miserable self.

3.

"I just can't go back there, you know that, Calendula."

Rebecca took a gulp of wine and flicked the filter of her Camel with her thumb nail. She lifted the cigarette to her lips, squinting against the smoke, and took a deep drag. She held it in a moment, and then sighed deeply, the blue smoke escaping her as she ran a hand through her short crop of hair.

"Not going back, I'm not," she said, tapping her foot.

They were outside the door to their hotel room in Eureka, the slightly rotten smell of the bay heavy in the air. A semi rushed by. A car horn honked. Somewhere in the distance two men were arguing, their shouts audible but the words just an angry jumble of noise. Megan was inside watching television and eating McDonald's french fries—by the time they'd checked into a room it was late and the only places still open were the fast food joints.

Calendula watched her take another gulp of wine from the plastic motel cup she'd filled with the box of Merlot she had insisted he pull over to buy as soon as they saw a liquor store. She leaned back against the cinderblock wall of the hotel, crossed her arms, and tapped her cigarette. The ash fell slowly to the ground.

"Not going back."

She was freshly showered, her short hair still wet and slicked back on her head, and Calendula could smell the cheap hotel shampoo she'd used, so different from the organic herbal products he was used to smelling on her. She wasn't wearing her glasses, and though her face was pallid and her lips colorless, she still looked smoking hot to Calendula, with her fierce eyebrows framing those almond eyes. Like a model in some edgy French fashion magazine.

He rubbed the flat of his thumb against his wart, feeling an eye twitch coming on, looking for some kind of in. Some way to make her come back with him.

"What's up with all the nicotine consumption? I thought big

tobacco was—"

"Don't fuck with me."

"I'm not, I'm just pointing out, that, uh, you know, we all make compromises."

"Look, don't try to change this around. This isn't about me. It's about Megan. And whether she's going back to that place. You go. Meet up with Coyote, do your little dog act. Lick his ass, follow him around, be his bitch and follow his orders. When you're all done, come back and get us. We'll be waiting."

"Waiting? Where? Under a bridge? In an alley?"

"No. Here at the hotel."

"We can't stay here for another night. I didn't bring enough cash."

"I don't believe you. You wouldn't go anywhere without that money. I know you."

"I'm telling you I left it. I didn't want to risk bringing it. Figured it was safer. Hidden there."

Of course he was lying. He had the money, that slim bundle of hundred-dollar bills. He resisted the urge to touch the lump in his pocket, but instead kept up a circular pattern on the wart, his eye twitching softly. He flashed her a wide smile and raised his eyebrows, hoping the gesture didn't come off as asinine and clown-like as it felt.

"Fine. I'll just call my mother. She already told me that Brett would come get us."

"Brett? You'd leave with Brett?"

"It's looking like my only option."

"If that's what you want. Go ahead." He knew she'd never do it, admit defeat like that.

Her eyes grew thin and she puffed on her cigarette, began tapping her foot again as two streams of smoke jetted out her nose.

"You know, you're looking more and more like a Manson girl every day. It's kinda sexy."

"Don't. Just don't."

An ambulance drove by on the highway with its sirens on, cars pulling over to let it pass. For a moment her face was bathed in spiraling red and blue light. He stepped toward her, touched her chin.

She looked away.

"Seriously, baby. I just wanna let you know I like your haircut. It was a bit extreme at first, but now that I've gotten used to it, you look really hot."

"Seriously? You think that will fucking work?"

"I'm being honest here. Give me a break."

"If we go back how long do we have to stay?"

"We'll just square up with Coyote," he said. "Figure out a plan, grab our cash, and then we can go."

"We don't have to stay and harvest and trim?"

"Hell, no. Square up. That's it."

She took another drag off her cigarette. "There are things happening there. Weird shit. We can't go back. It's not good. Not good."

"Honey. We've got no choice."

She kept her head averted from him, her eyes focused on something far, far away.

4.

Diesel's huge, ape-like frame was sprawled across the big white sofa. He was in his underwear, staring blankly at the TV and smoking speed from a glass pipe. *Wheel of Fortune* was on, an old woman clapping while eagerly watching the wheel spin round, but all Diesel could see was the time-worn image of his grandfather holding court before the general store, telling the locals that this was a great place to raise sheep. That the rolling hills of green prairie that remained after the redwoods were harvested were perfect for sheep, as long as they were locked up at night so that the mountain lions couldn't get to them when they crept down into the valleys from the hills of manzanita and tan oak.

Diesel had never raised any sheep. He'd always wanted to. But unlike his grandfather and his cousins he didn't have the patience to keep any livestock. Too much work keeping those fuckers alive. Responsibility.

Yet like his father he was a good hunter. He'd always wanted to take his son hunting with him, but after the boy's mother ran off to Eureka with him he never had the chance.

Now DJ showed no interest in hunting at all, barely gave him a "thank you" when he gave him the 30.06. Maybe it would be different with his grandson. No. It *would* be different. He was sure of it.

He took another hit of the pipe. It was growing hot.

What was it his grandfather always used to say?

When you get too old to cut the mustard you gotta lick the jar.

Diesel never understood what that meant but he loved it nonetheless. Somehow it seemed to make sense to him now, though, and he let the words spill out of his lips.

Gotta lick the jar.

The pipe grew too hot to hold and he placed it on the filthy end table beside a pile of crushed oxyContin and his trusty .22. He ran his fingers through his thick orange-and-gray beard and sighed.

Amber was gone and the place was a mess.

They'd gotten into an argument, over something stupid. High for days, at least a week, things got out of hand and he smacked her, something he swore he would never do.

To make matters worse, in a moment of blind rage he smashed all of her beloved Christmas figurines.

So, she stormed out of the house, jumped in his old Trans Am and tore off to town. Ended up running off with some biker she met at the Branding Iron. Kind of ironic, as that's where he'd met her.

Part of him ached with a gnawing, empty loneliness.

Another part of him said, Fuck it. Good riddance.

But most of him just wanted to get high out of his mind and forget it all. Forget that she'd even been here. He swallowed the last of his Budweiser. It was warm and flat. He tossed the empty can to the ground.

Without Amber around to keep the place neat with an iron fist the place was filthy. Dirty plates with unfinished TV dinners, cigarette butts stubbed out into them, lay on the armrests of the sofa.

Black scorch marks from hot speed pipes everywhere.

Muddy boot prints on the white shag carpeting Amber'd always been so adamant about keeping clean.

In the middle of the room the carburetor of his Harley lay disassembled atop a few sheets of newspaper. The stink of gasoline and ditch grit.

Piles of baby clothes and toys were everywhere from customers who'd brought them to trade for speed, knowing Diesel was so excited about becoming a grandfather.

His cellphone started chirping.

He picked it up, tiny in his massive hand, and looked at the screen, slipping his other hand into his underwear to scratch his balls. He didn't recognize the number and almost didn't answer, but that little voice inside his mind, telling him to *hustle, rustle and bustle*, caused his thumb to tap on Answer.

"Yeah, what's up?"

"You have a collect call from"—hysterical sobbing—"Katie, it's Katie, Pops"—beep—"Do you accept? Say yes or no."

"Yes. Yes, I accept. Katie, you there, girl?"

Unintelligible weeping followed by—"There was no one else to call, and...and...nowhere to go."

Diesel swung his feet down off the sofa and sat up straight, clutching the phone tight and pressing it hard against his ear.

"What happened?"

"It's not his fault. It's not. It's me. It's always me." More weeping.

"Okay, okay. Just calm down. Where are you? Tell me where you are and I'll come get you."

"I'm at the Last Chance Market, Pops. At the Last Chance Market."

"You hang tight, Katie. I'll be right there. Kay, honey?"

"Okay. Okay."

5.

Calendula and Rebecca drove back to the compound in silence while Megan slept. They'd let her stay up late watching the Disney Channel, and now she was in fathomless slumber.

They said nothing that long drive down the 101 from Eureka, then east on the 36, following the Mad River before turning up Alder Point road. Then Zenia Bluff road and eventually into the one-lane maze of potholed asphalt that twisted like a black snake through the hills and mountains, up towards the Trinity Alps.

Finally, bouncing along dirt roads that had no name, deep into the back hills, the wind whipped the little Subaru, swaying it, while above them a new storm blew in: black clouds of the El Niño, the child, blown up from the tropical heat of Mexico.

He knew something was wrong the moment he saw the gate hanging open.

"We shut the gate. I'm positive of it."

"It's Coyote. Probably just too lazy to shut it behind him."

"Coyote always keeps the gate closed. Always."

He began to drive wildly down the driveway and into the compound, slamming into potholes, the Subaru bouncing and its underside grinding.

"That gate was fucking closed when we left. Coyote better be here."

"Slow down," Rebecca yelled at him. Megan began whimpering from the back seat.

He came skidding to a stop in front of the chef house and threw his door open, leaping out. Through the moldering, moss-covered screen of the front porch he could see that the front door was open, hanging by its top hinge, the frame busted to shit.

"No."

He raced across the yard and leapt onto the porch.

"No, no, no."

His gut filled with something sharp and cold, like jagged chucks of ice. He sprinted into the bedroom, everything in slow motion, the edges of his vision blurred like a dream.

"No, no, no."

The hum in his ears was deafening and his head pounded so hard flashes of light and darkness strobed behind his eyes.

The grow-room door hung open and inside was darkness, only a bit of gray daylight seeping in from the bedroom windows, but even in all that blackness he could tell the plants were gone. That familiar canopy of foliage no more. He could see that lights were missing, too, the silhouettes of barren chains hanging limp from the ceiling.

He stepped inside. The hydroponic buckets were all lying on their sides, the floor flooded and littered with lava rock. As his eyes adjusted he saw that many of the controllers—the timers, pH meters, and thermostats—were ripped from the wall.

"No," he said again, whispering the word. "No."

Something inside him gave and fluttered away. He staggered out of the room. Rebecca was there, in the bedroom, clutching Megan to her chest.

"We have to leave, Calendula," she said.

Calendula groaned. "That's all I've ever heard come out of your mouth from the moment we got here and I'm so sick of hearing it."

"What if whoever did this comes back? What if they're still here somewhere?"

"They're gone, Rebecca. No one is here."

"We don't know that."

Calendula turned, and sent his fist into the ancient fake-wood paneling of the wall.

"Calendula, *please*?"

"Please what? Run away? That's always your answer. What about Coyote? We're supposed to meet Coyote here. Did you forget that?"

"We can meet him at the end of the dirt road. I...I don't feel safe here."

"Will you stop. Please, just fucking stop. *We have to go, we have to go*, I am so fucking tired of hearing you say that. All the hard work I do, all the effort and energy I put into this. And all you ever say is, *We've got to go.* You never wanted it bad enough, did you? You talk and talk but look at you. You never really wanted to live off the land."

"What does this have to do with living off the land? I don't even know what you're talking about. We have to go. Please. *Can we just go?*"

"I guess you'd be happy if I worked at a carwash. I could really write my own ticket then, huh?"

"What are you talking about?"

"You know what I'm talking about. Don't play dumb."

"Please, Calendula, please, I'm begging you. Can we just go?"

"No. We're not going, okay? Fuck, I've got to think. Goddamn it."

His head felt ready to crack, he could feel his mind pushing at the confines of his skull.

"Fuck. Fuck. Fuck," he said under his breath, feeling the panic begin to morph into anger, like a giant force of nature, water or fire or wind, grown gargantuan and out of control: a tsunami or inferno. He lashed out, turned, and began kicking the wall, the paneling bursting into dust and shattered chunks. He pummeled the cheap fake wood with his fists, howling, ripping the wall to shreds.

In one last burst of frenzy and frustration he brought his face careening towards the wall, head-butting it with all his might. But instead of sinking into the cheap paneling like he expected, his skull crashed into a two-by-six stud with enough force to make the house shudder. Then he fell straight backwards, not even aware of the sickening *thump* the back of his head made when it hit floor.

6.

When Diesel pulled his F350 into the parking lot of the Last Chance Market, Katie was nowhere to be found. The usual old timers were shuffling around: Banjo in his overalls, Billy in his ubiquitous cowboy hat. He gave them a wave as he parked and got out of the truck. She wasn't in the store. He made his way past the gas pumps and around back, the rain coming down in a drizzle now. He found her by the payphone. She was slumped on the ground, clutching her knees, weeping quietly, her bulging round belly sticking up prominently like she was ready to burst. Her hair hung limp across her face.

"Katie? What's going on?"

She looked up at him and he saw that her left eye was swollen shut and colored an ugly shade of yellow, purple and black. Her lip was fat and cracked.

"It's not his fault," she said.

"Jesus Christ." He quickly hobbled over to her, helping her up and wrapping his big arm around her tiny shoulders. "Did DJ do this to you?"

She nodded her head—her face a mess of snot and tears and hair—then sank into his embrace, the bulge from her pregnant belly pressing against him, the smell of her rain-wet hair filling his nostrils.

"Shh, shh, it's okay. Pops will take care of you. Pops will take care of everything."

He slowly walked her to his pickup, holding her up and steadying her as her shoulders shook, ignoring the stares from the old timers.

"Everything all right, Diesel?" Billy called out, pushing the brim of his Stetson up.

"Ain't nothing to fret over," Diesel said. "Family squabble. We'll sort it out." He opened the passenger door and eased the crying girl up into the truck.

Sliding behind the wheel, he slipped the key into the ignition.

Katie, curled up on the seat, hid her face in her hands as the engine started with a roar.

"I'll take you home to my place. You can rest up there. Get yourself together. I'll go have a talk with DJ."

"Please don't hurt him," she said. "It wasn't his fault. It wasn't."

"Don't worry, Katie. No one's going to get hurt."

7.

Rebecca stared at Calendula. He lay on his back. He wasn't moving.

She whispered, "Calendula?"

He'd scared her. Scared her bad. For a moment she considered running up to him, scooping the car keys from his pocket, and leaving him there. Take Megan away from this horrible place and just let Coyote find him. But no, she had to help him, get him to the hospital, he could have a concussion, a fractured skull. She set Megan down in the doorway and inched closer to him.

"Calendula, can you hear me? I think you're really hurt. We gotta get you to the hospital. Calendula?"

Again, the thought of the car keys came into her mind. Even if he did come out of it she would have to drive him to the hospital. She was going to need those keys. She slipped her fingers into his front pocket, felt the keys.

Calendula's hand shot up and grasped her wrist. "What are you doing?"

"Oh, Calendula, thank God."

"Are you trying to take my car keys?"

"No. I mean, yes, because I have to take you to the hospital."

"The hospital?"

"Yeah. You're hurt."

"I'm fine." He released her wrist and stood up quickly, swaying slightly when he got to his feet. He put a hand to the wall to steady himself. "Just fine."

She could see the burgeoning contusion on his forehead, a nasty purple ball with a fine trickle of blood leaking out from the center of it and running down either side of his nose.

"You're not," she said. "You're really not."

"Sweetie, I'm fine." He turned to her and smiled, face bloodied, eyes glimmering crazily, and she felt fear—sharp and unmistakable— erupt inside her. She could literally see the madness etched in his face.

She took a step away from him. "No, Calendula, you're fucked up. Just look at you."

"I suppose you're an expert, huh? Well, take a look at yourself. Crazy-haired-psycho bitch. Drunk, rolling around in the mud, throwing up on the floor."

Rebecca could hear Megan whimpering behind her, beginning to break out into a full meltdown. "Don't, Calendula. Please, let's just get out of here."

"We'll leave when I say we can leave. I have to go talk to someone."

"Listen to yourself. Do you even know what you're saying?" Rebecca was crying now too, stammering. "You're scaring us. Please. Please."

"Stop it. You're being unreasonable. And you're upsetting Megan."

"Calendula, please."

"I have to go and talk to Spider. He'll know what to do. Just take care of Megan till I get back."

"Spider? You have to talk to *Spider*?"

He brushed by her, out the bedroom door and into the hall. She followed behind him, into the kitchen. "What's going on, Calendula?" But he was gone, out the smashed-in door, slipping off the porch and disappearing into the darkness and rain.

8.

"You're going to have to excuse the mess," Diesel said, opening the door to the cabin and gently guiding Katie in. "I've gotten awful sloppy since Amber left. Been kinda depressed." He led her over to the sofa and sat her down. "You need anything? You want some water?"

She nodded her head.

"Okay, I'll get it for you. Here's the remote, you watch you some TV."

He disappeared into the kitchen and came back with a glass of water.

"Here you go," he said handing her the glass. "Purest spring water you can get, straight off the mountain."

She sipped at it. Sniffled. Put the glass down on the end table and stared down at her feet.

"You feeling any better?"

"Yeah," she said, and looked up at him, half her face a swollen mess. "Thank you, Pops. Thank you so much."

"Now, you ain't gotta thank me. Like I've been telling you, we're family now. Look at all the toys and clothes I've been a gathering up for the little one. We're going to have ourselves a right old family. Okay?"

She looked down again and nodded her head. He thought he saw a hint of a smile there.

"Okay, then. You stay put here. Make yourself at home. There's grub in the kitchen. I'll go talk to that boy of mine and we'll get this all straightened out."

He gently placed his big hand on her head and awkwardly tried to stroke her hair. Yes, he definitely thought he could see the beginnings of a smile on her face. He hoped so, at least.

"Be back, in a jiffy."

9.

The humming in Calendula's head had become nearly deafening, a brilliant white light made of sound that filled his skull.

Wiping blood from his eyes, he made his way through the ancient detritus of the dead—motorcycle parts and broken toys—the stagnant puddles reeking of rot and decay, and walked up to the last cabin on the trail. He pushed the door open and stepped tentatively inside.

"Spider?"

A voice from the shadows in the far corner: "I suppose you want to know who did it?"

Calendula nodded, his mouth suddenly very dry, a queasy sick feeling stirring in the pit of his belly.

The ghost stepped forward, greasy orange-and-black Harley bandanna wrapped tight around his skull, long gray beard, bloated eyes glowing in rotten sockets. Calendula could smell him, smoke and grease and a putrid decay.

"Who the fuck do you think did it?" Spider spat. "Who knew you were gone? Who's the cheap motherfucker that always looks for an excuse not to pay you?"

Doubt flooded Calendula's mind like a dark ink. No, no. And yet maybe it was true. Why would he lie? What could he possibly have to gain by lying to him?

"I can guarantee you one thing. When that fucker pulls up here, denying everything, he's going to have a duffel bag full of cash in the back of his ride. Money he made on your blood, sweat and tears. It's not a pretty picture, hoss. You just gotta decide what you're going to do about it. Do you get what I'm saying, son?"

Calendula nodded, throat constricting. He thumbed the wart on his finger and listened as Spider ranted on and on, trembling with some inner force, pulsating. He seemed to grow and inflate, stretching his boundaries like a balloon, his mouth opening and closing, within it a great chasm of darkness that seemed to swallow everything: the room, the back shack, the land, the earth itself slipping into that blackness between his lips.

Calendula's eye began to twitch like the legs of a sleeping dog.

"I told you not to trust him. To keep your eyes open. But you didn't listen. Did you, kid?"

He just continued expanding, bigger and bigger till he filled the room and his shoulders touched the sides of the cabin, spitting and cursing and yelling until Calendula felt certain he would explode.

But then Calendula blinked and Spider was just an old bearded man again, pulling out a chair and sitting down at the table, shuffling a deck of cards, the waxy, yellow rectangles flipping through his gnarled fingers, knuckles swollen and red. He dealt out a hand of solitaire, then kicked his chair back so that it leaned against the wall and he stretched out his legs, crossed his battered engineer boots at the ankles. He motioned with his sallow, hush-puppy eyes to the window.

"Ever notice how you can see right up the road from that big-old window there? That's why I used to sit back here in my day. Put your back up against the wall like this, and from that window you can see clear up the mountainside. Can see anyone coming down from the hills, and always have the drop on 'em. By the time they get here you're ready. Take a look up there now. What d'ya see?"

Calendula peered out the window. Through the lichen-covered branches he spotted the path twisting up to the chef house, and beyond that the road slinking off into the fog enshrouded hills, the arrow-head-like points of tall firs poking up through the mist. Then something caught his eye near the top of the mountain, a quick flash of light. He squinted and saw it again. Yes, two tiny beams of light snaking downward. Headlights.

Spider said, "See 'em?"

"Yes."

"Who you suppose that is?

"It's him, isn't it?"

"Sure as shit is. Now, if I was you, I'd go meet him halfway. Ask him a few questions pertinent to this here situation."

Calendula nodded. The hole in his head itched terribly and he abandoned his wart to finger the wound absently. He turned from the window and headed to the door, pausing to look at the bearded ghost kicked back on his chair, disinterestedly laying down and turning over cards on the dirty table.

"Thank you, Spider."

"Don't need to thank me, hoss. I ain't done shit for ya. 'Cept be observant. Something you shoulda been doing for your own damn self."

Calendula nodded and stepped outside. The buzzing in his head had dissipated to a low murmur and he felt calm. Very calm. An old shovel was leaning up against the wall of the shack. He picked it up and looked at it. The dirty handle was streaked in black and gray mold and the bucket was rusted up, flaking off chunks of orange metal. But it felt solid and strong. He hefted its weight in his hands, gripping it tight. A sturdy shovel, it'd probably seen a lot of use out here. Dug a lot of holes.

10.

Diesel's truck rattled up over the ridge and through the thick, wet fog that was spilling out over the road from the forest. He pulled up to the small flat where DJ's trailer sat perched on a few cinderblocks in a tangled nest of whitethorn and poison oak. Rolling up next to DJ's truck, he whistled a low soft breath through his teeth. Tapped the wheel with his big fingers.

Part of him just wanted to pummel the boy. Anyone who could beat a pregnant woman like that deserved a stomping. But he knew from experience that wouldn't help anything. He reminded himself that he, too, had fucked up in the past, remembering that night DJ's mother had left him.

He'd been so drunk and high on pills that the whole incident was like some foggy dream. He'd been fighting blind, swinging at the demons in his mind. When he came to, his wife was on the ground beneath him, bloodied and quivering, and he looked up to see DJ staring at him from the doorway of his bedroom with that strange, uncomprehending look on his little face. He was instantly speechless with regret and remorse but the room was spinning and he couldn't catch his breath, couldn't breathe, and he had to lie down, pushing past the kid and staggering to his bed.

When he woke in the morning he was alone. His family was gone.

He couldn't let that happen again. He forced himself to remember DJ as an infant in his arms, all those broken promises.

He could hear rap music blaring from inside as he hobbled up the wooden steps to the door of the trailer, rapped on it with his huge fist.

"DJ? You in there, son? Open up, boy. We gotta talk."

Nothing. Just the pounding of the bass and the growl of anger from the guy singing, if you could call it that. The kid probably couldn't even hear him out here with the music cranked so loud.

205

He tried the knob. It twisted in his hand and he swung the door open. The reek of freshly harvested weed hit him like an openhanded slap. There were string lines crisscrossing the small trailer, filled with the stuff, and garbage bags strewn around the room overflowing with herb. DJ was in the back corner, hanging branches on lines. He had his baseball hat on all sideways in that way that Diesel hated, his pants pulled low, boxers hanging out.

He looked up, mouth agape, jaw lowering and closing in surprise. He looked like a fucking clown. An idiot clown.

"What the fuck? Where'd you get all this?"

"Oh, hey, Pops. I, uh, you know, a friend needed some help. Told him I'd dry his herb for him."

"A friend, huh?"

"Yeah."

Diesel wrapped his hand around a cola, squeezed it, brought it to his face and sniffed it. "A friend who harvested weeks too early?"

"Yeah. Way it goes."

"Who's this fucking friend of yours?" Diesel asked, looking around, noticing the pile of speed on the table beside the glass pipes.

"Actually, it's none of your fucking business." DJ puffed his chest up, squared his shoulders. "Why are you here?"

"I'm here because you beat your damn pregnant girlfriend half to death and left her in the fucking rain. Now, I said, where'd you get all this goddamn reefer, boy?"

DJ stared silently back at him, eyes squinted.

"You rip off those kids down at the chef house? You did, didn't you? Answer me."

DJ spoke in a low hiss, spitting out the words. "If I ripped them hippies off, it was 'cause they had it coming."

"Had it coming?"

"Yeah."

"Had it coming how?"

"Coming here, where they don't belong. Not to mention, Coyote owes us."

"Owes me. Me. Don't you get that? And if he don't have his herb he ain't going to be able to pay me. That's why you're giving it back."

"Yeah, right."

"I said you're giving it back."

"The hell I will."

"The hell you won't, boy. You best do as I say or so fucking help me I am gonna give you an ass-kicking like you never had."

Diesel took a threatening step towards him and DJ stepped back. "I'm warning you. I'll fucking kill you if you don't get the hell out of here."

"What did you just say to me?"

DJ blinked, turned, and made for the 30.06 leaning against the wall in the corner. But before he could even raise the rifle to his shoulder Diesel had already stepped forward and grabbed the barrel. There was a momentary back-and-forth-tugging, and then Diesel slammed the gun into the boy's chest, knocking him backwards and off his feet, while twisting the rifle from his grasp.

DJ hit the ground and as he looked up—eyes wide and mouth hanging open—Diesel brought the butt of the gun down square into his nose.

Screaming, DJ brought his hands to his bloodied face. Diesel kicked him in the gut. Hard. The boy made a sound like a pierced tire belching air and curled up on his side.

"Pull a fucking gun on me, boy?" Diesel raised the rifle and brought the butt down against DJ's ribs. "Teach you to pull a fucking gun on me," bringing it down again, this time into his lower back. He kicked him once more and then set the stock of the rifle down. Leaned against the barrel, panting. "What kinda idiot tries to use a hunting rifle as a close-range weapon anyway?"

DJ moaned once from the floor and then began to cough in wet, pained sounding hacks as Diesel thought, Fuck, now I done it. Lost my goddamn temper.

But the boy needed to be taught a lesson.

"You're one stupid sonofabitch. I just came here to talk to you. To get you to man up and be a husband and a father. Look what you made me do."

DJ groaned, curled even further into himself. "Go away. Please. Go away and leave me alone."

"Fine. I'm fucking leaving, you dumb motherfucker." Diesel looked down at the gun he was leaning on. "And I'm taking this with me. You can come and get it when you calm down."

"Just go."

Diesel stomped out of the trailer, knocking branches out of his way, leaving the door wide open and swinging on its hinges.

Rain was starting to fall now and dirty brown puddles had gathered in the muddy yard. He pulled himself up into his truck, lay the rifle on the passenger seat and sunk his face into his big hands, rubbing his eyes with the tips of his fingers. He sighed heavily and set his hands in his lap. The rain began to pick up, pelting the windshield in a steady patter. He lit a cigarette and blew out a cloud of smoke, watched the fog and mist swirling down from the trees.

How had that happened?

The boy pulled a gun. That's how it happened.

Clutching the cigarette in his teeth, he pulled a Xanax from his pocket and tossed the whole bar in his mouth, chewing it, relishing the bitter taste. He needed to focus on the important thing here: the girl and his grandson.

Fuck it, for all he cared, his son could go straight to fucking hell.

11.

"Megan?" Rebecca called out for the third time, trying to stay calm, squinting into the shadows. Nothing. She peered around the dark bedroom. Megan was gone.

"Megan, sweetie, are you in here?"

Rebecca found herself whispering and didn't know why. When she tried to call out it felt wrong, it scared her, like she might awaken something sleeping. Something evil.

Could she have gone into the grow room? Why would she do that? As Rebecca approached she heard weeping. Quiet, but definitely there, coming from behind the open door.

"Megan?"

She tried to make her voice sound calm and reasonable, not a terrified whisper. A sniffling couple of breaths and more crying. Yes, something was in the corner, hidden behind the open door. She went to grasp the knob and was suddenly afraid.

What if it wasn't Megan? What if it was something else? Then resignation. She had to find her daughter.

She pulled the door back from the wall and there in the corner was Megan, clutching her bunny stuffy, curly hair draped over her round face.

"Megan, honey, what are you doing? Didn't you hear me calling you?"

"I'm scared."

"Scared of Calendula? Did he scare you, sweetie?"

"I'm scared of both of you."

12.

Katie sat on the big white sofa in the glow of the television. She shuddered, unable to weep anymore. She was no good. Everyone always told her so. She deserved it. Deserved it all.

DJ was all she had and now he didn't want her anymore.

It was always the same. When she was eight her father left. Just left. One day he was there and the next he was gone. She never heard from him again besides that one Christmas when she was ten and he sent her a Barbie Malibu Dream House. She was too old to play with dolls at that point and just left it in its box.

"Ain't you going to play with it?" her mother asked. Katie shook her head. "Ingrate," she said, sipping her Lord Calvert before putting a Benson and Hedges to her lips.

When she was fourteen her mother dumped her off on her Aunt Melinda and moved to Seattle with some guy who didn't want a kid around. Aunt Melinda was a bitter woman who drank too much and, when she did, never hesitated to tell Katie what a burden she was.

All through high school it was like she was invisible. She had no friends. Boys didn't notice her. But then she met DJ at the Alder Point store. He'd just moved back to Southern Humboldt from Eureka. He seemed so sweet and shy, asking her if she wanted to go to the County Fair in Ferndale with him. After that night of spinning on the twister, kissing in the shadows, the taste of cotton candy and pepperoni pizza heavy in his mouth, everything had been different. She was happy for the first time in her life.

She moved in with him. She was so proud: he owned his own land. Forty acres. Sure, there was nothing on it but a shitty little trailer, but they'd make it work. They'd build a real house one day. Then she was pregnant and DJ's dad was telling her to call him Pops. She shoulda known it wouldn't last. Nothing did.

She eyed the speed pipe on the cluttered end table. The gun. The crushed pills. Her face hurt so badly. She could feel her swollen eye crusting up. She pressed her finger tips to it. It felt foreign and not her own. She needed something. She picked up the pipe and took a hit.

Immediately, she felt better. Her heart began to race. She took a small snort of the crushed pills to calm herself. That was good.

A silly sitcom was on the television. A teenager being a smartass to his parents. And it was funny. Really funny. She found herself laughing and she felt so much better. Everything would be all right. Pops would work it out with DJ. She took another hit, this one a big, long one. Her skin flushed, heart pounding so hard it threatened to leave her chest.

Then she felt something shift inside her. Something jerk and move. Suddenly she was sick. She thought she might throw up. She stood up and a great gush of warm water fell out of her, running down her legs and splashing onto the floor.

13.

Yeah, the more Coyote thought about it the more fucked up the situation was. As he let his mind go over it again and again he grew seriously pissed off. Stupid fucking kids. If the weed came out bad he was taking it out of their cut. He'd been running that grow for years now and had never had a problem with the generator or the fuel line before. Christ, how many gallons of diesel had they dumped into the river? If the environmental protection people caught onto this he'd be screwed. Hundreds of thousands of dollars in fines. Fuck. He'd be ruined, probably lose the land. He was tempted to just get a big insurance policy and torch the whole fucking place. The way herb prices were dropping so fast, it seemed like the only way he was going to turn a real profit anyway.

And there was the gate, just hanging open. Hadn't he told those kids to always keep the goddamn gate locked? The SUV slammed into a pothole. He gripped the wheel tight and careened down into the driveway.

And all this rain. He was sick of it. And tired. So tired. Tired of the game. Tired of Northern California. Tired of Humboldt. Tired of dealing with all these idiots.

And Sunbeam calling him out of nowhere. Demanding her money.

Maybe the rain would keep her away. One could hope.

But if he knew her right, she'd go through rain, sleet, hell or worse to get paid. It was funny how a person could walk away indignant from cash one minute and then demand it back all high-and-mighty the next. Women. Just like his fucking wife. Whatever. Better to pay them early, he'd learned, then deal with them later. Always cheaper that way in the long run.

As he banked around the bend toward the Chef House, a figure emerged from the darkness, staggering up the road. It startled him and he jolted for a moment, but as he crested the curve and the headlights illuminated it, he saw it was Calendula, drenched, leaning on a shovel.

Look at this freak, Coyote thought, wandering around in the rain. Just what the fuck is going on around here? He eased the SUV to a stop and rolled down the window.

"Yo, dude, what the fuck you doing?"

"It was you. Wasn't it?" The whites of Calendula's eyes gleamed in the darkness.

Christ, what now? Coyote slipped the transmission into park. "Me what?"

"You that *did it.*"

"You best explain yourself, son. What the fuck is going on around here?"

"You took the weed. You took all the weed and then showed back up like you don't know what happened. I never should've called you."

"Whoa, whoa, slow down. What the fuck are you saying? The weed's *gone*?" Coyote swung the door open and stepped out into the rain. "Just what the hell are you talking about?"

"You know exactly what I'm talking about."

Coyote felt his body begin to quake, his ears begin to ring. He stepped toward Calendula through the pouring rain with a pointed finger, the wind whipping his hair into a frenzy. "I said explain yourself."

Calendula stepped up into the glare of the high beams. Coyote could tell right away that something was wrong with him. He looked demented and demonic in the harsh light: gaunt face stained with blood, a massive lump on his forehead.

"I'm not listening to your bullshit. You know the weed is gone. You're a fucking thief. Admit it."

"Fuck you. Fuck you." Coyote shoved his finger into Calendula's chest. "The weed is gone and you're accusing me? *Me?* How do I know you didn't take it, you little shit?"

"Don't even try and turn this thing around. I know it was you because Spider told me so."

The words sent ice down Coyote's spine. His anger dissolved. It was suddenly very cold out in the wind and rain. Very, very cold.

"What did you say?"

"Spider told me."

"Spider? You see him, too? I thought I was the only one."

"Yeah, I see him, and he told me all about you."

"You...you can't believe him. He's a liar. He's told me awful things. Things that I know can't be true. Jesus, I thought it was all in my head."

"Oh, no. He's real all right. And he told me to give you this."

With that Calendula raised the shovel up over his shoulder.

Coyote began to stumble backwards through the rain, shaking his head, mumbling, "No," as the shovel came crashing down towards him. He instinctively raised his arms to protect himself from the blow, then turned toward the SUV, its door hanging open, only a few feet away. As he lurched towards it Calendula brought the shovel down hard, right on the back of his head, and Coyote watched helplessly as the SUV melted into darkness and the ground came rushing up towards him.

14.

When Diesel swung open the door to the cabin he was startled to see Katie standing there, staring back at him with a grim and confused look. She almost seemed like a ghost standing there, silent and swaying slightly, one side of her face a swollen purple bruise, the other looking both very pale and very childlike. He stared at her blankly for a moment, frozen in the doorway.

"What is it, Katie?"

"Something's wrong."

She looked down at her belly.

"I don't feel so good. I think...I think the baby might be coming. I...my water. My water, yeah—I made a mess." She motioned to the floor with her hand. "I made a mess. I'm sorry. I'll clean it up. Do you have a rag or something?"

It was then he noticed the speed pipe in her hand.

"Katie, you ain't been smoking that, have you?"

"It was just a little bit. Just a hit to make me feel better. I never meant for nothing to happen to the...I never meant to hurt the..."

Her face crinkled and she began to weep.

"I'm sorry. I'm so sorry."

He rushed toward her and gently took her by the hands. "Come on, let's get you to the hospital."

"I'm so, so sorry."

15.

It was beginning to rain heavier now and Rebecca jogged the distance from the chef house to the old Dodge Ram pickup, Megan wrapped in her arms. Rebecca's chin jutted out over the girl's little head in an effort to shield her from the wind and rain. She could hear the voices of Calendula and Coyote arguing in the distance, just make out the headlights up the hill, aglow in the darkness. She slipped her fingers under the door handle and pulled the truck door open, and sat Megan on the busted-up seat. Megan's bottom lip quivered in the dim-glow of the dome light and she sniffled, her shoulders rising and falling in quick shudders.

At least she's stopped crying, Rebecca thought as she brushed the hair out of Megan's face, then used the hem of her T-shirt to dry the girl' eyes and wipe the snot from her nose, talking the whole while in the motherly murmur she'd used when Megan was just a baby and woke up in the middle of the night crying. "Okay. It's okay. Shhh. Everything is all right."

She knew Calendula kept the keys to the Ram on his keychain, but maybe Coyote kept an extra set in here somewhere. She searched frantically: in the glove box, behind the visors, the armrest console, under the floor mats. No keys anywhere.

How could she have not gotten the keys from Calendula? She had them in her fingers. Just one pull and they'd have been hers. But she'd been scared. *He* had scared her, the way he was acting, so crazy. She felt as if she was coming out of some kind of cloud, a blanketing dream state she was staggering out of. She hadn't felt this sober since she'd come here, all the adrenaline and terror setting her mind on an edge straight as a razor. She was going to get those keys, or get Coyote to drive her and Megan out of here. She was leaving, with or without Calendula. But she didn't want to bring Megan with her. It could get ugly and the little girl had seen enough insanity already.

"Sweetie," she said, "I'm going to need you to stay here while I go get the keys to the truck. Do you understand?"

Megan nodded her head, still whimpering, but beginning to calm down.

"Mommy is just going right up there to talk to Calendula and Coyote. I will be right back. Okay?"

"I want to leave, Mommy."

"I know, sweetie. And we will. Soon, I promise."

"I want to go back to Granny's."

Rebecca shut her eyes, took in a deep breath and held it for a moment before releasing it and opening her eyes again. Megan's hair was back in her face, snot already dripping back down her nose.

"Okay, Megan. But for now you have to stay here. Just stay here till Mommy gets back."

"I'm afraid to be alone." Megan began to shudder and Rebecca was afraid she was going to break into another sobbing fit again.

"You won't be alone. Mommy will be right up there by those lights. I need you to be a big girl and wait here. Okay?"

Megan nodded, breathing heavily.

Rebecca brushed the hair out of her face. *"Okay?"*

"Okay, Mommy."

Rebecca shut the door softly. Oh, yes, she would get those keys, come hell or high water.

16.

Katie moaned as Diesel steered the big truck down the switchbacks, the windshield wipers slashing back and forth against the onslaught of water pouring from the sky.

"Ohhh. It hurts. Hurts so bad."

"Just hang tight there, sweetie. We'll be there soon."

Everything was happening fast. Too fast. He wondered at all the times he had raced down these back roads before, tires shrieking, heavy truck lolling and threatening to tip, thinking what he was doing was so important. Had any of it ever been that important? No. Not compared to this. Just sketchy drug deals and drunken attempts at revenge. This was the first time anything seemed truly important in a long, long time.

He was sweating heavily and grinding his teeth when they finally pulled off the 36 and onto the 101. They got off on the first Fortuna exit and splashed through the wet streets, lines of cars queued up at the drive-thrus of McDonalds and Burger King, the rain falling in thick white lines against their bright headlights. They roared through the Safeway parking lot, up the hill and into the hospital parking lot.

Diesel parked and looked over at Katie, her head turned away from him, weeping quietly. "I'm just no good," she moaned. "It's all my fault. All my fault."

Diesel swallowed heavily, forcing himself to be strong. He had to be strong. He patted Katie's skinny leg with his big hand. "Now, now, everything's going to be fine. You'll see. We're at the hospital now. The doctors will take care of everything."

God, he wanted a hit. Needed something to keep him going. Why hadn't he brought his pipe and a stash?

He got out and hobbled as quickly as he could around the truck to the passenger side and swung open the door. Carefully, he helped her down, out of the truck, and into the pouring rain.

When her feet hit the ground, she grimaced and clutched her

218

swollen belly. A couple of long-haired metal-heads sitting in a van blasting Slayer and passing a joint back and forth looked up at them as they shuffled down the sidewalk. One of them, a skinny dude in a blue-denim jacket with black patches sewn all over it, made eye contact with Diesel and gave him a knowing nod. Diesel looked quickly away, not knowing what the nod meant, if it meant anything at all.

The asphalt and concrete stank of rain as they made their way past the ornamental shrubs—just dark amorphous shapes in the gray light of the evening—and around to the hospital's brightly lit entrance.

17.

Spider was right. Calendula found the money right where he said it would be.

He peered into the open duffel bag. It was brimming with cash. A few big bundles of hundreds, giant chunks of twenties clasped together with rubber bands. Had to be at least a couple hundred grand. Minimum. Off of pot *he* grew. That *he* harvested. Only to have Coyote sneak on back and rob him. The fucking balls, the sheer goddamn audacity, the fucking scum-bag piece of shit.

He zipped up the bag and swung it over his shoulder. He'd have to hide this somewhere, but first things first.

He turned back to Coyote, lying face down on the ground. "Motherfucking thief." He slipped a foot under him and kicked him over onto his back. A gurgling sound rumbled up from Coyote's chest as rain splashed down on his pale, bloated face. "Teach you to steal from me."

Calendula poised the blade of the shovel against Coyote's throat, balanced it on a lump there, and used his weight to press down on the shaft of the handle. The wet blade slipped off, slicing down through skin and muscle before striking the earth. Blood began to trickle out of the wound, pooling on the ground.

"Damnit," Calendula said, lifting the shovel and once again positioning it over Coyote's neck. As he steadied himself and prepared to thrust, Coyote's eyes sprung open, locking with his.

"Don't. Please..."

He reached up and grasped the shovel. A pathetic attempt, because it was too late. This time Calendula used his foot to send the blade down. He felt the cartilage in the windpipe crack, but again the edge slipped off, ripping a huge red gash into the side of Coyote's neck that released a violent stream of blood. Calendula was amazed how high the blood sprayed. A good six feet, two steady geysers, pulsing with Coyote's heartbeat.

Coyote's mouth opened and closed frantically in choked screams, then his arms and legs began to flail like an overturned insect's. Calendula fell down on top of the thrashing body, pinning Coyote's shoulders to the ground with his knees. "Fucking thief," he said again, slamming the shovel into his neck.

18.

The first nurse was an older black woman, stern eyed, with short graying hair. She had a clipboard and wanted all of Katie's information. The other one, who brought the wheelchair, was short with her hair in a tight French braid. They both made pained expressions and exchanged cross looks when Katie lifted her battered face to them.

The black nurse locked eyes with Diesel. "Who did this to her?"

He looked away, glancing down at his dirty hands, streaked with oil and grime, the tips of his fingernails chipped black crescents, thinking: It ain't supposed to be like this.

"My son. The father. He ain't here."

She nodded and jotted something down on her clipboard as the other nurse eased Katie into the wheelchair. Katie whimpered and put her head in her hands again.

"Let's get you to the maternity ward, sweetheart," the short nurse said, pushing her down the hall.

19.

Calendula gasped for breath, lying on his side, covered in Coyote's blood. He watched as the stars and dirty moon revealed themselves, and then were swallowed back up by dark clouds. Rain again began to patter the earth. The exertion involved in killing Coyote had not been unlike a sexual one; and with release, doubt and remorse began to flood his brain.

What have I done? What do I do now?

He noticed the bag of money was stained with splatter marks and lying in a puddle of blood. He pushed himself up off the ground, stinking of death, and standing upright, pulled the strap of the duffle bag over his shoulder.

Coyote's body lay before him, headless and still, no longer twitching. He stepped forward and grasped Coyote's head by the hair, lifted it up, and cradled it in his hands, staring down at it, mesmerized for a moment—the glassy sheen of his hooded eyes, the small trickle of blood leaking out his left nostril and dripping off his lower lip, such a deep shade of red—then looked away, a nauseous feeling boiling in his gut as Coyote's mouth began to slowly open and close, as if trying to speak.

"I didn't do it," Coyote said.

Calendula looked back at the head. "What did you say?"

Coyote blinked, licked the blood off his lips. "It wasn't me, man. It wasn't me."

Calendula felt his anger returning and shook the head. "Bullshit. If it wasn't you, who was it?"

"I don't know."

"I know it was you," Calendula said. "Spider told me. Who else could it have been?"

Coyote stared up at him, his sad eyes wet and glistening.

A sudden burst of lightning and the land was bathed in light. Calendula looked up to see Rebecca there, a few yards away, frozen, staring at him open-mouthed.

The thunder clap was almost instantaneous, the roar so resounding, so deep and penetrating, that the land itself shook, the vibrations rippling up into his knees so that he staggered. Then there was darkness.

20.

The maternity ward was packed. The halls filled with visitors bearing flowers and balloons, expectant mothers trying to walk down their babies, their partners at their sides nervously whispering to them, beaming grandparents looking slightly lost, doctors and nurses hurrying among them all. Katie could sense heads turning, feel their eyes looking at her, and she kept her head down, chin pressed down into her chest, covering her face with her spread fingers.

"It's a busy night," the nurse said, pushing her down the hall past bulletin boards covered in photos of newborns, the wheelchair rolling smoothly over the gleaming floor. "Haven't seen it this crowded in quite a while. You're lucky this room is available. We were booked solid last night."

Katie pondered that word "lucky." She didn't feel lucky. She felt terrified and desperate and, though Diesel was with her, she felt very alone and lost. And most definitely very, very unlucky.

The short nurse steered Katie into a brightly-lit birthing room where another nurse in bright-purple scrubs was already at work unwrapping instruments and devices from their sterile plastic sheaths. Katie peered through her fingers, watched as the nurse in purple glanced quickly from her to Diesel, her mouth a down-turned line.

As the short nurse helped Katie take off her blouse and pull off her jeans she asked her when she was due.

"I don't know. Can't remember. I think around now. It's February, isn't it? I haven't been to a doctor in a while."

The nurse slipped a hospital gown over Katie's head and helped her lay down on the bed. There was a poster of the human body pinned to the wall. Katie stared at the snaking strands of sinew as the nurse in purple rubbed an alcohol pad on the underside of her arm, inserted an IV, then went between her legs and began examining her.

"Oh, oh, it hurts," Katie moaned. "Ohhh…"

"That's just a contraction," the short nurse replied. "Don't push yet. Just let it pass."

"Okay, your cervix is dilated three centimeters. When was your last contraction?"

"I don't know. Coming off the highway into town maybe."

"About fifteen minutes ago," Diesel said. Both nurses looked over at him but neither said anything.

The short nurse disappeared out the door and then reemerged with a large Styrofoam cup of ice water, a straw sticking up out of it.

"Sip this, it will make you feel better."

Katie sucked hungrily at it.

"Okay, okay, that's enough. Not too much now."

Strapping a transducer to Katie's belly with elastic straps, the nurse in purple began to slowly move the device across the swollen hump, the tense look of concentration on her face giving way to concern.

"I'm not picking up a heartbeat."

21.

Rebecca ran down the road screaming. She looked over her shoulder, stumbled, fell to her hands and knees, and got back up again. He's crazy, she thought, still screaming, feet beating against the mud and gravel.

He killed Coyote. And then stood there with the head in his hands...talking to it.

When she'd walked up the sloping road toward the headlights, Rebecca had heard the fighting, the grunting and howling, the horrific cries. But she told herself they were changing a tire or trying to push the Navigator out of a ditch.

And then everything had gone quiet. So very, very quiet. Even the relentless beating of the rain abated for a moment.

It wasn't until that flash of lightning that it all became clear. In that brilliant pop of luminescence, she saw Calendula drenched head to toe in blood—such a bright shade of red, so unmistakable—and the amorphous shape steaming by the open door of the SUV. A body. Coyote's body.

It was like a dream, when you're paralyzed and unable to move. You struggle to do something, anything, the panic building and building inside you. But you're frozen.

Then she'd remembered Megan sitting back there alone in the old Dodge Ram pickup. She started screaming. Screaming and screaming as she turned and started running down the road.

—

Calendula was too tired to chase her. She'd come around. He loved her and knew she loved him. She just needed some time to sort it all out. Once she calmed down and saw the money, everything would be different. He just had to get her relaxed and show her the money. All that money. Then she'd realize it was all worth it. Everything was worth it. Now they could get their own land, their own piece of the dream. And they'd do it right. Organically, sustainably. Growing with the sun and not some diesel generator and high-pressure-sodium lights.

He tossed Coyote's head aside, leaned forward and put his hands on his knees, taking in great gulps of wet air. It'd taken nearly everything he had to kill Coyote like that. Some inner fury that unleashed itself. It felt good. Powerful. All that rage and hate that swelled within him released in a sudden rush, a frenzy where he was in control, he was the one calling the shots. He just had to somehow convince Rebecca of his logic.

The contusion on his forehead itched and he dug at it with his fingernails, wondering if a hole in his head like this could be letting in the ghosts that seemed to be seeping into his brain.

Then he laughed. Silly delusions.

He had to get rid of the body. Drag it out to the woods and bury it deep, with all the others that littered the property. Spider would tell him how to do it. Where to put it. He'd miss Spider, but he'd be glad to be gone from him.

He licked his lips, salty and metallic with blood, his left eye twitching again.

Time to get to work. He could have all this straightened out by morning. No one would be the wiser. As Spider had told him, the cops let folks out here settle their own problems.

Then, from up on the hill, another set of headlights. What the fuck? Who in the hell could that be? This was not a good time for visitors. Not a good time at all.

22.

"This is fucked. I can barely see." Ivy squinted through the rain-streaked windshield, struggling to see past the wipers beating quickly back and forth. "I hope we can get back out of here."

"Don't worry," Sunbeam said. "I've seen worse. You've got four-wheel drive. We'll be fine. Nothing more than a good old Humboldt County winter and a muddy dirt road. Just think, in a couple of days we'll be sitting on a beach in Kauai."

"Jesus. I can't wait."

"Yeah, this fucker just better have my money. Look, we made it. Here's the gate."

The Four Runner bounced and shuddered as they passed the gate and pulled down the driveway. As they veered around the bend, the headlights cut through the darkness and there was Coyote's Navigator parked on the side of the road, interior lights glowing, the driver's door and back hatch open.

"Huh. There's his car. Pull up behind it and I'll go see if he's there."

Ivy pulled to a stop behind the Navigator. Sunbeam slipped on her parka, pulled up the hood, and ducked out into the storm.

"Hello? Coyote?" She struggled to make her voice heard over the metallic beat of heavy rain smacking down against the Navigator. "Coyote, are you there?" It was empty. She went around the other side and looked around, shielding her eyes from the whipping wind and downpour. "Coyote?"

Lightning cracked the darkness and she spied a shape lying on the embankment, the rough outline of a body. Was that Coyote lying there? What the fuck was he doing?

"Coyote?" she asked. "Is that you?"

23.

"Let me see that," the short nurse said, taking the monitor and moving it across Katie's belly. "Let's try it with her on her side."

"All right," said the nurse in purple. "We're going to need you to lay on your side."

They eased Katie over on her side, sliding the monitor against her belly. The short nurse looked at the nurse in purple. "Go get the doctor."

Katie couldn't stop crying. "What is it? What is it? Is my baby all right? Is my baby all right?"

Diesel felt helpless in this sterile room with its spotless, shiny instruments. Dirty and foul. Wrong. Even worse because he wanted a hit. Wanted a hit of speed so bad it tightened his bowels, strained his eyeballs, and made him set his teeth against each other till they hurt.

"It's going to be okay, sweetie. Just hang tight. The doctor is coming."

He watched as Katie bit her lip and nodded her head.

The nurse came back into the room with the doctor, a young, handsome guy with closely cropped blonde hair and the beginnings of a beard. A stethoscope was slung over one shoulder. He went to the sink and, as he washed his hands, asked Katie her name, age, due date. Drying his arms up to the elbow with paper towels he slipped on a pair of rubber gloves, explained to Katie that his name was Dr. Fleming, and approached her while slipping the ends of the stethoscope into his ears.

He placed the metallic bell on her swollen belly and began to slowly move it back and forth, up and down, his head cocked to the side, eyes half shut. He took a deep breath and looked up at the nurse. "Do we know who did this to her face?"

"The father. This is the grandfather."

The doctor glanced up at Diesel quickly and then back to the nurse. Diesel did not like the way he looked at him, as if he was some kind of insect that had found his way into the doctor's kitchen.

"Have you taken any blood yet?"

"No."

"Okay. Do that. I want a drug test done." The doctor looked down at Katie. "Have you been taking any drugs?"

Katie began to weep harder.

The doctor gave a stern look at the nurses. "How far apart are the contractions?"

"Nine minutes."

"And how dilated is she?"

"Three centimeters."

"When the contractions get to be five minutes apart come get me. If it takes more than a couple of hours we might need to do a caesarian, so alert the surgeon. I want to get this thing out of her."

Diesel shuddered. His grandson had just gone from being a baby to a thing.

24.

When Rebecca reached the Ram pickup a wave of shock ripped through her, leaving her shuddering and numb. The door was wide open. Megan was gone.

"No, no, no. Megan? Megan?" She searched the truck, growing more and more desperate, crawling through the front seat and then frantically into the back bed. "Megan? Megan?"

"Mommy?"

Did she hear that, or was it the wind?

"Mommy?"

Yes, she definitely heard it—Megan's sweet, tinny voice—coming from down the escarpment. She raced over to the edge of the steep embankment, looked down, blinking into the night, and saw two shadowy figures: Megan and another child, walking hand in hand towards the darkness of the rushing river. Megan looked over her shoulder, blank faced, and called one more time, "Mommy?"

25.

Diesel stumbled backward till he hit the counter, glancing around in a daze. The jars of cotton balls, the red biohazard waste bin, the gauze and napkins, they began to dance and jitter. His mouth filled with water and specks of light flickered before his eyes. The room was spinning and he was going to be sick. The nurses were busy hovering over Katie, telling her not to push. Not yet. Just chew on this crushed ice.

He ducked out the door and into the hall, racing past startled people and pictures of newborns, and ran to the bathroom.

Falling to his knees before a toilet he wretched up yellow bile. He hadn't eaten in days. He shuddered and dry heaved. Again he spat up a slop of yellow slime that burned his throat and left a foul acrid taste on his tongue. A cool sheen of sweat lacquered his body. He trembled slightly and then braced himself, clenching his eyes tight. He focused on his breathing, lifted himself up, went to the sink, and splashed cool water onto his face.

He could hear laughter outside in the hall.

Keep it together, he told himself, keep it together.

The girl needed him. He had to go back, but he was shaking badly and needed a smoke.

He remembered the night DJ was born, holding him in his arms, so tiny. All those promises he'd made to himself. All the promises he'd broken.

First, it had just been celebrating. Then it was a bender. Then getting on the speed so he could keep it together at work, jamming the shovel bucket of his excavator into the ground to haul earth up out of those deep black holes.

He needed a smoke. Just one quick smoke and he would go back to the girl.

He headed out towards the exit, shuffling past the doctors, nurses, pregnant women and families, pulling a rumpled pack of

Marlboros from his front pocket. He stepped out into the rain.

The overhead lights in the parking lot glimmered in the downpour, halos of dull blue light. He found a small balcony to stand under and, as he took a drag of his cigarette, he noticed two uniformed Fortuna police officers storming hurriedly into the door of the maternity ward.

He knew where they were headed.

He had no choice but to leave. He didn't want to end up down at the station answering questions, possibly even see his ass thrown in jail again. And he still had that goddamn hunting rifle in his truck. He was a felon, he'd end up back in the joint if the cops discovered it.

He hobbled back to his truck feeling ashamed and beaten. But he didn't see any other choice. Starting the engine, the truck roaring to life, he felt a deep and utter emptiness within him: a chasm so deep he could see no end to it, only darkness, eternal and black.

26.

"Megan?" Rebecca rushed to the edge of the embankment. "Megan?"

The little girl stopped and looked up at her, a blank, questioning look on her face, as if she was unsure which direction she should head: to her mother or to the river.

"Mommy?"

That same word, loud enough not to be taken by the wind but quiet enough to barely make it up the ravine.

The dead boy grinned dementedly over his shoulder and raised a hand in a friendly wave. How had they gotten down there? Not seeing a path, Rebecca rushed off the edge, sliding down the cliff face feet first through the chaparral and rocky clay, slipping faster, for a moment her belly rising up into her lungs, and then her feet slammed down on the sandy bank.

Megan stood there before her, crying, a futile look of hopelessness on her round, doll-like face. The little boy stood beside her, pale, black-haired, clad only in cutoff jeans cinched around his waist with a rope. He was smiling.

Rebecca leapt at Megan and pulled her—limp as a bundle of rags—into her arms, taking a step back and hissing at the boy. "You stay away from us. Stay away."

The ghost simply grinned, black hair plastered to his head, beaming at her with a look of bemusement, his eyes large and dark in his pallid face, head cocked jauntily, something green and viscous leaking out of his mouth.

Scared to turn her back on him, Rebecca backed away, snarling like an animal. "Stay the hell away from us."

Then the boy spoke, a sweet, high-pitched voice, filled with amusement. "Take your time. The river will be waiting. It's not going anywhere." His eyes twinkled and his smile grew bigger, black lips, stained in slime, stretching over impossibly white, square teeth.

27.

Ivy watched Sunbeam circle the Navigator in the glare of her headlights, the pounding rain beating a cacophony against the roof of the Four Runner.

At first she thought the movement she noticed in the darkness was just a trick of the shadows. But when she squinted she saw it was a hunched figure, sneaking slowly up behind Sunbeam. She screamed as she saw it rise up, raising something long and skinny over its head. All the tiny hairs on her arms and neck went erect, a coppery flood of saliva filled her mouth as she slammed both hands down against the horn.

The blare of the horn startled Sunbeam and she turned around just in time to see the rusted blade of the shovel come swinging through the rain.

Her face exploded in pain, her nose shattering into a bloody pulp of cartilage and snot.

Staggering back, she lifted her hands to her face in a brief moment of disbelief before the shovel rose back up and slammed down again, this time on the top of her head, sending her into darkness.

—

Rebecca clawed her way up the embankment, scrabbling for purchase in the soft dirt and clay, pushing through a tangle of whitethorn and huckleberry that scratched at her face, one hand digging into the wet earth while the other clutched Megan to her chest. Megan whimpered and shook. They were both covered in mud and drenched to the bone, shivering violently. Rebecca pulled herself to the crest of the embankment. Exhausted, trembling, and gritting her teeth, she managed to heave herself up to the road.

Collapsing to the ground, she lay there, struggling for breath. The fear and rush of adrenaline-filled panic subsided into an utter fatigue. Lightning flashed and she cradled Megan tight as thunder came bellowing behind it.

She had to think, had to find some way out of here.

The sound of a car horn.

She turned and looked up the road, her cheek pressed into the cold, wet gravel. Was that another set of headlights? Was she hallucinating? Seeing double? No. A new set of headlights and then the car horn again.

Someone was here. This was her chance.

She pulled herself up into a sitting position, scratches and bruises screaming, and shifted Megan so that she sat on her lap. She stroked the hair from her face.

"Listen to me, Megan. Listen." Megan trembled, her breath coming in quick, awkward gasps. "Megan, please, you have to listen to my words. Are you listening to me?"

"Yes."

"You have to be strong. It's time to be strong. Do you hear me?"

Megan didn't respond, so Rebecca took her by the shoulders and shook her, trying to make contact with those big, brown eyes. "Now is the time for us to be strong."

28.

"Can't you mind your own business?"

Calendula watched Sunbeam crumple to the muddy earth.

"Always sticking your nose where it don't belong. Let this be a lesson."

He lifted the shovel over his head and sent it rocketing down against the side of her skull. It struck with a loud crack and he felt something give. A trickle of dark liquid leaked out her ear and began to form a puddle on the muddy ground.

Breathing heavily, he raised the shovel up again.

—

Inside the Four Runner, Ivy howled, fumbling with the door latch, watching the shadow figure strike her friend down.

"No. No. No," she whimpered, pushing the door open and falling out onto the gravel and dirt.

Leaping up and barreling out into the rainy night, she sprinted up behind the figure as it raised the shovel again. She grasped the blade as the shovel rose and yanked hard, using its upward momentum to pull the shovel free from Calendula's grip.

"What?" He spun around, fire in his eyes. "What are you doing? I'm trying to work here!"

Terrified, Ivy slowly retreated, holding the shovel up defensively.

When he lurched forward and came at her she turned to run, but it was too late. He grasped the shovel handle, slamming it against her so that she stumbled backwards, and quickly yanked it free from her grasp as she fell.

She hit the ground hard, the wind escaping her lungs and leaving her breathless for a moment. Then she squirmed onto her belly and began to crawl away. Casting a panicked glance over her shoulder, she screamed in terror when she saw him behind her, readying the shovel, eyes wild and demented.

As the shovel came plummeting down Ivy spun away, onto her back. The shovel whizzed by her head, slamming into her hand. The thin bones cracked and she bellowed in pain. Frantically she began to crab-walk away, gasping for breath.

Calendula lifted the shovel, his stubby, rain-soaked dreadlocks poking from his head like demonic horns. He grinned.

—

When Rebecca saw the silhouette of Calendula in the headlight beams, she thought of her mother. Her mother drunk. Sprawled on the sofa, smoking, slurring her words. Telling her men are pigs. Fighting to enunciate each word as she sipped cheap vodka from a plastic cup.

"Men will hurt you. Fight back. They'll be all hands and try to take away what isn't theirs. Stick it in you. You fight back, girl."

And her mother had locked eyes with her, her face heavily made-up, lipstick smeared. She pointed a finger at Rebecca, just a little girl, only eight or nine, and said, "If one of those bastards tries to hurt you, go for his eyes. You claw his damn eyes out. You understand me?"

At the time she had just nodded, incapable of understanding what her scary, drunken mother was rambling on about.

Now she understood.

—

She had just been saved by Joan of Arc. Joan of fucking Arc had just come howling out of the darkness and saved Ivy. A short-haired crazy woman: mouth open, bellowing some primitive war cry, tendons stretched tight at her throat, leaping onto her attacker's back and spearing his face with her fingers.

Joan of Arc. It was a miracle.

—

Rebecca clawed frantically at Calendula's face, searching with her fingers, scrabbling with her nails, for his eyes.

He dropped the shovel and managed to push one of her hands free, shrugging violently to get her off his back. But her other hand found purchase and she dug her fingers into his eye socket, twisting until she felt them sink in.

As she tried desperately to tear his eye free from his face he bucked wildly and finally managed to break free, throwing her from his back. When she hit the ground her teeth clacked together so hard she thought they might shatter.

—

"My eye," Calendula moaned, gently trying to push it back into his head as he stumbled towards the escarpment. "Why? Why would you do that?"

—

Ivy, seeing him on the edge of the overhang, pushed herself up from the ground, the pain from her crushed hand causing white triangles of light to dance before her, and ran at him, intent on pushing him off the edge and into the river. She slammed into him, but instead of falling backwards he simply crumpled around her and they both tumbled to the ground and rolled through the mud to the edge of the embankment, the black water of the rushing river below them.

—

Calendula struggled with Ivy. The bitch was going crazy, clawing at him, kicking, all knees and elbows as she writhed on top of him. He filled one hand with her hair and groped at her face with the other, sinking his index finger into her ear. He worked his finger in, squirming, the pressure of the trapped air building, swelling the canal, until he felt the soft *pop* of her eardrum and the warm flood of blood. He watched her clench her eyes shut and shriek in pain, rain slashing against her face. Turning, he pushed his weight against her with his knees so that he came up kneeling on her chest and, releasing her hair, began to pummel her face with his right fist while, with his other hand, he ground his finger deeper into her ear, the slick, warm fluids lubricating the descent as he wiggled it further and further in.

—

Gasping for breath, Rebecca got shakily to her feet and grabbed the shovel. Limping over to where Calendula and Ivy grappled on the edge of the embankment, she lifted the shovel over her shoulder like a baseball bat and swung it with a grunt.

It smacked into the side of his head, striking his skull with such force that the metal rang like a church bell. He crumpled and Ivy squirmed free from under him, screeching, her hand to her ear, running off towards her Four Runner.

Calendula lay on the edge of the embankment, blinking confusedly, mouth opening and closing in like a fish out of water.

Rebecca stood above him with the shovel in her hands. He had to be put down. He was dangerous. Like a sick dog. She gritted her teeth and raised the shovel over her head, preparing to bring it down into his face when her concentration was broken by the sound of a pleading voice.

"Don't, Mommy. Please, don't hurt him."

Megan, suddenly there, grasping ahold of her leg, looked up at her with those huge brown eyes.

"Don't do it. Don't hurt him, Mommy."

—

Lights danced around the periphery of Calendula's vision. He thought he could hear Megan somewhere. His head hung over the embankment's edge and the sound of rushing water filled his ears.

Looking up through the blood and rain he saw Rebecca above him, the shovel poised to strike.

He struck out instinctively, snagged the hem of her jeans in his

241

grasp, and quickly rolled over, pulling her feet from under her. He could see the surprise in her face as she fell, heard her grunt as she hit the ground.

Megan—tangled in her feet—tumbled down with her, the ledge of the escarpment quivering. He sprang up onto his hands and knees, teeth bared, and leered at her with his single eye.

Rebecca scrambled to put herself in front of Megan, then crawled forward to face him, the two of them like wild animals in a standoff.

"Don't," she said. "Don't you hurt us."

His leering expression broke. Cracked like parched earth. The viciousness, anger, and insanity slipping away. He sat back on his haunches, looked at her pleadingly.

"How could you say that? How? I would never hurt you or Megan. I love you. Love you more than anything. Can't you see that? Don't you know you're my everything? My world? Everything I've done, I've done for us. For the dream."

He rose up and held out a hand to Rebecca.

"I love you," he said, and then there was only the roar of an engine and the blinding light of high-beams.

—

The Four Runner hit Calendula just as he was beginning to stand and stretch out his hand to Rebecca.

The bumper slammed into his left leg, pulverizing his pelvis and snapping his femur in two—the jagged ends of the broken bone pushing out through the muscle and flesh of his thigh and nearly severing his leg—while simultaneously throwing him upwards, off his feet, and into the windshield, the impact of his neck and shoulders shattering it into a spider-web pattern of tiny white triangles.

Rebecca watched as the Four Runner skidded to a halt and he thumped down, rolling off the hood, smacking the ground in a heap, like so much dirty laundry. She thought she saw him look up at her, extend his hand in a pleading gesture, and mouth something. But she couldn't hear what it was.

And then the world turned upside down. Everything was moving, sliding, and tumbling as the embankment gave way and crashed down into the river.

Rebecca fell for what seemed like a long time, spinning through the torrent of mud and clay that fell all around her, finally slamming to the earth by the shore of the river with Megan on top of her, feeling ribs give and break. She moaned, her side on fire, and wondered for a quick moment if she was going to puke, then looked up to see the blinding lights of the Four Runner falling through the air towards them.

She threw herself away from the vehicle as it crashed headfirst into the shore, front end exploding, radiator erupting in a torrent of steam and hot water, horn suddenly blaring. It hung there for a moment, suspended and balanced on its smashed nose, then slowly tipped over into the river with the wrenching sound of twisting metal. It landed on its roof, the sides collapsing in on themselves and the windows shattering.

As she rolled blindly away from it, shielding Megan with her body and arms, Rebecca was suddenly at the bend in the river, slipping off the shore and into the water, the icy cold of it making her gasp as the current engulfed her.

Turning over and digging her feet into the sandy bottom, she lurched for the shore, still clutching Megan to her. Crawling through the shallow rapids at the river's edge, she slipped on the slimy, moss coated rocks and fell onto her side, cracked ribs shrieking in pain, the icy water rushing over her. Fingers numb, her teeth chattering, she felt Megan slip from her grasp, screaming, as the current pulled her away. Rebecca shot out an arm and grasped Megan's hand.

"Hold on," she said. "Hold on."

She could see Megan's tiny face contorted in effort as she gripped her hand, her jaw set tight, teeth clamped together, eyes wincing in concentration.

"Don't let go, baby. Just don't let go."

Calendula went sweeping by them, pin-balling against rocks and boulders, looking bent and broken like a discarded doll. His head bobbed above the water line, the dark silhouettes of his stubby dreadlocks giving him an absurd and clown-like appearance. Was he looking at her? Staring at her as the black water swept him away?

Megan's hand began to loosen in her grasp and a surge of terror ripped through her. She strained to hold it—slick, slippery and wet—squeezing, locking eyes with her little girl, panic flooding her body. And then the tiny hand was gone and she was watching in horror as Megan disappeared into the rushing maelstrom.

Desperation overwhelming her, she threw herself into the freezing, black water, yearning to somehow save her baby, but knowing it was too late, that she was gone.

29.

Diesel pulled the old 30.06 out of his truck and stumbled through the rain and dark to his house. Once inside, he gathered up some oil and some rags, sat down on the couch and began to clean and polish the rifle.

The piles of baby clothes and toys made him sick and sad in a strange, fucked-up way that tasted of defeat. The feeling made his eyes go wonky and everything felt distorted and fake. Like this was all a dream. He wanted to cry. He couldn't remember the last time he'd wept. Maybe when his father died? Did he cry when his father died? He couldn't remember.

He packed his glass pipe with a huge shard of speed and watched it melt, inhaling deeply as the flame danced around it. His heart rang out and sweat beaded on his forehead, running down into his eyes, but it didn't give him that jolt of hope he'd been looking for.

He ran the grease-soaked rag up and down the barrel of the gun till the metal gleamed.

The police would be here soon, asking questions. He was sure of this.

He should empty out his safe, get all the crank, pills, money and guns out of here, to his hiding place in the woods, those old fifty-gallon barrels he had buried on the far side of the hill.

But what was the point?

What did anything matter anymore?

His dreams of a new start and a family were gone. His son hated him. His grandson dead.

The girl, Katie, would probably end up in prison for killing her little unborn baby. He'd heard of cases like that before. Prosecutors always went for the jugular when it came to dead babies and meth.

He was tired. He couldn't go back to prison. But didn't have the strength to keep up the fight to stay out. He was just tired. Down in his bones, deep in the sockets of his eyes. In his fingers and arms. His aching fucked-up leg. Tired. So tired. Sleep. He just wanted to sleep.

He looked at the rifle, the gun his son had tried to kill him with. The gun he had inherited from his father. That had belonged to his grandfather. He envisioned sitting in a tree stand with it. Remembered being a kid and lining up a buck in his sights for the first time. Hidden behind a mesh of barren branches, high above the animal that had stopped to lap at the saltlick his father had secured to the earth with a tent stake. The ring of the shot and the moment before it fell. It looked so beautiful dead there. The proud laughter of his father and uncle. Hanging it by its feet in an old shed. Using a sharp knife to release all its guts.

He went to his bedroom, the gun held lightly in his hands, pulled the sheets back, and lay down on the big bed, his muddy logging boots leaving clumps of dirt on the white sheets. No, he wasn't going back to prison. Never. He was going to sleep.

He took a deep breath, closed his eyes, and put the barrel of the gun in his mouth, the cold steel resting on his lower teeth—taste of grease and dirt—the front sight jammed up against the back of his throat.

With his arm fully extended, he was just able to reach the trigger.

EPILOGUE

"Sometimes I live in the country,
Sometimes I live in town,
Sometimes I have a great notion to jump in the river and drown . . .
Good night, Irene. I'll see you in my dreams."
—Song, circa 1932,
Sung by Huddie "Lead Belly" Ledbetter
Author unknown

"Duck, duck, goose!"
—Children's game

1.

Doctors speculated whether the severe hypothermia Rebecca experienced—lying washed up on shore all that time, half in the river half out—had caused some brain damage, but they were never able to either prove or dismiss this.

Calendula was dead. Sunbeam. Ivy. Coyote. But these were nothing. Mere drops in a pond, compared to losing Megan. This loss, this gaping hole in her life, this sad abyss that threatened to swallow her whole, was what now defined her. A cavern and ache that was always with her and would never let her go. That now gave form and definition to her being, made her what she was.

But it wasn't until the grand jury investigation that she truly began to feel she was losing her mind.

Sitting up on that chair in the courtroom, answering their questions, their implications and grave stares. Her mother was in the audience, weeping the entire time. A Kleenex permanently affixed to her face. She said she was there for support, but her presence provided only guilt. Rebecca knew she blamed her for everything. Had warned her and told over and over her it wasn't safe there.

She wanted to tell them about the ghosts.

How the land was haunted and determined to take them all.

That it was a miracle she survived. That she wished in her heart that she hadn't been washed up to shore unconscious but breathing. That she wished she was there still, with her daughter, even in death.

She wanted to tell them about the little boy she'd seen. How he told her that he and the river would be waiting. She wanted to say so much, but her lawyer told her to just say that all she knew was that there was a landslide. That's it.

And so, that's what she did.

It seemed men weren't attracted to her anymore. Her hair grew in weird, it was always trying to tangle itself back up into dreadlocks again and she'd get frustrated and brush it all out so that it had a wild, bird's-nest look.

But most likely it was the desperation in her eyes, the sadness and edge-of-panic look that lay within them.

It was scary.

Those eyes which once held such determination and stubborn strength now radiated only madness. The madness of a drowning swimmer who in her flailing and desperation to survive will surely take you down with her. She often thought of the little girl who lived in a boat in the bathtub. She'd tried to change the ending of that story, but she couldn't. It was fate.

Church bells.

Rebecca could hear the sound seeping in from outside the bar. It was noon and she was falling-down drunk, leaning heavily on the brass rail, dangerously close to toppling off her stool. The ground looked very far away.

"You hear them church bells?" she said to the balding guy sitting two stools down.

"Yeah, I hear 'em. They ring all the time. Especially Saturdays and Sundays. All damn day. Catholics and their bells."

"Church bells," she said. "Church bells." Their ringing conjured some distant memory, like a puzzle piece whose awkward sides refused to fit into the rest of the picture. What was it? When had she heard church bells like that? When she was four? Before her dad left. God, could it have been then? Easter Mass. She put her head down into her hands and began to cry.

"Fuck, lady, relax." The guy stood and started away with a disgusted shake of his head.

"Hey, where you going?" she said, looking up, startled. Then shouting, "Don't you leave me. Don't you fucking leave me."

The guy stopped before the door. "Lady, you must have me mixed up with someone else. I don't even know you."

"You bastard. Bastard!"

And then, as the blinding-white-light of the afternoon came streaming in she was falling, falling down off the stool, a slow-motion tumble to the floor, where she lay with the taste of blood in her mouth.

The bartender came around from the bar, a short, older guy with a graying beard and big hands. "Come on," he said to her, "let's get going. You've had too much and you're scaring away the customers." He pulled her up to her feet and walked her to the door. "That's it. That's it. Let's get going, Miss It," and he shoved her out into the heat of the day where she floated down the street like a ghost.

She was somewhere in downtown San Diego and the church bells were ringing for Sunday Mass. She didn't know how she'd gotten here. She'd lost her phone, or broken it, or just thrown it away. She couldn't remember anymore. Lost her glasses, too, so that everything was an unsteady blur.

She briefly wondered where she was going to sleep that night, though dusk was still far off. She was tired and needed a rest. Just a little rest. A nap. She veered off down a residential alley that seemed quiet, stumbled down past some trashcans and leaned up against an old brick building, sunk down against it, slipping towards the ground as the church bells chimed a terrible cacophony, something distorted and wrong, playing at the wrong speed, horrifyingly strange-sounding.

She put her head between her knees and covered her ears with her hands, rocking back and forth, strange images blooming up before her eyes.

A homemade birthday cake with only a handful of candles.

A Christmas without a tree.

Making out with some boy in an Iron Maiden shirt in the dark corner of a roller-skating rink.

And there were songs. Phish and the Grateful Dead, Charlie Manson and the themes to sitcoms and soap operas: *Friends*, *Seinfeld*, *Days of Our Lives*. And through it all, entwining all the notes and melodies, was that old sixties song Megan used to sing: "California Dreamin'." And with it all those other songs of California as well: "Hotel California," "Estimated Prophet," "Mendocino County Line," "Promised Land," "Going to California."

And everything smelled of earth and rain and piss and garbage and tasted of blood.

Curses and fights, doors slammed and walls kicked, digital photos posted and lies told on Facebook. She realized she'd never loved Calendula. Just a lie she'd told herself in order to get to some place she wanted to be. Had never loved her mother either. No one. She'd loved no one. No one but Megan. She was the only thing she'd ever loved. The only thing that ever mattered or meant anything to her. The only beam of light in a world of darkness. And she was gone. Gone, gone, gone.

She heaved and spit up bile. Drenched in sweat, she put her head between her knees and tried to vomit. But there was nothing left inside her.

2.

The land went for sale on a one-day online auction. DJ sat hunched over his laptop and waited for the bidding to slow down. He wasn't stupid. When it grew to a reasonable pace he started bidding. He had plenty of cash. He'd cleared his father's coffers after he went there and found the old man in bed with his muddy boots on, his head in pieces, brains splattered all over the headboard. He had everything now: tweak, guns, cash. And land. He'd even inherited his father's land. His granddad's old hunting cabin turned into a tweaker palace by his so-called Pops. He was a rich man. And now, now he'd have the neighboring land as well. He ended up casting ten bids. The last one sat for the final three minutes of the auction and the land was his.

Katie was in prison. She'd pled guilty to manslaughter and gotten five years. He was lonely, but he didn't really miss her that much. She was a good girl. Kept her fucking mouth shut. About him, about everything. Never pressed no charges or said a thing. Just quietly doing her time.

Did he wonder about the landside? Care about all the bodies found there, encased in a tomb of dirty mud and red clay? No. Did he question why Coyote's head was missing? Ripped off his body? That the coroner had found conclusive evidence of induced trauma? Fuck no. Not at all. None of his business. This was his inheritance. His birthright. Why should he question any of it?

He grinned and slapped his hands together. Hell-motherfucking-yeah, dog, it was all his now. All of it. Homicide Hill was all his.

3.

Spring. Megan and the little boy walked hand-in-hand down the river bank. The rain was long gone, just a distant memory. The sun glared across the earth, bright and blinding. The sky was an impossible blue, vast and infinite. The tan oaks and whitethorn were flowering and gusts of yellow pollen danced through the air, caught on a warm breeze.

They followed the path up the hill, the lush grasses—cocksfoot and oat straw, plantain, fescue and junegrass—a gleaming ocean of green about them, dotted with the fuzzy, yellow heads of blooming dandelions.

A butterfly fluttered by, its flight erratic and fitful. Megan chased after it, lifting her tiny pale hands in the air, laughing happily as it beat its wings crazily and was whisked away into the trees. The boy watched her and smiled. They passed the garden, which was now a dense tangle of fava bean stalks, heavily laden with plump seedpods.

Stopping in front of the chef house, they watched the man unloading equipment: huge lightbulbs, long, black coils of wire thick as snakes. Tanks, buckets. Trays of tiny green plants with fang-like serrated leaves.

A raven swept past, its shimmering, black wings beating loudly against the air. It perched high atop an oak and stared down at them.

Megan turned to the little boy, her magic owl. "Will we stay here forever and ever?"

He grinned and blinked his large, dark eyes. "Yes."

ACKNOWLEDMENTS

To my darling wife, Tara, who read this chapter by chapter, draft by draft. I couldn't have done it without you. To my son, Dylan, who gave me lots of creepy ideas and allowed me to use his story "The Little Boy who Lived on a Boat in the Bathtub."

To the entire Southern Humboldt community. A strange and wonderful place like no other.

To Amanda Blaine who read my rough drafts and gave me incredible suggestions.

To my dear friends, Laurel and Tanner, who beta read the rough drafts. And Laurel's amazing parents Fred and Leigha.

To Darryl Cherney for giving me permission to use his and Judi Bari's song "Trim a Bale of Ganga."

To the LitReactor community, both teachers and students. In particular, David Corbett whose classes on the craft of character changed how I viewed the art of novel writing, Chuck Palahniuk who showed me how "creative" creative writing can be, J. David Osborne who gave me great advice on my rough draft, and John Skipp who helped me choreograph my violence. Also, Ania Ahlborn, Suzy Vitello, and Emily Schultz.

To the Creepypasta Wikia community whose help and support has been such a boon to my writing. ShadowSwimmer77, Empyrealinvective aka Travis Kuhlman, Mr. Dupin, RuckusQuantum aka Charles Resurreccion, Jay Ten, Diexillius aka Alex NIȚESCU, Thomas O, Banningk1979 aka K. Banning Kellum, Blacknumber1 aka Michael Waight, Umbrello, Dr. Frank N. Furter, Tiololo/Rinskuro13,

ChristianWallis, SoPretentious/TenebrousTorrent, Dorkpool, The Koromo, DerpySpaghetti, Doom Vroom, KillaHawke, Natalo, ShawnHowellsCP, Ameagle aka Jasey Roberts, GarbageFactory, SnakeTongue237, Underscorre, Raidra, Mmpratt99, Supersatan25, FrenchTouch, Rainboh, AGrimAuxiliatrix1, Hopefullygoodgrammar, Atonal Anthem, Spoopy Christie, RisingFusion, RomanRage, HawkWD and the site's founder ClericofMadness.

To Mark Spencer, who helped me with my rough draft and let me use his comments as a blurb.

To my writing group: The Circle of Darkness, an incredibly talented bunch who not only helped and supported me, but talked me through the nervous breakdown I had during a rewrite, lol. Repo Kempt, GD Dearborn, Kristen Peterson, Brian Asman, Johnathan Nash, Wendy Maxon and Claudia Quint. Thanks so much, guys.

And to my wonderful parents, Roland and Lorraine. Thanks, Mom and Dad, for everything. I love you so much.

matthew v. brockmeyer

BLACK THUNDER PRESS

matthew v. brockmeyer

Made in the USA
Lexington, KY
19 July 2019